The Battle ahead...?

Dr. Sonia Sharma

Invincible Publishers

First Printing: 2019

ISBN: 978-93-88333-93-1

Invincible Publishers

Registered Address: 201A, SAS Tower, Sector 38, Gurgaon - 122003

Dedicated To

All The Daughters Of Jammu And Kashmir

The forced second class citizens of the state, for their identity depended on the status of their fathers and then their husbands?????? till yesterday

To the perseverence of people living along the Border and LOC as does the west Pakistan Refugees (now our own)

To the sacrifices of the thousands of martyrs and their Families among the forces

And those living, who have sacrificed their youth guarding the people and territories of J&K

Finally, to the changing face of politics in India that has infused the hope back in the people who believe in the idea of one-India

A Note from the Author

'PERSPECTIVE' is a war constantly fought in our heads toying with varied narratives overflowing through the intellectual word stream.

A good 'STORY' is a potent tool to live another life through its characters to understand a perspective that might be dissimilar from what we have always believed in. And with that promise, I put forth my narrative about an otherwise empowered young girl's life and the burden of expectations she had to face in a socially and politically challenging scenario.

Writing this book was both an emotional and a challenging journey. Emotional, because it brushed past a few good memories and some not so good, dating back to the times when the turmoil had just begun to surface.

Challenging, because forming an opinion about the situations and people long dead and gone, basing them on the plethora of literature in the public domain, reconstructing a chronicle of events as told and passed down to generations what was never noted down in history and finally doing a psychoanalysis of the conversations in the space of time, we can only retrospect.

With these thoughts, I thank my Readers who take out time to acknowledge my Stories, my Books.

A Special Thanks to my First Reader and my First Editor Dr. Himani. Her enthusiasm motivates me to keep writing.

Many thanks to Mr. Ajay Setia and the entire team at Invincible Publications, especially Tamanna, who is always ready to address any concern whatsoever, Senior Editor Chandni, Cover Designer Ashish and all the rest who worked at the backend to make this book a reality.

Not forgetting to thank the family, the three most important men in my life—my Father Mr. Lila Karan Sharma, a man I idolize for his values and who has shaped my thoughts the way they are, my Husband Dr. Anil Sharma, who has always let me be 'Me' and my son Agrim, who made me realize unknowingly that I had in me the flare to write and express myself. Thanks to my Mom Mrs. Nirmal, for pushing me to work harder to achieve my goals and finally, my lovely daughter, Apeksha, for bringing in the sunshine and optimism into our lives.

On that note, I handover this Story to you and introduce you to Srishti to accompany her on her journey from a dreamy teenager to a formidable woman.........

Dr. Sonia Sharma

Chapter 1

'Life is not what we always plan it out as, but the beauty of life lies in its unpredictability, the exuberance that accompanies the surprises, the fear of the unknown and the passion that drives us uphill to conquer what was thought to be unreachable; an Eldorado before someone got there for the first time.'

On the historic day of 5th of August 2019, that marked the renaissance of the State of Jammu and Kashmir as the Bill for Reorganization of the State of Jammu and Kashmir is tabled in Rajya Sabha, Srishti stood in front of the portrait of her late Grandfather, touching it tenderly with her fingers as a few stray teardrops made way out of her eyes and she whispered. *'It is happening, Dada Ji. Finally, the integration of Jammu and Kashmir is happening with the rest of India. Your constant endeavors, your struggle did not go waste. My Dad's supreme sacrifice did not go waste. I'm free to exercise my choices today and so are all the daughters of the State.'*

She'd chosen the rocky path straddled with the age-old mindset, the misogynistic ethos and the laid-back attitude of the society that paid little attention to things, which didn't matter to it in the short term. Knowingly she'd taken it upon herself to dismantle the hurdles she felt on the way creating a concrete road for the rest to follow, for how so long she could go on.

Srishti didn't know if she would be the one who could bring in the change or even witness one, but she sure knew that she would be one of the milestones on the way to the Battle Ground that held the key for her liberation and of the rest who wanted to join her.

She knew, rather had faith, that one day, the sun would rise to clear the clouds that shrouded a sizable population of her State from getting their legitimate rights. Be it with the complete abrogation of Article 370 or 35A, or maybe at least recognizing that 50% of the population in all the regions of the State, the women of the State, the daughters of the State got their lawful share at par with the sons, for they share the same DNA, the very basis of the Hereditary clause stated in the Archaic Law.

Though the High Court judgment of 2004 stood in favor of the daughters, it was not enough. Rights are not about getting them as crumbs. They needed to be a full meal, holistic and fulfilling. How could they be termed Hereditary if they can't travel down the generations just because the DNA happens to be that of a woman? A mother can't feast on the gourmet while her children stay hungry.

But the happenings of today, two years after that fateful day which changed the course of her life brought back the memories of the Battle she'd embarked upon. The abrogation of the outdated law, Article 370 and 35A was unquestionably a win for her and hundreds of thousands of the people in the State, but her celebrations would have multiplied if she hadn't lost what she lost on the way. She knew that the struggle was far from over, and much was still needed to be done for the confidence building among the masses. But it was time; she needed to give her pace a pause and reflect upon where it all began.

The year 2012

A Quiet Town of R S Pura in Jammu

"Congratulate me, Dada Ji. I've been selected at IIM Indore for a five year integrated management course!" A jubilant Srishti, all of eighteen, came running to her large bungalow amidst the vast paddy fields.

The house came alive with her energy every time, she was happy.

Srishti was an eighteen years old daughter of an Army Major who was martyred while on duty in Poonch sector when she was just a three years old baby. Her father, Major Jasvinder Singh was the only son of Colonel Jagjeet Singh, her grandfather and Kamalpreet, her grandmother.

Her mother, Neha, Srishti learned, was a broken woman when the misfortune struck her. Neha was the daughter of a Brigadier, who had met Srishti's father when he was posted in Delhi for a cool-off. They had fallen in love during their stay at the Army cantonment when he was a regular visitor to his superior's house. They dated for about two years, and after Neha completed her studies, they got married. Neha couldn't survive her husband's loss, and left little Srishti orphaned at a very tender age. Ever since, she lived with her paternal Grandparents, her loving Dada Ji and Dadi.

She had no bonding with her maternal grandparents, who maintained a very formal and impersonal relationship with her. They sure didn't forget to greet her occasionally and sent gifts her way on her birthday or festivals. They lived a high profile social life, and Srishti's small town grooming could never fit into their metropolitan lifestyle.

She had gone to stay with them for a month for the first time when she was fourteen. Her school was shut owing to the high-pitched agitation on Shri Amarnath Shrine Land Controversy. Naina Masi, her mother's twin had come to Delhi from California with her sons; Saksham, eight and Shreyansh, six and had invited her to join them for a family bonding. Srishti was too excited to meet her younger cousins for the first time and Naina Masi after a very long time. Dada Ji was a little unsure but her Dadi, the darling that she was, had convinced him to send her over for a month.

Naina had tried convincing Srishti's Dada Ji to send her alone by air, promising she would pick her up at the Delhi airport stressing on the fact that Srishti was a big girl now.

He'd not argued and gave her the flight details as she'd asked for. But Dada Ji being Dada Ji had booked a ticket for him as well along with the return ticket on the same evening. Srishti had breathed easy knowing that.

She'd traveled extensively with her grandparents during her summer vacations, as they'd made sure Srishti did not miss the things a child does with his/her parents. They'd gone to the mountains and the seas, Jungle Safari's, Adventure parks as well as overseas for their various vacations. Her grandparents had been actively involved in her growing up. But the prospect of traveling alone had perturbed her. With Dada Ji beside her, she knew she could conquer the world.

Srishti had felt lost in the elite looking house of her maternal grandparents, rather missed the warmth she always felt with her other set of grandparents. She'd shrugged it off thinking, she barely knew her Nani and Nana Ji. Her Nani had quickly admonished her when Srishti had called her Nani.

"Oh! Please, Srishti. Call us Granny and Grandpa like Saksham and Shreyansh do. Don't use that tacky language here." She felt sheepish and had nodded quietly. Naina Masi had pulled her to herself and made her comfortable.

"Should I call you aunty as well?" Srishti had asked her hesitatingly.

Naina had smiled very sweetly and said. "No way. I've got only one niece who can call me Masi. So, for me, Masi is just fine." Granny had cringed and had left them alone. She had felt very awkward in that house. She played with her cousins, but a lot of time, she'd to stress upon her mind and ears to understand their very American accent. Naina Masi was the only saving grace who shared stories with her, took her out for shopping and recreations.

Srishti had initially thought that she might get to know her extended family during her stay there as well as would know little more of her mother through them, but their indifference had not allowed her to broach the topic. The impersonal setting of the house, decorated with art pieces from different parts of the world and the various certificates, trophies, and medals of her grandfather who had retired as a General had very few family pictures. She just kept looking around to find a little of her mother's memories in that household, but all she got was disappointment. It had her thinking that maybe her grandparents, her Granny and Grandpa were not happy with her mother marrying her father. But both her parents were dead now. They could at least respect their memories. Was their resentment towards her mother, the reason for their indifference towards her as well, she couldn't say?

It had been only twelve days since she was there when Dadi had felt her unease as she spoke to her one evening. The next day itself Dadi and Dada Ji were there to pick her up. Srishti couldn't ask for more. She'd left happily promising Naina Masi that she'll be in contact. That day, she knew, if there was anyone she could call her own, it was only her Dada Ji and Dadi, and the home was where they were. She could argue with them, could act stubborn or ask them for anything, and they would only do what was right for her.

Dadi had come out rushing with Dada Ji right behind, hearing her energetic voice. Srishti had literally swirled Dadi around as she shared the news with them.

Dada Ji had looked happy and proud, little concerned but content. He had raised her fine.

"When do we go for counseling?" He had asked.

"In two weeks." She'd come now and hugged him, and he had embraced her back, a little tighter than usual.

"Hmm..." He had said and gone inside quietly.

"He doesn't seem happy, Dadi." She had asked getting emotional.

"He's happy, very happy indeed. He's probably disturbed at the prospect of you going to the hostel. This house would be so dull without you." Dadi had said wiping her eyes, and she'd hugged her back, misty eyed herself. The thought of leaving home hadn't sunk in till then.

Dada Ji had come out looking happy this time with a box of sweets in his hands and the latest model of I-phone 4S, with 32GB storage, she so wanted for months now.

"Oh. My. God! When did you get this?" She jumped with joy, snatching the box of the phone from his hand.

"I love you. I love you. I love you." She chanted as she hugged him dearly.

"Well, I knew my daughter would get admission in a good college. So I was kind of ready. It would be this good, I didn't know. Congratulations, my child. You have made us proud, very proud. Your father, wherever he is, would be so proud of you." He said, wiping his eyes. "And your mom, very happy at her daughter's excellent performance. God bless you."

She had simply stayed in their warm embrace that moment. The moments of triumph in her life always brought in the fond memories of their son and daughter-in-law to her grandparents and to her, a fruitless desire of sharing her achievements with her parents.

"So, when do we go shopping, Dadi." She'd asked to cheer up the mood.

"We will very soon. Now you go and share the news with your friends. Go and party." Dadi said, handing her a generous amount of money amidst Dada Ji's glare and she ran away with it laughing.

"Call up your Nani and Nana also to share the news." Dadi had shouted from behind.

"Granny and Grandpa, Dadi. Don't be so tacky." She'd halted and responded with a borrowed accent.

Her Grandpa was pleased to hear about her admission. They now had something to flaunt about her too. Granny was not far behind and in fact, had invited her over.

"Congratulations, Srishti. Why don't you come over? Now that you're going to college, let me take you shopping. You would want to stock up on the latest fashion stuff, you see." She'd asked.

"I will, Granny before I join the college. See you soon. Bye." She said politely. She could never be rude to anyone.

She'd gone out with her friends to the City Square Mall, the only Mall in Jammu then. She was going to miss all this; her grandparents, her friends, this city, her school, and the carefree life she'd spent there. The dread of unforeseen is always there at the juncture where Srishti stood.

That night, she'd called up Naina Masi as well. Naina had been in constant touch with her ever since she'd spent time with her in Delhi and Srishti loved sharing her anxieties with her, things she could not share with her Dadi.

"I got through IIM Indore, Naina Masi." She had literally shouted into the phone in excitement.

"Oh My God! I can't believe this. Did you?" Naina had said sounding surprised. *"I'm so proud of you Srishti. I'm sure everyone is. God Bless you, sweetheart."* Naina choked on her words.

"You're crying, Masi. Aren't you?" She asked.

"Oh! It's nothing. Neha would've been so proud of you today if she was alive to see this day. So would your father be? I'm so happy for you. All I wish to do right now is to take you in my arms, and that's what is bothering me. Come over for a vacation, if you can Srishti." She had said getting emotional. Srishti was teary-eyed talking to Naina.

"I will, someday, Masi. Right now, there's a lot of running around to be done. Bye for now. I'll call up again." She'd said and then cried her heart out after she hung up.

Chapter 2

Naina poured another cup of her morning tea on a lazy Saturday morning. Her brew had gotten cold while talking to Srishti. She felt happy and content with her. Living so far away from the country, she once called home, Naina had wondered, at times, how Srishti was doing. Her own mother was very critical of Srishti's upbringing but was not willing to contribute to making it any better. She'd finally felt happy meeting her after ten years when Srishti was a teenager.

Naina remembered how she had rushed to the airport, but Delhi traffic was just too unpredictable. She was worried sick thinking about Srishti waiting for her, all by herself for the first time at the huge T 3 Terminal. She tried calling her to remain in the lounge itself till she arrived and failing to get the call connected; had messaged her same. Srishti had appeared unaffected by the delay when Naina had seen her, trying to ascertain her identity, as they faced each other after many years. Naina went and took her in a tight embrace instantly. Srishti looked tomboyish, very innocent, and extremely beautiful in her black denim and a grey T-shirt worn with Nike sneakers. Naina soon knew why she was so relaxed, when she saw Col. Jagjeet Singh come from behind pulling her suitcase along.

Naina went and touched his feet, and he blessed her lovingly.

"You could have told me, you were coming along, uncle. I wouldn't have stressed so much." Naina had said wiping the beads of sweat from her forehead.

"I just wanted her to be safe, Naina. Please take good care of my daughter. She's all I have. I know, you would always look out for her, but I couldn't let her be on her own. Not till she's ready. I've protected her all along and will do so till I believe she's capable of taking care of herself. Call me whenever she wants to come back, and I'll personally come to pick her up. Please don't send her alone as Jammu is on the boil right now."

Then he had hugged her and kissed her forehead. "Call me every morning and night, sweetheart. You know that our day doesn't begin till we hear your sweet voice and doesn't end until you kiss us goodnight. Let me know, dear when you want to come back. Your Dadi and I'll come; we'll shop and go back. Okay, baby? I will miss you."

Then looking at a shocked Naina, he smiled and informed her, "My return flight leaves in another hour. Bye." He had put both hands on the girls' heads to bless them and left. Naina was taken aback by the extent of his involvement and his devotion in taking care of Srishti. Her own parents couldn't have done a fraction of it for their own granddaughter. She was glad; Srishti lived with her Dada Ji and Dadi. Her parents always found flaws in her upbringing and had complained about it every time, she'd asked about her wellbeing. Srishti looked like any other teenager, untouched by malice, with the posture of a sportswoman, charming, talkative and full of life. Well, her accent and the liberal use of Hindi, when she spoke, could be improved, Naina had thought and had grinned at her happily as she exited hand in hand with her niece.

Naina couldn't believe, it had been four years when she last met Srishti. She'd formed a bond with her; she'd missed having in her own household, being the mother of two boys. Srishti was any mother's delight. Now Naina didn't depend on her mother to get any information about her. She would call her up regularly, connect with her on social media, and would often give her heads up regarding what was in and out of fashion or lifestyle. She recommended her good TV shows and Hollywood movies that she could watch, which facilitated her in improving her fluency in English language. She would often send the study material she needed to get through business studies and economics. She taught her how to use social media constructively and not get affected by cyber bullying and cyber criticism.

Srishti had high regards for her too. She often confided in her about her friends, her latest crush, her PMS. In all, through the distance of thousands of miles between them, they'd learned to bridge the gap in their relationship.

Naina was glad that Srishti had a very well rounded personality, all thanks to her grandparents, who had not let the paucity of her life shadow her personality. How she wished, Srishti didn't lose her parents even before she was big enough to know them or maybe what she didn't know wouldn't have hurt her as much.

Naina didn't know, she'd zoned out till she felt a sprinkle of water on her face. Shreyansh was shaking his head in front of her face, having come back from swimming.

Saksham, her older son was walking back along with his father, her husband, Shivesh. Shivesh worked in the capacity of the Vice President in one of the software companies in Silicon Valley. Naina herself worked with a multi-media company, her being an MBA in Mass Com.

"What's for breakfast, Mom? I'm so hungry." Saksham asked.

"It's waffles with top pour of your choice, chicken sausages, and cold coffee. Now, you would want to run and get dressed before it all got cold." She said as both the boys ran to their rooms to change into dry clothes.

"What's up? You look happy. Who was on the phone?" Shivesh asked, pouring some tea for himself.

"It was Srishti, Shivesh. She's gotten into IIM Indore." Naina informed.

"But she needs to be a graduate before she did an MBA. She was in Class XII, I guess." Shivesh had asked, getting surprised.

"IIM Indore has started an integrated five years management course from last year. I'm so happy for her." Naina said, bringing him the fresh information.

"That's great then. But… forget it." Shivesh was about to say something but thought otherwise. He hardly knew the girl, and making ascertains about her didn't seem right to him.

"But what, Shivesh?" Naina probed. She didn't like the way he left his conversation midway, that too about the girl, he knew very little about, only what was told to him by her.

"Nothing significant Naina; just an observation. It felt as if she is shown the vastness and magnificence of the sky, about to learn to fly but then what. When she would be ready to take the flight, wanting to choose her direction, her wings would be clipped. Would she ever be able to or be allowed to leave the place her grandfather worships?" Shivesh said and got up to go inside to change.

That shook Naina and had her thinking. Shivesh's words were reverberating in her ears, harsh but true. Naina couldn't fathom the day; little, soft-spoken Srishti would stand in confrontation with her indomitable grandfather. There was nothing she could do, and right now, she didn't want to. Everyone was happy and proud of her. It was time to let ner live her dreams. How life changed course, no one could predict and five years was a long; very long time, something she didn't want to ponder over now.

Her very hungry kids and husband would be back soon. She did better get on with feeding them for now.

Chapter 3

Back at Col. Jagjit Singh's house, the phone wouldn't stop ringing. The relatives and friends, who came to know about Srishti's achievement, kept coming to congratulate them. Well, to someone living the fast life in metros, it might appear as an intrusion and overtly overbearing, but the slow-paced life in the quiet suburb of Jammu; it was a tradition.

The human-to-human connection and face-to-face interactions still weighed more than mere Facebook likes. Maybe, the distance in terms of travel time was the contributor or the social framework of intricate and interlinked relations made their interactions possible as well as necessary for their survival. Yet the mutual rivalries, extreme sense of unnecessary competitiveness and an urge for one-up-man-ship existed just as much, like any other society.

What Srishti had found abhorrent was the fact that when people came to commend her for her success, they didn't come alone. They came with the success stories of their own children, children of their friends or even the distant relatives who'd done equally well or may be better. Her young mind wasn't able to comprehend the thought behind. Was it to showcase their own accomplishments or to belittle the efforts of the one, they'd taken the time out to come and laud—she wasn't sure.

She thought about it for a while and left it at that. She had grown up with them and knew well how her society functioned. Each one of them, at some point or the other, was a victim of those comparisons, but no one did anything to make it any better. Maybe, it was just a harmless banter, only meant to prolong the conversations. After all, not everyone could discuss business or politics, state of the economy, or foreign policies. Or maybe, the ones who discussed that had little time for such social interfaces. Wasn't a similar mindset at play in the very elite congregation of her Granny's clan? She had nothing to complain of. They were her people, people who knew her and loved her all the same, people she identified with.

Her shopping spree was endless. After all, she was getting out of the rigmarole of wearing the same old school uniform for years now. Her anxiety peaked, as well. What kind of children rather people, she would be among, in the college? Would they be just like her, children who had burnt the midnight oil to get ahead of the cutthroat competition or would they be as snobbish as some of the children she'd met during her inter-state sports meet or debate competitions? Her bravado was gone for a toss, and the fear of alienation, acceptance, and re-integration was playing on her mind. Her grandparents were mindful of her apprehensions and tried to address her concerns as best as they could. Naina Masi had helped instill confidence in her. At this juncture, she really wished that she'd gone to her Granny to get the much-needed polish, to get an extra boost for her confidence and it sure did happen.

Granny had insisted that Srishti spent at least a week with her before she joined college.

Granny appeared much more forthcoming this time. The years had added a few more wrinkles and a visible sense of despondency in her outwardly active life. She might have missed having Naina and her children closer and might as well had felt at a loss for keeping an unwarranted distance between herself and her only granddaughter for years. She had taken Srishti to all the happening places and malls in

Delhi and NCR. The exposure to the different cuisines and top of the class restaurants taught her dining etiquettes, whereas the frequent trips to the designer boutiques for clothes and accessories made her aware of the right way of adorning them. She had grown up being a tomboy and the little tips she got there added to her feminine finesse. She was much less critical of her Granny now, and so was the older woman. The two women bonded well surpassing the barrier of two generations between them, and Granny also introduced her to her friends with pride. Looking back and comparing the conduct of her maternal Grandmother from then to now, Srishti wondered, why people always got caught in the slugfest of their imperious aspirations?

Dada Ji and Dadi had stayed in Indore for a week, till she settled down well. The vast campus spread over 193 acres of land built over a hilltop looked breathtakingly beautiful, especially at night overlooking the Indore skyline. The infrastructure was good that provided comfortable living facilities and daily need stores. Rest would come automatically. The home away from home had to cater to the basic needs that came with living on one's own, probably for the first time for most students joining college. Srishti had made friends instantly. She realized that everyone was just as apprehensive about the new surroundings and an independent lifestyle as she was, which brought them all together. Those were the very bonds that would see her through the unsheltered life that she was going to march ahead with.

Dadi would call up every morning to wake her up, and she would call them back before bedtime to tell them how her day was. Her Granny was making amends and called her up regularly. She did feel good to have her extended family back on track. But talking to Naina Masi was still the best. She often gave her advice about making friends, on understanding the advances of the fellow boys or anything in general. Naina would often share her own experiences with her to bring out the similarities and the dissimilarities of their times. A generation-long gap was bound to have made certain things better. Whereas some of the values, she had found were deteriorating and even missing. At times like these, Srishti wished, if she also had her parents to share her anxieties and dreams with. But she knew it too well, what she has got was the best she could get in her circumstances.

The life on campus made her realize that maybe she came from a small town, but her outlook towards life was as accelerative as anyone else her age, if not more. She owed it to her grandparents, who had always allowed her the freedom to take her decisions and stand by them, right or wrong. It let her live her life, the way she'd wanted. Her Grandfather had instilled leadership quality in her, and she wasn't afraid to take the difficulties head-on. She was a freethinking girl, a quality, she'd found missing in a lot of her friends.

Her roommate Aradhana lacked self-confidence and was always looking up to someone to simulate his or her actions. Her overbearing parents would keep on loading her with advice regarding hypothetical issues she might face in her college life. Aradhana always tried finding excuses to finish their prolonged conversation sessions. Srishti often felt that Aradhana might be feeling suffocated with that kind of upbringing.

Vanya, her best friend, was one of her kind. Her parents lived abroad, and she was one feisty girl but that Srishti could handle. Srishti possibly could not be with someone who would sit and brood all day about their haves and have not's. Rest of them was a mixed bag that she would come to know about in due course of time.

She was the part of this big group of newcomers, and they all moved together for fear of ragging and intimidation by the seniors. Soon their phobias were washed away as they settled into their daily routine. Life had started looking up on the campus, and they all were getting used to the mess food. The weekend trip to the local market where they stocked up on their weekly tucks was what all of them looked forward to. Before Srishti knew it, she was at home with her campus. Furthermore, studying the subject, she was always interested in was what made her resilient towards the shortcomings of her cushy life.

And then her first term was over. She was on the moon to go home for the first time after her college had begun and had instructed Dada Ji, not to come to pick her up. He had booked her on a connecting flight from Indore to Delhi to Jammu, and for the first time, she traveled alone, albeit her friends went with her to Delhi.

Before Srishti realized, it was already two years. Time flew as the workload, and field sessions increased. The calls back home would be limited to nights alone. She did keep on feeding her family with pictures of her and her friends amidst several college fests and their outings. Her summer vacations went busy with her internships, which were mostly in Delhi and that, was the time, she got to stay with her maternal grandparents. She'd felt a lot less awkward with them lately.

And then she met Vineet.

Chapter 4

Srishti was back on campus for the third year, the year she completed her Bachelor's degree. The new breed of freshers was around and she along with her friends was eyeing the possible victims for their ragging session, which they had conveniently termed as 'Socials.'

They'd found Vineet walking all alone towards the Admin Block. He was a tall guy with a wheatish complexion and looked extremely athletic. He had an air of arrogance around him and had appeared a little too confident for a fresher. She was ogling at his looks when her friends had dared her to go and rag him. Her throat dried up at the prospect of going up to him and conversing with him, leave alone rag him but she wasn't the one to back down. She'd walked up to him nonetheless.

"Hey there! Fresher?" She mustered up the courage and pointing a finger towards him, asked.

"Yeah. That I'm and Vineet's the name. You are?" He said containing his amusement, throwing a question her way.

Srishti felt sheepish. Her knees went weak, but she held on, keeping a straight face, and responded.

"A senior. And that should do for you. Why don't you come over to my gang and introduce yourself?" She asked, trying to be bold. His demeanor was affecting her, and she knew, she couldn't continue conversing with him for long.

"Well, I'm running a little late for submitting my papers for admission. I guess, your gang would've to wait for that." He said, looking straight into her hazel eyes.

"No worries. Won't stop you from completing your formalities and we'll be around anyway. Will catch you at some suitable time." She said.

He turned to leave as Srishti breathed a sigh of relief to finally get away from him.

"Besides, don't you know, ragging is a punishable offense?" He turned back and looked at a flushed Srishti.

"Yeah! It is. But only if someone complains, and you don't seem like a guy, who would go crying to the Dean or hang himself for being asked his name. Are you?" She almost dared him.

"Damn right, you are. I won't, not if the tormenter is just as beautiful as you are. Can't wait to introduce myself to you. But admission first." He signaled at his file, squeezed his eyes and scrunched up his nose displaying the urgency and ran towards the Admin Block.

Srishti took a deep breath and kept standing there, looking at him disappearing into the office building. Just as she was to turn towards her friends, she saw him leaning backward from behind the wall and waiving at her.

She quickly turned and got back where her friends were sitting.

"Hey, Srish! Looked like, he was the one ragging you." Raman asked.

"Did he look just as yummy from the close up as well?" Trisha asked.

"Stop it guys. Now you don't rag our otherwise Jhansi Ki Rani." Vanya pitched in, and Srishti didn't know if she was pulling her leg just as well or rescuing her. Her friends were mean; to have thrown her in the harm's way and were now enjoying her displeasure.

"You know what, Go. To. Hell!" She got up and left while everyone was laughing at her antics and calling out for her.

Her heart was thudding, and she needed to be alone for a while, to ponder over what just happened. She had always been among guys, in the Army school earlier as well as in the college. The harmless crushes that she'd had in her adolescent years appeared too frivolous compared to what she felt today. It was nothing like anything that she'd experienced before. She fell straight on her bed and closed her eyes to tame her fray nerves, but the horses of her desire went running amok, unbridled and pulling her to the unfamiliar terrains.

She sat up, getting agitated. She can't be thinking about a junior in such a way. He didn't look as young as a student fresh out of school, though. Maybe, he'd taken a gap year or so. He might be of her age. She admonished herself for thinking along those lines. She would have to train her mind not to drool over him when she saw him next. This wasn't happening, and she felt threatened by her own heart. She got up quickly, freshened up, and left to go for her afternoon class.

The next few days went uneventfully. Srishti hadn't seen him around. Her eyes kept searching for him amidst the old and new students, but it seemed as if he'd evaporated into thin air. Her friends had forgotten about him as well. Life was as usual, but as soon as she closed her eyes, the naughty smile stretching his plump lips showing an enormous amount of his pearly white teeth gnawed at her sensibilities, and she had an urge to feel them beneath her fingers. She didn't want to think beyond. Those deep brown eyes piercing through her soul threatened to drown her in them. It had been the end of the week, and she wasn't able to get over her infatuation, instead was diving deep into it. She'd never felt this distracted before and her friends too had not lost a chance to make her realize that.

But then, the inevitable happened. Srishti's last class was canceled, and she was walking back to her hostel, taking a detour to the Pi store.

"Hey, Gorgeous." She heard the notorious voice that had been resonating in her head for days now and was making her lose sleep for almost a week.

She turned, only to see him standing casually against a pillar, his both hands in his pant pockets and that infectious smile playing on his lips. Srishti's cheeks burnt with a sudden flush as her heart raced dangerously in her chest.

"We had a date, I guess." He said again.

"No, we didn't." She mustered up some courage and said.

"A ragging date then." He asked.

"You're pardoned." She retorted and turned to leave quickly. His presence was affecting her big time, and she wanted to run away before she did something silly.

"I couldn't stop thinking about you all these days." He shouted from behind her.

Her feet froze, and she heard his footsteps approaching her, her body engulfed in the warmth that his proximity exuded.

"Talk to me Ms…," He pleaded as he came in front of her keeping a safe distance between them.

"Srishti." She said, restoring a little of her self-confidence and extending her hand. "3rd Year IPM."

"Vineet. First-year PGP. I'm a BS in Economics from IIT Kanpur." He said firmly holding her hand.

"Oh! That's why you weren't among the IPM freshers." She blurted out and repented just as quickly.

A wide grin broke on his face listening to her admission as he tightened his grip on her hand.

"You had been looking for me. Didn't ya?" He asked, reducing the distance between them.

"The ragging date. Remember? Only, I didn't know, you weren't the fresher, we thought you were." She said, trying to make amends.

"You can still rag me. I'm technically a fresher. But the privilege is extended to you, singularly. Wanna take it?" He said, his voice turning husky.

"I'll let it pass. You are my senior nonetheless." She said, trying to pull her hand out of his. He let it go.

"Meet me, Srishti. I want to know you, and as of now, you want it just as well. Come for a friendly date and then if you don't like it, I won't bother you ever. I'm not going to stalk you against your wishes." He pleaded once again.

"OK." She said resigning to his wishes and to her heart as well. She wouldn't have wanted anything more than this right now, and she would have to give it a shot, at least.

"OK, then. Take me wherever you want to take me." He said.

"Now." She asked, surprised.

"What better? It's the weekend. You've got some other engagements?" He asked.

"NO... I mean, nothing is planned, but this was neither. Give me some time to freshen up. I'll see you in an hour at JAM." She responded.

"Sure." He then took out his phone and extended it to her. "Just punch in your number if you don't mind."

"Can this wait, Vineet, till after we meet? I mean..."

"Yeah. Sure. I know what you mean." He said. "See you in an hour," and left.

She also ran away, back to her hostel, completely forgetting what she'd gone to the Pi-store for. She'd to mind her sprinting heart before it exploded with joy right then and there.

Chapter 5

Once in her room, Srishti breathed easy. She gulped some water to cool herself down, trying vainly to shush her bouncing heart, reminding herself, it was just a friendly date. It might not mean anything, once it was over, but today, it won't listen to her.

Srishti rummaged through her wardrobe to find something suitable to wear, something that was not outright be suggestive of her internal upheaval as well as wasn't just too plain to display her indifference. She hadn't known, finding **that** right dress was just so frustrating, more than ever before.

She scrubbed her face clean and did make do with a little moisturizer for her face, accentuated her hazel eyes with brown kohl and applied some lip-gloss on her soft pink lips. She settled for a black pair of Levi's jeans and teamed it up with a fitted black sleeveless vest worn over with a grey lace shrug falling a little short of her toned waist. Leaving her waist length hair loose, wearing her sneakers and a sling bag, she was all set to go. Srishti looked into the mirror once again to approve of her looks and then at her watch. She still had 15 minutes.

Vineet saw her walking towards their designated place. She was early, by ten minutes. A soft smile crept up on Vineet's lips, sensing her urgency. He, himself had reached there half an hour earlier. She looked pretty and confident, very much at ease with herself unlike before when she was too taken aback having confronted by him suddenly. He knew it in his heart that he was affecting her just as much as she was affecting him. There was an unmistakable attraction between the two, and it was too evident in their conduct.

Vineet walked up to her as she smiled at him tentatively.

"Hey." He greeted.

"Hey." She responded.

"Where to?" He asked, and she motioned him towards the outer side of the sports complex.

"Don't want to eat something?" He asked again.

"I'm good. Grab something if you want." She said.

"Let's go then," Vineet said, putting his backpack on his shoulder.

"How do you like it here?" She asked in an attempt to start the conversation as they walked.

"From one campus to another, well... This one's more picturesque." He said, looking intently at her, and she wondered why she had even bothered to ask. Would he ever give a straight answer?

He understood her unease and deflected the topic. "It's quite pleasant and breezy as well; a good living place. How do you like it here?" He asked.

"Great. It's been home for the past two years and still going to be for another three. Haven't had another experience to compare it with. I'm here straight from home." She said.

"Where are you from?" He asked as a sweet smile broke on her lips.

"I guess, I was given the privilege to interrogate you by someone, just a while back and not the other way around." She said with a-tongue-in-cheek, and he burst out laughing.

"Yeah. That you have, so shoot. What do you want to ask?" He stopped, looking over the vast skyline of Indore from where they stood. "Shall we just sit here?" He asked.

She nodded and sat there, looking in the direction he sought.

"This place looks so beautiful, so alive at night. Those twinkling lights spread across the city just keep encouraging and instilling the faith that once we are equipped with our desired knowledge and required skills, we would be adding an equally bright glow to the society." She said, looking dreamily into the infinity.

"A dreamer. Aren't you?" He asked, looking at her intense face.

"Yeah. You can say so. But aren't we all? It's our dreams that keep us awake at night, push us to work harder than our peers, and sustain us among the people we would never have known otherwise. You and I and all the rest out there are only striving to make their dreams come true." She said, turning her face towards him.

"You miss home, don't you?" He asked, his eyes turning soft.

"Yeah. I do. Don't you?" She asked this time.

"Nah! Not much. Been in the hostel since class VI. Dad being in Indian Foreign Services had been traveling across the globe, and Mom accompanied him wherever she could. There hadn't been a home per se. It was more like transit camps, the really posh and five-star transit camps." He said, looking far away.

"On the flip side, you've probably seen half the world or even more. Isn't that awesome?" She asked excitedly.

"Yeah, it is. But that excitement comes with a shelf life, you know. You soon grow out of it. It might seem stimulating to an onlooker, but when you don't have a home to go to in your short breaks and when you don't know where your roots belong, it's terrifying for a child. It's OK now. You learn to live with it." He said.

"You don't have siblings?" She asked.

He laughed vainly.

"Nah. My parents were too busy to give me one. They discharged their biological obligation towards procreation by bringing me to life and got on with what they were born to achieve in life." He said bitterly and asked, "I'm sure you have. Don't you?"

"Nah. Mine didn't live long enough to give me one. I wish they did." She said, looking into oblivion, searching for the stars that were her parents.

"Oh! I... I'm sorry, I... I didn't know." He said stammering, knowing not how to respond.

"That's OK. You won't have known until I told you. That's what we are here for, to know each other. It's just a part of the process, and that happened a long time ago, even I don't remember when." She said, finding her smile back.

He pulled his backpack and took out a bag of chips along with two cans of coke.

"I'm sure we need it now. Hungry, aren't you?" He asked.

"For chips and coke, anytime." She grabbed the can from his hand and opened it to gulp some quickly. She was thirsty, she didn't know.

He kept quiet, trying to find words. Srishti's admission about her parents had put him in a fix as to how to ask about anything, where she grew up and how she managed her life so far. Srishti appeared to have a very well-rounded personality, extremely difficult to attain, in circumstances anyone would think, she lived in.

Srishti sensed his curiosity as well as his dilemma on how to broach the topic. She stated herself to save him the jitters.

"My paternal grandparents have brought me up. Dad was an army Major and was martyred while on duty. Mom followed him shortly to the heavens leaving me behind. But my grandparents are extremely chilled out, so I grew up fine; thoroughly loved, and spoilt. Dada Ji is an ex-army man, a Colonel and Dadi retired as a Principal from Army school. So, there're no complaints from life. I got the best, one could, in those circumstances." She said, bringing back the cheer in her voice.

Vineet took a deep breath and closed his eyes for a while.

"Knowing that you are loved is what makes you who you are. You are lucky that your grandparent's love has touched your heart unlike a lot of those who've had everything but had to feel the vacuum in their lives." He said sighing.

"Listen Vineet. Sometimes we are unnecessarily objective about others because we expect too much. As children, we get angry about what we don't get, and we are justified in our emotions, but that feeling should not and must not survive beyond childhood. As adults, we would have to look beyond, look into the reasoning, and allow others to explain their position but more often than not, our anguish resists us from doing that. It would only hurt you and hurt the ones who care for you." She said, placating him.

He kept looking at her face with awe.

"I guess you're right." He said and then asked suddenly. "Dinner?"

Confused, Srishti looked at her watch. It seemed a bit early for dinner. She felt perplexed, somewhat dejected. Did she upset Vineet? Was she a bit too overbearing with her observations and opinion? Did she overstep her boundaries?

"It's a little early for dinner, I guess. But carry on anyway. I'll see you around." She said, containing her disappointment and started walking to go back. Vineet kept standing where he was, looking at her retreating.

Chapter 6

"I'm sorry if I said something, I shouldn't have." Srishti turned with an afterthought and said.

He knew now what she felt at his sudden change of stance. He kept looking at her, trying to articulate a narrative, to let her know; he didn't mean to hurt her or get away from her, but he couldn't.

She turned and started walking again.

"I'd fall in love with you if we'd stayed the way we did back there, Srishti." He said gruffly.

She stiffened, hearing his words, not knowing whether to feel pleased or distraught. She'd certainly not wanted their first meeting to end so abruptly but to acknowledge his love; so early in their acquaintance was almost suicidal. Srishti didn't have the courage to face him, but her feet wouldn't budge to take her any further away from him.

He came in front of her and looked at her face, confusion, and trepidation written all over.

"I didn't mean to startle you, but you left me no choice. You misunderstood my intention when all I wanted was to prolong our time together for as long as I could but certainly at a place that was a little less intimate and a little more distracting." He said pleading.

"I'm sorry, Vineet, but we just met. We barely know each other." She muttered almost inaudibly, but he heard her.

"My point Srishti. That's why I suggested we left." Vineet said, lifting her chin to look into her eyes now.

"I'd been on dates before, but the connect, I felt with you was a first and I'm sure that you might not believe it or maybe you shouldn't, but that's true. We got here to know each other. It doesn't really matter what color you like or what's your favorite food or a movie or all that crap people talk about on their first date. What we spoke about was straight from the heart, something that you guard against the whole world for fear of being judged. But here I was, with my guards down, baring my insecurities, allowing you in a space where no one has set foot ever before. I felt threatened and expectant all at once, but I knew that you wouldn't understand and would need more time to feel what I felt. Please forgive me and I'll make amends. Take your time. Give us some time. You don't have to rush, and you don't have to do it at all to oblige me if you don't want to. But do promise me, you will think about me, about us." He said, his voice cracking now.

"I will. I would have to if I were to get some sleep." She said, smiling now. "Dinner."

"Yeah. I'm famished. Let's go." He said, taking the phone out of her hand, punching in his number and then giving a call on his phone to save hers. She didn't resist. She didn't want to. Life was opening another door at her, and she was swamped with the feelings of a cosmic pleasure.

They had dinner in one of the canteens.

"So where are you taking me tomorrow." He suddenly asked.

"What's tomorrow?" She asked.

"It's Sunday, and you can show me around Indore city." He said.

She smiled. Vineet appeared too impatient, and she needed to check his speed. He did seem decent, well spoken and well mannered but she wasn't a pro at judging people so quickly. She had only one heart that she'd guarded for so long; she couldn't let it stray away so hurriedly. She needed time, time to think things over, time to analyze his behavior and time to ascertain whether she was ready to let go of herself, to allow someone to share the space she had called her own so far.

"Some deep thoughts." He asked, looking keenly at her taking a bite of his food.

"No, not really. Just thinking about the assignment, I have to submit on Monday. I would need to work on that tomorrow and a seminar that's lined up in a couple of days. Had thought of starting it today but...." She said hesitatingly.

"But I kept you busy for an entire evening. Sorry." He said.

"Don't be. I wouldn't have let you if I hadn't wanted, but yeah, work comes first. So I'll let your offer pass for a while if you don't mind. We can meet sometime in the evening if you are OK with that." She said.

"Beggars can't be choosers, I guess." He said, acting a bit dejected.

"Come on now, Vineet. You don't expect me to usurp my entire schedule because you just happen to come into my life all of a sudden." She said, getting miffed this time. She could handle a boyfriend but not someone who would derail her from her goals, not the must-do types and definitely not the clingy kind.

"Hey. I'm sorry. I was just joking. Get some sense of humor, girl. Loosen up." He said. "But thanks for acknowledging that I've finally come into your life. That would do for now, and we meet in the evening."

She flushed with the realization of what she had just said.

"Aren't you going out with your friends somewhere?" She asked.

"It's too soon to call them friends, classmates - yes. But yeah, there's some plan they were hatching for tomorrow. Will go and find out now that you have chickened out." He said lazily.

She laughed heartily at his boyish quirkiness.

"You know, you're looking like a little boy who's been refused a candy for some reason." She said laughingly.

"Now stop analyzing me. That session is long over, to be resumed tomorrow." Vineet said, taking her dainty hand in his and rubbing it gently with his thumb. She lost all the humor, as an electric current of undefined magnitude ran through her veins, making her aware of him gaining control over her body. She got up with a start.

"I.... I need to go. Go...Good night." She said hurriedly.

"Yeah, you should, before... I mean, good night. I'll call you up tomorrow. Can I?" He asked with an equal unease, feeling the sensations, he wasn't privy to either. Touching her was wrong, very wrong. The more he came closer, the more he wanted her, and it wasn't doing him any good. Besides, he was only making her flustered, something too hard for her to comprehend this early.

She nodded, and they walked towards the hostel complex. Vineet dropped her close to hers before walking back to his.

She saw him walking back, suddenly feeling bare of his aura that had veiled her unknowingly and she'd felt protected and safe with him. She smiled at her own admission and face-palmed her forehead to make such conjectures so soon. She needed to divert her mind. Srishti entered the hostel to be greeted with Vanya's high pitch voice.

"Where the hell had you been? Been trying your number infinitely. Your Dadi had also called. Have you lost your phone?"

"OMG. I'd forgotten to turn it on. I'll tell you later but let me first go and call up Dadi." She said and ran towards her room.

Srishti took the phone out of her pocket. Vanya was right. There had been 22 calls from her and another 8 from home in the last two hours. Damn, she'd forgotten to turn it on after her classes in a hurry to get ready and meet Vineet. She didn't realize that earlier, and when Vineet had taken her phone, there had been no missed calls in the call log. She looked at her watch. It was already 11 pm. Dadi and Dada Ji must be worried. This was not done. One date with Vineet had made her forget about everything and everyone else. This wasn't happening. She won't let it. She made the call home.

Chapter 7

"Sorry, Sorry, Sorry. This won't happen again. My ringer was off." She shouted into the phone as soon as Dadi picked it up.

"Stop it Srishti. You know, I had been so worried, and your friend also didn't know where you were." Dadi reprimanded her.

"I know, and I'm sorry. Was in the library working on an important assignment first, and then we all went for dinner. I simply forgot to turn the phone on. Did I wake you up?" She lied.

"No, you didn't. We had gone out for a pre-wedding cocktail party. We just got back, and before you talk to Dada Ji, know that he doesn't know, I'd called. I told him, my phone had died down, and he had been so busy socializing that he also didn't nag me. Here he comes. Talk to him." Dadi rescued her.

"Hey, Dada Ji. You forgot about me today. Your cocktail party was more important, I guess." She turned the table.

"It's a weekend girl. We have some life too, so chill and let us chill too." Dada Ji was in a light mood, and she knew why.

"Good then. Now you go and rest. I'll call you tomorrow when you are a little soberer." She said, laughing and cut the call. She felt a lot lighter.

Vineet was right. To know that you are loved, and there's someone to guard your back gives you the confidence to face the world differently.

She hated lying to Dadi, but it was too early for any kind of admission. She could talk to Naina Masi about it, but that also would have to wait.

She had to make her own opinion first before she gave anyone the right to peek into her personal life. This was a little too personal, and she didn't want to call for unnecessary advice that could influence her own opinion. However insecure, she had felt treading along that path in the past, she knew one thing that when the time comes to take the leap, it would be her personal decision. She couldn't be spoon-fed on this account and whether it worked or not, it had to be her own doing.

She sat on her bed, contemplating something when Vanya opened the door. She had been her roommate since last year.

"Where are you lost, girl? Heard that you had been with some drop-dead gorgeous senior if the grapevine is to be believed." Vanya came and patted her back.

"That was quick. Wasn't it? The news does travel fast on the campus." She said, leaning back while looking at her.

"Didn't you know that? But yeah, it's different when you are on the other side of the fence. So tell me, who is he?" Vanya asked impatiently pulling a chair to sit close to her.

"You remember the guy, near the admin block, I'd gone to rag a few days back, thanks to you all. I met him this afternoon and ..." She said, but Vanya cut her short in the middle with excitement.

"That fresher. But I heard he is some senior. How?" She asked.

"Yeah, that fresher. Vineet is a PGP fresher and thus our senior. So if you are done with your interrogation, I'll go and freshen up." She got up quickly to end the conversation, but Vanya was quicker. She pulled her hand down and got her to sit on the bed.

"No dear. I'm not done yet. So tell me the juicy details. How did you meet? What he said and how you responded? What did you both talk about? Is he just as sexy to talk to as he looks? Damn, I should have gone to rag him myself that day, if I knew he was a senior." Vanya's enthusiasm was contagious, and Srishti had to calm her down.

"Hold your horses' girlfriend. He's taken now. Besides, it was just a friendly date. What do you expect would have happened? We just talked." Srishti said.

"Taken! Already! That too on the first date or rather a friendly date. Mind your own words Srishti, you are contradicting yourself." Vanya said.

"So... What do you want, I tell you? Oh Yeah, Vanya! We held hands, snuggled up real close, kissed and blah blah blah. Would that do to calm your over-excited brain? You know, you need a boyfriend too, to cater to your overactive imagination." She laughed, but Vanya wasn't the one to back down.

"Yeah, I too need a boyfriend. Too. Seriously Srishti. He's already your boyfriend. Is it? Show some restraint girl. Don't be so easy? Guys judge the girls very lowly, who give in this soon. You must...." Vanya went on, but that was what Srishti didn't like.

Opinions and more opinions She cut her in the middle and cupped her cheeks.

"You know, I'll take your advice when I need it. Right now, I'm tired and happy, and I just want to relive what I felt today. So don't disturb." Saying that she ran to the washroom.

"OK, Ms. Smarty pants. I'm around when you need me." Vanya shouted from behind.

"I hope I don't need to. But if I do, I will." She shouted excitedly from behind the closed door of the washroom before Vanya could hear the sound of music from her phone and turn on of the shower.

Vanya plunked on her own bed, feeling happy for her friend. She put on her headphones to watch some random video. She had to let her friend soak in the newfound feeling of love or whatever it might be.

Srishti came out in her pajamas, feeling fresh.

"You know, he wanted to..." She was about to tell her something but seeing her busy watching the video, she smiled at her best friend's gesture, to let her be on her own. She went up to her and kissed her on the cheek and lipped a quiet thank you. She then came back to lie on her own bed, turning the lights off. Sleep was far away, but she could try.

Her phone beeped with an incoming message. It was Vineet.

Vineet: *Will be going to the city after breakfast. Would it be possible to meet before dinner, if you are done with your work?*

Srishti: *Yeah. Sounds good.*

Vineet: *Hope I didn't bore you today.*

Srishti: *No, you didn't. In fact, I forgot to call up Dadi. There were thirty missed calls from her and my roomie together while we dined. Proves, I undoubtedly was pleasantly engaged.*

Vineet: *Also proves that I still have a chance.*

Srishti: *Don't count your chickens before they are hatched.*

Vineet: *A guy can dream. Right. Besides, someone just told me how important dreams are.*

Srishti: *So, would you allow us now to plunge into them, and that would only happen if we slept.*

Vineet: *Some dreams are seen with eyes wide open. You are one of them. Yeah, and we'll surely sleep someday (?) but right now, let's get some sleep. Good Night.*

Srishti: *You are incorrigible, and you know that. Right. Good Night, anyway.*

Vineet: *I wish I could see that blush on your face. Some other time, maybe. Good Night. Finally.*

She exited the chat but kept holding the phone close to her chest. To say Srishti was blushing would have been an understatement. Her entire body felt on fire, in anticipation of what the future held for both of them.

She wasn't the only one whose mind was sprinting way ahead of their relationship status.

She was hardly sane enough to comprehend her own reaction leave alone his. But she could very well dream and dream she did.

Chapter 8

Srishti got up lazily as it was a Sunday. It was a bright morning and even a brighter day ahead. She tried waking up Vanya, but she refused to get up. Srishti freshened up quickly to go for breakfast so that she might be able to see him around before he left for the town. The urgency of her demeanor surprised her as well, but she didn't want to rein in herself just yet.

She ate her breakfast half-heartedly talking disinterestedly with her friends present there when she couldn't meet him.

She definitely had the option to go out with him, and she'd pretty much lied to him about the work she needed to do. She thought it only necessary to check his speed, but right now, her heart was revolting against her brain. She shrugged the depressing thoughts away and indulged in the gossiping, her friends were doing or the pranks they were playing, things that always gave her pleasure.

It was then; she realized if all of what that had given her joy all along, was it worth sacrificing for an instinctive relationship, she was so looking forward to forming with Vineet. The friends who had been there for last two years and each one of them had helped shape her ideas, views, and imagination towards some aspect of life, should she be intending to let go of all that because she found a chance at falling in love with a guy she just met. It felt risky, and in her heart, she knew, she would never be able to be selfish enough to distance herself from the very people who adored her.

She took the resolve right then and there that she would not let Vineet or his thoughts break her away from her friends. They had been her support system for all the time that she'd spent on the campus and would remain so until they were together or maybe more. They split after a while to go their separate ways.

Srishti completed her assignment quickly, she knew she would have and finished her seminar topic, which only needed a few observations to be written. It took her max a couple of hours. Vanya then roped her in for their spa session, helping each other with the face and head massage, doing their nails and epilating their arms and legs, finally finishing with the face pack. It was their usual Sunday routine. Vanya was high on keeping herself well groomed, and in the last two years, Srishti had learned to be just as feminine. They grabbed a quick lunch to complete their sojourn. Before the evening fell, they were squeaky clean, but the glow on Srishti's face told a different story, her attention focused entirely on any vibration in her phone. Vanya kept on pulling her leg.

She took out the long one-piece number in the abstract shades of blue, her granny had insisted on buying when they went shopping during her summer break. She had thrown it at the back of her cupboard thinking; it was too girly. Today, she found it flattering. It fell a little above her ankles. The collared neck dipped down to a modestly deep V with buttons running in the middle down to her waist. She clinched her slim waist with a narrow belt in black and teamed it up with black bellies. Vanya did her hair in soft curls. She completed her look with an eyeshade in pale blue and blue eyeliner and a lip-gloss in pink. Vanya had joked that her cheeks looked too colored to shame the blush on, so she did without it. Srishti's heart thudded in her chest, waiting for his call. After pacing her small room for about half an hour, she sat down disappointed. It was already six, and he hadn't called. She felt like calling him up, but Vanya snatched her phone. She didn't resist.

Just when she thought of changing into her pajamas, her phone vibrated with a message. It was Vineet.

Vineet: *Hey there! I just got back. Can we meet in another half an hour? Need a shower badly.*

Srishti: *Yeah. Same place. See ya.*

She found the spring back in her gait. She got up instantly and swirled Vanya around in excitement. She was finally going on a date.

Her enthusiasm was killing her, and that took her to JAM 5 minutes before time. She knew that she was making her keenness to meet him too apparent and though Vanya had suggested her to exercise restraint, she didn't care. She'd missed him, and she didn't want to shy away from the fact. The magnetic pull she felt towards Vineet was unprecedented, nothing like she had ever felt before.

After waiting for 5 minutes, she saw him running towards her, and her heart skipped a beat. Vineet looked breathtakingly handsome in his green T-shirt and blue denim, his freshly washed face misted with the droplets of water from his wet hair, he had probably forgotten to comb. The expressions on his face were priceless as she felt his urgency to reach her and for a moment, she thought, he might come and take her in his arms. Her face flushed at her own thoughts as a breathless Vineet came and stood in front of her mouthing a quick Hi.

"Hi." She responded.

They left from there to go towards the Sports Complex where they sat the previous day.

"Missed me?" He asked, looking hopefully at her face.

"Yeah. Kind of." She said, looking at him briefly before averting her eyes.

"But I missed you definitely." He said as they walked.

"But you were with friends or like you say, your classmates." She asked.

"That doesn't change anything. I wasn't with you is reason enough to miss you. Isn't it?" He said.

"Well, I'm hardly in a position to comment on that." She said and continued. "So, how're your classmates. I'm sure a few of the girls must have made a pass at you. Didn't they?"

"Jealous. Already?" He asked.

"Nooooo. Not jealous. Curious maybe." Srishti said as he motioned her to sit.

"Well, in that case, I didn't notice even if anyone did. My indifference might have signaled my 'Not interested' intent to them." He said. "What did you do today?" He asked.

"Just finished my work and then spent a little girly time with my roomie and best friend, Vanya." She said, thinking about how impatiently she had waited to get a call from him, her cheeks turning red again.

"It shows." He said, looking intensely at her face.

"Meaning?" She asked, looking up at him as his eyes tried boring into her soul.

"You are very beautiful Srishti, on the outside as well as inside but the efforts that you have put in to look the way you do right now, I can't take my eyes off you. I had so wanted to take you in my arms, the moment I saw you standing there. Your looks aren't helping to contain my desires. Please don't do it, at least until the time you are ready to acknowledge and reciprocate my Love." Vineet said, closing his eyes and lying down on the grass with his both hands under his head.

She didn't know how to respond. The constant conflict between her head and the heart was making it impossible for her to react rationally. She merely looked at him, his face looking innocent and composed all at once. She wanted to trust him and tell him; she felt all those emotions just as well, but there was something that restricted her from admitting it to him. Was it her upbringing, where Dadi and Dada Ji had always coached her not to trust strangers, especially boys or was it about the omnipresent stories of betrayal of the guys that left the unsuspecting girls to bear the brunt of their wrong judgment? She didn't want to stand in that queue.

Though Vineet looked trustworthy, she was sure, most people do before they break that trust. After all, the trust can only be broken if it was there in the first place. How could she be sure about the legitimacy of Vineet's words? Would she be able to feel the extent of heat without burning her hands in it, she didn't know?

"Hey. Sorry if I startled you, yet again." Vineet suddenly brought her out from her deep thoughts as he sat up beside her, coming out of his own contemplations.

She looked sideways at him and smiled.

"You are good with words, Vineet. I don't know how to make a distinction between your compliments and your objections. Great deal to learn but I guess, I'll get through, even if it took some time." She said.

"Hey, don't bother. I wasn't complaining. You might not believe it Srishti, and I agree that it's too soon to profess my love, but that's exactly how I feel. Your dilemmas are justified, and I won't contest them or try to persuade you into giving in to my wishes but allow me to express them as I desire." He said.

Then he looked at the ever-changing expressions on her face and took her hand in his rubbing it gently.

"You have touched my heart and believe me; no rulebook tells you as to how long should you see someone before you fall in love. It's instinctive. You might not, but I think I can make a distinction between what a crush feels like and what

I feel for you. As far as you are concerned, you would have to take the call yourself, whenever you want." He said, and she nodded quietly.

"I...I do feel something along those lines Vineet, but I'm scared, actually terrified. I can act all brave and confident when it comes to studies or sports, but I'm not just as emotionally strong to bear the heartbreak. I want to believe you, but this rational side of me keeps checking me, stopping me all the time. I'd been thinking of you, about you ever since I saw you first. I did feel the connect howsoever I might want to believe otherwise but....." She tried articulating her thoughts, but Vineet was quick to cut her halfway.

"Say no more Srishti. I got what I wanted to know, and now I'll make sure that I make my love, our love believable, to you and to all those who matter to both of us." He said quickly turning towards her balancing himself on his knees and continued. "I'm into this for a long haul girl, a very-very long haul, the forever kind. You better not chicken out now."

He held her face between his palms as she lowered her eyes, her cheeks; a deep color of red. But then she lifted her lids to look into his eyes.

"We barely know each other Vineet. What if we didn't like certain things about us? What if I didn't turn out to be the girl you thought I was or the other way around? What if...." Her confusion dripped out in her words. Vineet kept his finger on her lips.

"Shhh. No what-ifs Srishti. Life is too short for what-ifs. Love is not about finding the right blend of desired attributes in a person. It is a journey to discover the other as well as yourself and to accept each other with the flaws, the imperfections they come with. Loving me would not mean that you have to like everything I do or say. The relationship that takes away the identity of the other person or stifles the other is not love, it can't be." Vineet said, shushing her doubts.

"You are from Mars or what Vineet? I haven't heard someone say so or do so. Everyone I know of seems trying to over-shadow the other until their identity is totally obscure, especially the women being the victims of it. What you say is all idealistic, something that no one follows." She said with a sarcasm laced with bitterness.

"Well, I can't dispute that in a larger context, but maybe you haven't met or known those women who have broken out of the mold. On my account, I can promise you that. Take it as my **First Vow of Love** that 'you would never lose your identity as long as I'm with you rather as long as I'm alive' because I'm never going to leave you till my last breath." He said, sitting beside her again, resting his palms on the grass behind him, stretching his neck to draw a deep breath as a feeling of contentment washed over his face.

"That's a quite a promise Vineet, too good to be true but you know what, I'll take your word for it. I would follow my heart from now on." She said sitting crossed legs now tilting her head back to look at his face.

A soft smile crept up on Vineet's lips, and he sat upright and put an arm around Srishti's waist to pull her closer and left a tender kiss on her head. She rested her head on his shoulder, and the two kept sitting in silence for a while. Too many words had been spoken already, and too many emotions exchanged. It was time to immerse in the aura of their newfound Love.

Chapter 9

Vanya was eagerly waiting for her when she entered the room after having dinner with Vineet.

"Hey, baby girl. How did the date go?" Vanya shouted as soon as Srishti closed the door.

Srishti came close and hugged her tight.

"He said he is so in love with me. I'm in love too, Vani and I don't want to hide it from him." She said dreading Vanya's lecture about how soon was it to accept that, but on the contrary, Vanya surprised her with her enthusiasm.

"Really. Vineet professed his love. You are one lucky girl, babe. For a guy to actually commit to a relationship this early, it's a first of the ones I've heard of. Most of them simply like to fool around. I must meet your Casanova. Wow!" Vanya said coming out of the hug her hands still resting on Srishti's shoulders.

"So you don't think it was a bit too early to make such proclamations?" Srishti asked, looking totally shocked at Vanya's words. She had actually come prepared to get a lecture from Vanya when she told her about what happened between the two of them.

"You don't plan to fall in love, Srish. Love just happens, and if you two are sure about your feelings, time, or timing is hardly a subject worth debating. Just remember, he'll be leaving the campus a year before we do. Watch your steps and tread carefully." Vanya said, very thoughtfully.

"I know that but what should I be careful about Vani? I can't tell him to stay back after he's done in here. He would have to take up the job that he's been offered. And that is still two years apart. Should I not go around with him?" She asked, totally confused.

"Hey, no. I didn't mean that silly. You won't have to do anything. Just listen to your heart, and it will guide you rightly. I only want to see you happy always, as happy as you are today." Vanya said, hugging her again. She felt calmer now. Vanya's approval meant a great deal to her.

"So when are you introducing him to the gang and to me?" She asked excitedly.

"Very soon." Srishti chirped and ran to the washroom to freshen up.

That night, Dadi was quick to catch the music in her voice, but she simply dodged her by telling that she was happy to participate in some play for the college fest. She knew Dadi would believe her. Though she felt awful keeping a secret from her, but these were early days to announce her relationship status.

Having packed her bags and readied the dress for the next day, both friends dived into bed and started looking up for Vineet's profile on Facebook. Vanya's enthusiasm was infectious, and Srishti wanted to know what kind of life did he lead before he met her. Why didn't she think of doing this earlier, she didn't know?

Vineet looked too hot in his profile pic taken on a beachside somewhere abroad. His white linen trousers folded up and his sunrise yellow linen shirt unbuttoned, his toned muscles peeping out of it and the sleeves folded way above the elbows resting at the peaks of his inflated biceps with his hair gelled back. She wondered if that pic was taken professionally for some modeling assignment.

"Oh My God Srish! He's too hot. Though I'm tempted to look into his picture gallery, I'm not sure if I could handle it without getting dirty thoughts in my mind. I hope you won't mind that. Would you?" Vanya asked jokingly, getting away from the laptop and sitting up.

"Hey. Vineet is officially taken now. Back off." Srishti laughed back, turning her head towards her, and both the friends broke into a fit of laughter.

Just then, Srishti's Facebook account pinged with an incoming notification. It was a friend request from Vineet. She excitedly added him and went back to his profile. Something had changed. It was his relationship status that stated; *'Taken...Forever'*.

Her heart skipped a beat. Was it for real or she was needlessly hallucinating? Vineet's enthusiasm concerning her was both mindboggling and terrifying at the same time. She wasn't still able to decode his impatience; if it was the honesty of his heart or the childlike eagerness to own something just instantly because the latter had a tendency to let go of it just as soon as they got it. She wanted to believe the former.

Her chat box appeared with the incoming message.

Vineet: *Hey! What's up?*

Srishti: *Just stalking you.*

Vineet: *Quite rightfully! So what did you find?*

Srishti: *Couldn't stop ogling over your profile pic to proceed further.*

Vineet: *No worries, babe! I can arrange a live performance just for you, anytime you want.*

Srishti: *Shameless.*

Vineet: *Whatever. Did you see my relationship status?*

Srishti: *Quite in a hurry; aren't you?*

Vineet: *It's called time management. Sooner we begin, more time we get to be with each other. Would you want it any other way?*

Srishti: *I guess, not.*

Vineet: *Then stop worrying and start missing me.*

Srishti: *There are other things to do as well, Mr. Casanova. And yeah, this is the name given to you by Vanya, my bestie.*

Vineet: *I already like her. Say Hi to her for me.*

Srishti: *She says Hi as well. Don't you wanna get some sleep now. We've got a class in the morning.*

Vineet: *Good night, then. I'll hang around for a while to check you out on your profile.*

Srishti: *There's nothing too exciting to sacrifice your sleep over.*

Vineet: *I'm a man of simple needs, Srishti. Your carefree smile is the most interesting thing for me. You're looking so innocent, so pristine in the photographs taken probably at Golden Temple with your grandparents.*

Srishti: *Yeah. It was during the vacations.*

Vineet: *I don't know what you are doing to me, babe. All I want to do now is to think about you, and it's a first.*

Srishti: *Don't overthink, Vineet. Sleep now. We'll meet tomorrow. Good night.*

Vineet: *Good night. Love you.*

Srishti: *Love you too.*

Vineet: *OMG, Srishti! Should I take a snapshot of it?*

Srishti: *Would you stop embarrassing me Vineet? Good night.*

Vineet: *Thanks love, for acknowledging my love and reciprocating it as well. Good night.*

And she turned off the chat box looking sheepishly at Vanya who was giving her accusatory smiles.

"Happy," Vanya asked.

"Very." She said.

"I'm happy for you too. I sincerely hope it does work out well for two of you." Vanya said.

Srishti raised her hands to show her the fingers crossed, and Vanya shook her head in amazement, looking at the expressions on her friend's face. They wished each other good night and went to sleep on their respective beds to sleep.

Srishti closed her eyes to sleep, but Vineet's words and his drop dead gorgeous looks in the pic were sure to keep her awake for a while.

She so wanted to run her hands through his messy hair and touch those luscious lips. Her hands itched to feel his naked torso under them, to explore the heart he professed that beats for her. She shook her head to get over her wild imaginations as she felt a sudden impulse, the longing in her core. She took a few deep breaths to help her tide over this new found yearnings, she better be away from as long as she could. Her body and mind needed to be reined in now, and she knew where she stood as far as her boundaries allowed her to be.

On the other end, sleep was eluding Vineet. He had looked her up on Facebook and sent her the friend request. She'd responded within moments, and that had pleased him knowing, she'd trusted him to allow him into her personal space. He was so amused to look at her profile. The girl was far from malice and was innocence personified. Her liveliness exuded from her pictures taken with her grandparents, both paternal and maternal, with her college friends and those with the school friends. Even the single ones were charming and cute. It did not seem, she had put an effort to look attractive or sexy, but her carefree attitude and her simplicity coupled with her beautiful face and athletic built were oozing with sex appeal. At that moment, all Vineet wanted was to hold her close to his heart and protect her from the world full of deceit. He wanted her badly, and he knew she wanted him too. Only, they would have to let their relationship gain the much-needed confidence to further their proximity. With these thoughts in mind, Vineet held his pillow in an embrace, wishing for the day, it would be her in his arms, and her scent would surround him making him forget the shortcomings of his life.

Chapter 10

Mondays were hectic with back-to-back classes and workshops. She dropped on her bed tired by the evening. Since morning, she hadn't had time to think about him. He had also not called. Maybe, he was just as busy, she thought. It was 5 pm already, but she needed to take a shuteye if she wanted to hang on till dinner. She set the alarm to get up after half an hour and dozed off. It was the vibration of her phone that broke her slumber five minutes before her alarm was to go off. She groggily looked at her mobile. It was a message from Vineet that brought her out of her woozy state suddenly making her alert. She opened the text messages and found that there was a string of them from him. They read,

7.35am: Good Morning, sleepy head.

8.33am: Hey! Wish me Good morning, babe. Still sleeping or what?

11.32am: Too busy to reply, I guess. Hope your assignment went well.

2 pm: Hellooooo. Where are you? Aren't you having lunch?

5.25pm: I hope, you are back from college. Look at your phone for a change. Someone is dying to hear from you. I hope I wasn't merely a weekend crush.

Srishti looked at the chain of messages, her mind entirely puzzled on how best to respond to him. She'd been busy throughout the day, and the phone had been on silent during the college hours. Vineet is supposed to know that, she thought. The morning message was fine, but he didn't need to do that repeatedly like an obsessed lover. But next moment she softened her stand. Shouldn't she feel happy that he cared? That's when she responded.

Srishti: *Hey there! Sorry. Got up a little late, so rushed for classes in a hurry. Had a very hectic day. The assignment went well. Thanks. And no, you sure aren't a weekend crush. See you in an hour to prove the point.*

Vineet: *Waiting.*

Vanya was back by then equally tired.

"Hey! God, I'm so tired. How was your day?" Vanya asked, dropping herself on her bed.

"Too packed. Want some tea. I'm going down. Should I get some for you too?" She asked.

"Please. You are an angel." Vanya said, throwing her face into the pillow and Srishti left.

Having freshened up in a while, when Srishti got ready to go out, Vanya asked her where she was going.

"To meet the lover boy. He's been texting since morning." She said ruffling Vanya's hair.

"So from now on, are you going to spend all free time with him. What about our time together? What about spending time with the rest of the gang? Don't you think you'll alienate yourself from everyone else?" Vanya asked.

Srishti looked at her puzzled and sat on her bed with a thud. Vanya had suddenly given her the reality check; she, herself, had taken a resolve to take care of it.

"You know, I want to be with you guys too, to spend our free time but I guess this relationship is too new. Allow me some time. I'm sure, this eagerness, this restlessness will eventually subside once we've known each other a little bit more. I'll be with him for an hour or so and join you all for dinner. Promise." She said pleading. Vanya opened her arms, and the two of them hugged each other before Srishti left happily. She knew what Vanya had said was right, and she would want to be mindful of her fears just as well.

She saw him closer to her hostel block from where they left to explore the length and width of the campus to find a much-needed quieter spot. There were students all over; some in groups, some couples and some merely strolling all by themselves. Srishti waved at a few as they passed them to proceed towards the place they knew, they would find calm.

"Too busy or just avoiding." He asked.

"Why? Don't you believe me?" She asked.

"I want to but just wanted to make sure." He said shrugging.

"What if I lied?" She asked.

"Well, that, I'm sure you won't." He said.

"Too much confidence." She asked.

"You are too transparent to hold on to a lie." He said, pulling her closer and holding her by her waist as they walked.

She felt a shiver run down her spine. The picture of Vineet showing his toned abs and biceps from his profile pic crossed her mind, and she closed her eyes and took a deep breath to tame her mind.

"You. All right." He asked.

"Yeah. I'm good." She said.

"You can tell me if you don't like me holding you Srishti." He said, leaving her and standing in front of her.

"It's OK, Vineet." She said, looking down, her face streaked with the color of love, his Love. How could she even tell him that his mere touch had made all her nerve endings stand out and all he did was to put an arm around her back? His proximity, his scent, and his touch were sending her imaginations wayward.

He held both her hands and motioned her to sit down.

"Are you comfortable? You look a little restless today." He asked again.

"It's new Vineet. All these feelings, they are too new. I'm apprehensive and confused." She said.

"About us." He asked.

"Nooooo. It's about the things that I'm capable of feeling. I've been with boys all my life, in school, in sports activities and here in college as well. I've never felt anything, you know. Their patting on the back, those friendly hugs, they never felt like anything but with you, I feel like a different person, the girl I never knew I was. It's threatening." She said, trying to explain.

Vineet took a deep breath and smiled and then took her hand in his.

"You know, you are priceless. This is what love is. This is the chemistry between two people that bonds them together. If it weren't there, I would have been just another of your friends, Srishti and that I'm not. Just enjoy this bliss. Not many people get this in their relationship and trust me, I would never push you to move out of your comfort zone until you are ready." He said gently rubbing her hand with his thumb.

She looked at his face, honesty dripping through his eyes and she knew, she could trust him on that. She came closer and sat beside him, keeping her head on his shoulder, and he smiled at her gesture putting his arm around her. They talked about the random stuff, about college and other things till her alarm beeped.

"Why have you set the alarm for now?" He asked, surprised.

"Because I've to go. My friends are waiting." She said, running her fingers through her hair.

"Noooo. So early?" He complained, his eyes questioning her decision.

"It's been over an hour Vineet." She said justifying.

"Exactly. Just about an hour. Stay for a while longer." He pleaded.

"Our **Second Vow of Love** Vineet. 'I will not let myself be excluded from my core group of friends, and I guess the same goes for you too.' Being an only child, I have learned how important your friends and your peers could be to you. You and I can't live in isolation. So please, go out there and make friends. This relationship that's brewing between us is going to take long before it culminates into a forever like we would want it to be but in the process, don't let go of the other good things that you can have from life." She said thoughtfully.

"You know, you speak like a grandmother sometimes. Where do you get so much of wisdom from?" He said, looking at her, surprised.

"The successes or achievements in life never teach you as much as the failures and losses would Vineet. Everyone looks at the surface as to how happy I am and perceive me to be content, but no one looks deep inside. Probably I don't let anyone see in there to gain sympathy, but the loss of my parents is the biggest shortcoming of my life.

Life is so unpredictable Vineet. I survived because I had my grandparents who came across as my anchors. We need these anchors in life as Life has this funny way of springing those surprises or maybe shocks when you least expect them. Don't invest all your energies into one relationship howsoever strongly you might feel about it. Go and make friends and spend time with them as well. I'm not going anywhere. We'll keep meeting." She said getting up now giving him her hand to pull him up

He got up as well.

"I'll miss you." He said still holding her hand and bringing it towards his lips looking intently at her face all the while. The blush returned to her face, but she didn't make an effort to pull her hand back. He placed a lingering kiss on her hand, all the while, feeling the tremor in her body. Vineet pulled her closer into a protective embrace as she stood cuddled to him, her palm resting against his heaving chest. Srishti closed her eyes and took a deep breath to contain the rush that had erupted in her own heart.

"Shall we?" He asked when she didn't move for a while.

"Yeah." She said coming out of his embrace and nodded, her eyes still lowered.

He lifted her chin, urging her to look up. "You, all right."

"I am. Let's go." She said, smiling, and they left.

The mess was abuzz with high-pitched conversations like always when she entered it. She looked around for her friends before Meenakshi called out her name loudly to attract her attention, and she proceeded to go to their table. There were all of them, Ronit, Trisha, Vanya, Meenakshi, Naman, Smita, Brijesh, Satvik and Ishan, all nine of them. They made a group of a perfect ten. Meenakshi and Naman were going around, and so were Trisha and Satvik. Ronit was trying to woo Vanya for quite some time, but she wasn't interested. Though they had made sure it did not come in the way of their friendship.

"Missing in action babe. What's this we hear about?" Ronit asked.

"And what would that be that you heard, if I may humbly ask?" She said, pulling a chair and sat.

"Oh come on Srish. The whole world knows. Tell us what happened?" Smita asked.

"Your definition of the world seems quite misplaced. There's a lot more beyond the campus." She said, teasing them.

"Stop fooling around and tell us the details," Ishan said with finality.

"OK. If you insist, all I can say is 'Love Happened.' His name is Vineet, the guy you all had pushed me to rag the other day. Seems like I was the one who got ragged, but you know what, I don't mind." She smiled.

"That junior, that fresher we spotted a few days back," Brijesh asked wrinkling his forehead.

"Turns out, he sure was the fresher but not a junior. He's a PGP fresher, a graduate in Economics from IIT Kanpur." She said now looking at the amazed faces of her friends.

"Can we eat something if you are done grilling me? I'm famished." She said.

"That's why you hadn't had dinner with us for the last two days. And how come you came in early tonight?" Satvik asked, pulling her leg.

"You know what, I have decided that no one can take the place you all hold in my life. I'll spend some time with him, but I certainly can't let go of what we all have between us. It means a lot to me." She said on a serious note, looking at all of them. That made them a bit too emotional as all the friends got up to envelop her in a group hug.

At the far end of the mess, Vineet stood looking at her table, and he knew what she meant when she spoke about her friends. Maybe she was right. He never thought about life the way she did. Vineet knew what he had to do now before he waved at his own group of classmates that he should start making an effort to call them and bond with them as friends.

Chapter 11

Life on the campus got busier by the day with one event or another. Between the classes and workshops and outdoor activities, Srishti and Vineet tried finding time to spend with each other.

It was the first year when the cultural fest called 'Atharv' was organized on the campus, and all the undergraduate students were making sure, it was a success. It was time to celebrate life with friends and showcase their talents among peers from the other colleges. Srishti participated along with her other friends with zeal. Vineet contributed wherever he needed to as she kept on pulling him into doing something or the other. All in all, the fest was a great time to bond with her and her friends as well. It probably was the first time he enjoyed himself in a cultural fest, her enthusiasm rubbing on him.

They spent an hour or so together every evening and went for some movie or lunches on the weekends. Vineet loved Srishti's easy-going nature, her smile that could light up any dark space and she loved his unwavering love which came with a restraint, Vineet exercised to not push her into physical intimacy, something, she wasn't yet ready for.

Before they knew it, the exams started, and it was the time for the term break after that.

Her flights were booked two days after her exams got over and so were his along with most of their friends. They called it the buffer period, to enjoy, after the term before leaving for home.

"I'm gonna miss you." He said, putting an arm around her squeezing her sideways when they met after their last exam.

"I won't have it any other way. Of course, you are gonna miss me and so would I, but we'll talk on the phone." She said, resting her own hand on top of his around her waist.

"I'm going to Wellington, to Mom and Dad. I'll stay over in Delhi for three days and then fly off to New Zealand." He said.

"Wow. That's great. But why do you sound so low, Vineet? I'm sure your phone would work there. We can chat or call. Go home happily. They are your parents. Just reciprocate their love without judging them." She said.

"I'll try. Thanks. Stay with me for a day before we leave. We can get a hotel room in the city, or you can stay at my house in Delhi if you are breaking the journey in Delhi. I'll have your tickets altered." He said, looking hopefully in her eyes. She looked stunned.

"I can't Vineet." She said, coming out of his arms.

"Why, Srish? Don't you love me enough? Don't you trust me with you?" He asked.

"I don't think, I'm ready to take the leap, not as yet, Vineet. I don't feel adequate to take such a huge decision about my life. I'd rather wait till I know, what I'm doing would have consequences, consequences that I can handle if something were to go wrong." She said, sitting down on the grass.

"What consequences Srish? We love each other, and you know what you mean to me. I can handle whatever it might be. Trust me. And you are one big girl. You will be 21 in a couple of months, many years beyond the minimum age of consent." He said, sitting in front of her and cupping her face in his hands.

She smiled ruefully and held his both hands, taking them away from her face.

"What's with the minimum age a criterion, Vineet? The minimum marks needed to pass an exam is 40% or so. Do we strive to attain that? We don't. Then, why fuss? One needs to be mentally ready to take that call. I know I'm not." She said and closed her eyes and said with an afterthought, "I'm sorry if I disappointed you. I won't hold you back, though. You are free to exercise your liberties with whomsoever you thought fit as long as it was no strings attached. Just don't tell me about it."

"**Are you crazy woman? Who does that? What am I, some sex-craving maniac?** I love you Srishti, and I can wait for you, for as long as it takes. There's a difference in wanting you and simply wanting a sexual release. But I guess, you would never know till you felt it the way I do. Take your time." He said, sitting beside her encircling his knees with his arms and continued. "When I asked you to come and stay with me, this was not what was on my mind, Srish. All I wanted was to stay close to you and hold you in my arms for as long as possible or maybe kiss you. I'm sorry if I came across too strong." He said, looking at her sideways.

Srishti softened. Did she jump the gun in reading too much in Vineet's proposal? Yeah, he was right. Merely sharing a space with him wouldn't lead her into submission if she didn't want to. She too wanted to spend some quiet time with him without having to rush back to her hostel. She did trust Vineet to respect her wishes, even when they were in a closed room.

"When do we leave Vineet?" She asked, looking back at him, a soft smile playing on her lips.

"You don't have to do it if you don't want." He said.

"I wouldn't if I didn't want." She said.

"Tomorrow afternoon. Spend this evening with your friends." He said, suggesting.

"Yeah. That would do. Now cheer up. Sorry for misunderstanding you." She said.

"I'm good. But tell me honestly, why did you think, I wanted to go all the way when I suggested that we stayed together?" He asked, mocking her.

"What else would that mean?" She confronted.

"That's what you think. Okay. Your mind wouldn't wander there if you weren't thinking about me, fantasizing about me." He said, lying back on the grass smirking.

"Vineet. Stop mocking me." She shouted and got up to go, but he was quick to hold her hand and pulled her down. She sat back miserably, failing to hide her silly grin behind her mock anger.

"Come on, Srish. Take it easy. Wanting someone is not a crime, and it sure is not in our control not to think about it. To make it happen is surely a matter of choice." He said, pulling her closer and left a peck on her lips for the very first time. Her eyes opened wide in amazement as her body craved for more. She simply pulled her hand out of his and ran away. She was going to have all the time in the world with him come tomorrow, and now she was looking forward to it.

Srishti spent the entire evening with her friends. They went shopping, watched a movie and went out for dinner but all the while she was with them, her mind wandered around Vineet. He was invoking new feelings in her day in and day out. She didn't know how she would live the next month without as much as seeing him. Spending time with him had become a habit for her now, and she was dreading her own reaction towards him when she was alone with him in the secure confines of a room, a place too intimate to exercise restraint.

Vineet was right. Not thinking about him was hardly an option, but not having him knowing when she could, was just as hard. She hoped, he was the strong-willed partner in their relationship to not let them stray away on a path they must not tread in a rush.

Vanya had fallen asleep as soon as she hit the bed as they had gotten exhausted, but sleep was away from her. She was so tempted to call Vineet up, but it was already a little past twelve. She kept her phone on the nightstand and tried falling asleep when her phone beeped with a message tone. She hurriedly lowered the ringer volume so as not to disturb her friend and opened the chat box to read his message.

Vineet: *Hey. I know you aren't sleeping. Should've called if you wanted to hear from me.'*

Srishti: *Now that's assuming too much. I was about to sleep, and no, I wasn't thinking of you.*

Vineet: *Liar. I've been sneezing for an hour now. Stop missing me already and let me sleep.*

Srishti: *You know, you are incurable. Stop texting me if you want to sleep.*

Vineet: *Tell me, what were you thinking when you thought of me.*

Srishti: *That's a little too personal Sir. Stop trying to trespass into my personal space.*

Vineet: *I'll know someday.*

Srishti: *Patience. What's the hurry then?*

Vineet: *I can't wait for tomorrow when you'll be sleeping in my arms. God, I just can't wait for this night to be over soon.*

Srishti: *Vineet?*

Vineet: *Hey, what happened?*

Srishti: *We'll be okay, right. You sure, nothing would go wrong. I'm scared.*

Vineet: You trust me, babe. Don't you?

Srishti: *I don't trust myself.*

Vineet: *Then trust me more. I Love you, Srish, and I won't let you down. Ever. Sleep now, and we'll meet tomorrow. Love you.*

Srishti: *Love you too. Good night.*

She left the phone aside and her fears too. Vineet's words were reassuring enough, and she wanted to believe him. Maybe, that was the only option she had, and she could possibly not run away from the desires, a relationship came bundled together with.

She bid goodbye to her friends the next morning and left with him. Vanya had shown skepticism, but she assured her that she would be careful. They checked into a posh 4-star hotel where Vineet had already booked the room. She felt too awkward, walking in with him as if all the eyes were on her. Vineet completed the formalities at the front desk. She had thought that he might have booked the room with some fake ID like most of the youngsters who use the facilities for their clandestine affairs, but he hadn't. She admired his honesty. The bellboy took their suitcases to a luxury deluxe room that was going to be their nest for the next 24 hours. Her heart beat rapidly in her chest, being alone in a room with him while he tipped the bellboy generously and closed the door behind him. She kept standing in her place looking out of the window that opened towards the poolside, not knowing how to act. She heard his footsteps coming closer as she closed her eyes and held the edge of the curtain tightly.

He came in front of her, understanding her nervousness, and held her hand, loosening her grip on the curtain.

"Hey. Relax Srish. Come and sit." He said, motioning her to sit on one of the high back chairs.

She nodded and moved towards the chair, but the very next moment, she turned and collided with him, putting her arms around his torso and clung to him like a lost, scared child.

Chapter 12

Vineet took a deep breath, trying to make sense of her anxiety and put his arms around her gently rubbing her back to let her calm down.

"I'm scared Vineet. What will everyone think of me? What will Dadi and Dada Ji say if they know I'm staying here with you? I'm feeling very guilty now." Srishti said almost on the verge of crying.

"It's okay. No one's judging you, Srish and no one's going to say anything to your grandparents. We aren't doing anything wrong. Calm down, baby." He said, cupping her face trying to quell her fears.

"Lunch? Let's go down and have lunch." He suggested. It only felt right to take her to a more public place to distract her. Srishti was a bundle of nerves, and he was almost regretting, thinking if it was a wise decision to bring her out of her comfort zone.

The physical intimacy that is fairly an essential aspect of a couple's relationship and indulging in it was something, Vineet had never thought to be of much significance, was turning out to be a no-go area from where she stood. He had to do right by her if he were to instill confidence in her about his intentions.

They had lunch and went to the poolside for a stroll. Srishti felt a lot better by the time they made their way back to the room.

"Do you want to watch a movie Srish?" He asked.

"Yeah. Do you have any?" She asked.

He took out his laptop, and they went about trying to settle for one.

"Not an action film Vineet. Let's watch something ro.... I mean light." She said looking at the list of his favorites ranging from x-men to Captain America or Hunger Games. Guys could never get tired of these, she thought.

"There's no harm in saying romantic, Srish. It's not such a taboo word." Vineet said smirking and putting his arm around her and then pulling the laptop towards himself.

"How about ''The Faults in Our Stars?' I've been dying to watch it." She suggested.

"There's no fault in our stars, sweetheart, and you can watch it later. How about 'Me before You?' Have you seen it?" He asked looking hopefully at her.

"Haven't heard about it? Is it nice?" She asked, not knowing what it was all about.

"You'll love it." He said plugging the laptop into the LED TV in their room to play the movie.

She was so tempted to lie down comfortably in the bed, but she wasn't sure if it was the right thing to do. She didn't know what message would it carry to Vineet and she didn't want to raise his hopes yet.

He turned back after setting up everything and looked at her sitting cross-legged with her arms folded around a pillow on her lap.

"This is how you sit and watch movies." He asked, narrowing his eyes in half astonishment and half despair. The girl needed to catch up on a lot of etiquettes, he thought.

She didn't say anything and kept the pillow aside sliding back to sit against the headrest, her eyes still lowered, her trepidation very visible on her face.

Vineet went and sat beside her reclining on the pillows and pulling the duvet over their legs to make them comfortable. She slid back too and kept her head on his chest. He put his arm around her to secure her closer to his heart, and in no time, they were totally immersed in the movie.

She was sitting upright again and was in tears by the time the movie got over.

"Hey. It's just a movie, but yeah, that's what love is all about. Did you like it?" He asked, sitting up and lifting her chin, wiping her tears with the other hand.

"I want a happy ending in my love, Vineet. Promise me that happy ending." She said, looking deep into his eyes, her anxieties long gone as she cupped his face with her palms.

"A new beginning is what I promise you, Srish. All you'll have to do is to believe in me. It breaks my heart to see you looking scared or apprehensive when you are with me. I want you to feel absolutely secure and confident when I'm with you." He said, reassuring her trying to see beyond her insecurities as his fingers crawled through the thick mane of her hair to hold her neck, his other thumb rubbed gently on her lips.

"Kiss me, Vineet." She said, her breathing getting heavier. Her eyes looked pleading, and her lips quivering with longing.

All he wanted right then was to close the distance between them and plunder her mouth to his heart's content knowing, she desired him just as much as he did, but he took a deep breath and tried reigning in his urges.

"Are you sure, baby?" He asked, trying to appear in control, unsure of what he would do if she retracted from what she said a while earlier.

Her lips moved vainly to form some words before she gave up and leaned forward to end their misery. Vineet held her head firmly going slowly to taste the untouched petals of her lips, her inexperience tickling the depth of his desires. He didn't know if he was capable of this much of tenderness and was almost unaware of how delightful a gentle kiss could be if two people shared it out of pure love.

"I Love you, Vineet." She murmured.

"I Love you more, more than anyone I've ever loved in my life, Srish." He whispered as he left a trail of kisses along her cheek to her ear and took her in an embrace trying to ebb the thunder within. She clung to him, her own body aching in an unfamiliar spurt of yearning.

"I want more Vineet, all of it." She whispered.

"No. You don't." He said firmly in control of his own cravings.

"I do. I surely do. Look at me, Vineet. Do I look skeptical anymore?" She said coming out of his embrace, holding his face in her hands.

He held her wrists, bringing each one to his lips and left lingering kisses on them before looking at her eyes, now a whirlpool of desire.

"I Love you Srish, and I'm glad to see the skepticism all gone but now is not the right time. This much is enough to tide us through this month-long separation. Let's not rush." He said.

"Why, Vineet? The other day, you lectured me about the age of consent, and now that I'm willing, you are stepping back. I don't understand." She asked.

"I promised you Srish and more than that I promised myself; I won't let anything go beyond what you always believed in." He said.

"Beliefs change all the time. I changed mine." She said stubbornly.

"You're greedy and impulsive now. Stop testing my patience. I'm not planning to give in anytime soon." He said, slipping out of bed and going towards the restroom.

She only fell back on the bed hugging her pillow hard trying to shush her agitated nerves wondering if what she asked was a bit too much. A part of her rejoiced over Vineet's commitment while as a deep sense of unfulfilled desire gnawed on her mind.

"Come on, Srish. Stop acting like a baby. Let's go out for a walk, and we'll come back after dinner." Vineet said coming out of the washroom looking all ready to go out.

"Noooo. I just want to laze around Vineet. Can't we order food in the room?" She pleaded.

"We will but let's first get out for a while." He said, trying to pull her out of bed.

"You know, you are acting too bossy." She said, making a grumpy face.

"And you are acting like a tenacious child." He said as she walked lazily towards the washroom.

The evening was beautiful as they walked around the lush green lawns looked over by the dark starry night enveloped in the chill of December.

"Let's go inside. I'm freezing, and I'm hungry." She said, rubbing her hands, and they proceeded towards the restaurant for dinner.

She felt more relaxed now, moving around with him.

Dadi had called up to ask if she had packed up for the next day. She quickly updated her about her flight and cut the call saying that she was out with friends. Lying to her felt awful, but what else could she do? She kept eating her food quietly after the call, not able to look Vineet in his eyes.

"You. Okay." He asked after a while when she didn't say anything.

"Yeah. I'm good." She said.

"You don't seem to be," Vineet said, taking a bite of his food.

"Don't you think, I've become a habitual liar?" She asked.

"No. The reason you don't like to do it is the reason enough to tell you that you are not one. It is just a cultural barrier that restricts you from owning up to your relationship in front of your grandparents. There's a gap of two generations between them and you, and as long as you have regards for their values, you have no reason to feel guilty." He said, looking at her face.

She smiled politely and nodded her head, trying to make sense of his words.

"Thanks, Vineet." She said, looking up at his face again.

"For what?" He asked.

"For reminding me of my beliefs and for not giving in to my impulsiveness." She said, holding his hand from across the table.

He just smiled, pursing his lips and rubbing her hand gently with his thumb and nodded in agreement.

The night was cozier as she snuggled up to him and they talked about the random stuff before falling asleep peacefully in each other's arms.

The loud ringing of alarm woke them up to a sunny morning after a night spent like never before.

"Good Morning." He said still lying sideways looking at her sleepy face.

"Good morning." She said, opening her eyes and smiled, realizing where she slept last night.

"Slept well." He asked.

"Like never before." She said, her eyes asking him the same question.

"It's the best morning I've had in my life so far," Vineet said, putting an arm around her and trying to pull her closer for a kiss.

She jerked back and said abruptly. "I haven't brushed yet."

His lips broke into a smile.

"Then let me know how you taste in the morning." He said, pulling her closer again.

"What if you didn't like it?" She asked.

"We'll decide then." He said as his lips hungrily grabbed hers and within moments, she forgot her anxieties trying to get enough of him as he plundered her mouth with a raging need.

Before they knew it, it was time to leave as their flights were scheduled around the midday, for a journey she wasn't sure, that took them away from each other or brought them closer.

Chapter 13

Vanya and her other friends waited for her at the airport. She caught her and took her aside as soon as Srishti entered the airport lounge.

"You all right, Srish?" She asked with a lot of concern

"Couldn't be better," Srishti reassured her, but the doubt in Vanya's eyes won't budge. Srishti didn't know how to calm her.

"Did he....?" She tried asking but gave up looking at some people approaching.

"No. Vineet didn't, even though I wanted him to," Srishti said firmly all the time looking intensely into her eyes. Vanya's eyes welled up, but her lips broke into a smile of satisfaction. "Relax, buddy. He loves me, OK." She said again hugging her this time. Vanya just nodded and hugged her back before her flight for Mumbai was announced.

"See you at the other end of vacations. Stay happy." Vanya said and took her leave, happily rushing towards the Security check. Srishti waved her goodbye before coming back to where her other friends were stationed and exchanged pleasantries as everyone took to their respective queue for their flights. Vineet joined her shortly in the line after meeting a few of his friends.

"What happened, Srish? Why was Vanya so disturbed?" Vineet asked after they'd gone through the security check. They still had an hour before the boarding started.

"She just wanted to know how I was." Srishti replied, looking at Vanya running to board her flight. She had merely lounged around waiting for her as her flight had already started boarding.

"What? Is she your guardian here?" Vineet asked, laughing at her.

"Stop it Vineet. She's my best friend. She looks out for me. What's the harm?" She reacted.

"Nothing but I don't understand why you need to give so much of power to someone to interfere in your very personal matters." He objected.

"It's called care, you know. Vanya has a reason. I'm not quite sure if I must be discussing it with you, but she's been in a bad relationship before she came here. 'Once bitten twice shy'. Besides, I'd been pretty naïve when I came in here. My friends had always treated me with kids gloves and trust me you, I don't mind as long as I know they do that out of care. Vanya especially had been quite protective and has saved me from a lot of embarrassing situations. I owe it to her." She said assertively.

"OK. I'm sorry." He said.

"It's all right. You've just come into my life, Vineet. She'd been there all along. She'll take some time in trusting you, and I'll make sure she does because it means a lot to me." Srishti said, holding his arm trying to reassure him of his importance in her life.

"Yeah. I guess I never had friends like that. I always thought it to be an intrusion, but that was I. We are different people. We are bound to react differently to similar situations." He said.

"Would that be a problem in a relationship?" She asked.

"Not if we don't let it be. That's what personal space is all about, Srish. I don't have to like everything you do or the other way around, but that is our individuality, and that is something we would have to respect, to let us be ourselves without imposing our opinions upon each other." He said.

She looked at his face in awe and said. "Is there a book that you take all this wisdom from? Pass it on to me as well."

He smiled at her innocence.

"That book is called life sweetheart. I'm glad you didn't have to read it by yourself so far. Just collect these pearls of wisdom from wherever you get." He said, putting an arm around her squeezing her in briefly, and she laughed at his jibes. They proceeded to board their flight.

Her Granny was there to pick her up as she was staying in Delhi for a couple of days before she left for Jammu. She left his side to go over to her. It was a bit too soon to introduce him to her family.

She called up her Dadi to let her know that she'd arrived in Delhi and was on her way to her Granny's house.

The evening went well with Granny and Grandpa fussing over her. She'd gotten her favorite dishes cooked. Her room that she always stayed in looked freshly painted and decorated in the shades of lavender and white, her favorite and smelled good. It felt good to know, she was anxiously waited upon, and there were people who cared about her. Her Maternal Grandparent's love was something new for her that she had discovered only after she'd gone to college, but she couldn't complain. They must have had their reasons for their earlier behavior, she had thought.

"I love the room, Granny. Thanks. It looks so good now." She had chirped when she set foot there as Granny watched with bated breath for her reaction.

"Thanks, Sweetie. I'm glad you liked it. Now freshen up and come out. I want to show you certain other things I made changes with, and there's some stuff, I bought for you. I hope you would like it." Granny said.

"Oh. I love you, Granny." She said coming and hugging the old woman who embraced her back with a similar eagerness.

At night, Vineet had texted.

Vineet: *Hey. Sup.*

Srishti: *Missing my cuddle.*

Vineet: *So am I.*

Srishti: *What to do?*

Vineet: *Should I sneak in? I'm too close by.*

Srishti: *You are crazy.*

Vineet: *And you are beautiful.*

Srishti: *Is that a reason enough?*

Vineet: *No. But I love you, and that is.*

Srishti: *Won't work.*

Vineet: *Meet me tomorrow then. I leave two days later.*

Srishti: *I'll try. Will text you where I'll be going out with Granny. Would that do?*

Vineet: *That would. Good night and miss me.*

Srishti: *Good Night and not missing you is an option I don't have. Love you.*

Vineet: *Love you, sweetheart.*

She hugged the lovely Teddy bear that always sat on her bed and immersed into his thoughts when her phone rang with an incoming call. It was Vineet.

'Now what?' She asked as she picked the phone up.

'Just wanted to hear your voice.' He said.

'What do you want to hear now?' She asked.

'Just say anything. Gawd. Never knew that I'll feel this miserable after spending a night with you.' He said.

'That was a night to remember Vineet. I'll never forget it all my life.' She said.

'I'll give you better ones. Just wait for the right time.' He said sighing.

'I'm sure you would but last night was when you earned my trust Vineet. I'll never forget that.' She said.

'I guess you are right. I earned it back for myself, as well. Your love is doing things to me; I never knew I was capable of. Thanks for making me turn around.' He said.

'To me, you were always like that, Vineet. Why do you say so?' She asked.

'I'll tell you someday. Good night, Love. Do remember to text me your plans for tomorrow.' He said.

'I will. Good night. And good you called. I think I can sleep better now.' She said.

'So would I. Bye.' He said, and cut the call.

Vineet's words had confused her. Was she missing something, something that was right in front of her and in her extreme love and devotion to him, she wasn't capable of pinpointing that. He'd never given her a reason to doubt his credentials, but now, she felt very strongly about the missing part of their equation only if she could tell what it was. She wasn't sure if it was the right time to discredit Vineet and after what he meant to her just because his words had confused her. She felt embarrassed about her own contentions as if a side of Vanya was rubbing on to her. Srishti took a deep breath to cool her mind, tried thinking about all the good things they'd done together and would be doing in times to come. This time, it came easy, and soon she was submerged entirely in his dreams, the dreams that defined them together.

Chapter 14

Granny was taking Srishti to her Ladies club meeting for lunch, and then they would proceed to Select City Walk for shopping in the evening. She texted Vineet, and they planned to bump into each other there at the Mall.

By seven in the evening, she was so exhausted having gotten in and out of around two dozens of dresses. Granny was peculiarly choosy about what she bought. Srishti only prayed to finally see him after a daylong wait. He'd texted, he was somewhere around already and then she saw him entering the boutique she was in. She cursed herself for telling him exactly where she was. It would be too apparent for her Granny to put two and two together if he came in straight and spoke to her. She turned her head and walked toward the changing room to avoid the direct confrontation.

She heard him speaking to the lady at the front desk dreading if he was asking about her. She quickly came out.

"What happened Srishti? Aren't you trying that dress?" Granny asked.

"I'm good, Granny and very tired as well. Can we leave?" She asked, looking obliquely at him.

"Yeah. I guess. I'll settle the bill." Granny said and moved towards the billing counter where Vineet already stood tapping his fingers on the desk. Her heart came to her mouth.

"If you are done son, can I get my stuff billed?" Granny asked, looking at him.

"Yes, Ma'am. They are taking some time getting my stuff. Please proceed." He said humbly getting aside as Granny thanked him for his gesture. He then turned towards her and winked.

"Hi, Srishti. What are you doing here? Thought, you were to go to Jammu." He suddenly asked her.

"Oh, Hi. I'm here with my Granny. I'm leaving day after tomorrow. How about you?" Srishti replied with an equal amount of surprise in her voice.

"Oh. I'm leaving for Wellington day after tomorrow as well. I'm here to pick up some stuff Mom had ordered." Vineet said, and on that note, one of the sales girls brought three huge bags of clothes for him. He smilingly gestured towards them and proceeded to pay right behind Granny whose half attention was on their conversation. Granny smiled at him knowing that he knew her Granddaughter and Vineet wished her again with Srishti coming and introducing the two. Srishti breathed easy.

They came out after paying their individual bills while Granny tried calling the driver who had gone to pick her Grandpa from some meeting and was now stuck in traffic somewhere.

"I guess we'll call the cab Srishti. The driver is too far away. He'll take forever to come." She said after she ended the call.

"I can drop you guys if you don't mind. Where do you stay, Ma'am?" Vineet asked.

"Where do you stay?" Granny asked the counter question.

"Def. Col." He said.

"That'll be on the way then. We stay there, as well. Would that be okay, Srishti?" Granny asked her.

"Yeah. I'm so tired now that all I want to do is put my feet up somewhere." She said.

"This way then." Vineet showed then towards the lift that would take them to the parking bay where his car was parked.

Srishti stood perplexed as of where to sit in his black Toyota Fortuner as he beeped it open, but Granny came to her rescue motioning her to sit in front while as she took the rear seat. Vineet struck an easy conversation about nothing in particular and kept her and Granny pleasantly engaged for almost about 45-50 minutes that they rode together. Granny invited him to join them at their place and after a little hesitation; he agreed to go in to meet her Grandpa.

"Why don't you make him comfortable here, Srishti? I'll just go in and freshen up and come." Granny said and walked towards her room. Grandpa was still on his way back.

"Can I use the restroom please?" Vineet asked while Granny was in earshot.

"Sure. This way." She said, motioning him towards her room while she looked at the retreating back of Granny. She'd partially slowed down listening to Vineet but continued to go in. Srishti followed him to her room, and as she closed the door, he was quick to pull her in an embrace as the two aching hearts united after an agonizing wait.

"I missed you so much already, Srish. How am I gonna live away for nearly a month?" He said, holding her face in his hands coming out of the hug.

Srishti put her arms around his neck and pulled him closer to grab his lips hungrily. She had no words to give respite to his aching heart, but she could make the most of what they had. Vineet responded with equal urgency. They separated quickly, though, knowing where they were, and he went into the washroom while she smoothened her hair and wiped her face before she went out.

He and Granny emerged almost simultaneously from the respective rooms just as they heard Grandpa's voice saying something to the driver while he came in.

"Ahh. Hello young man. Thanks for bringing my beautiful women home." He said, looking at Vineet as he entered the living room in his signature style.

"That was hardly a bother, Sir. I was anyway headed home." Vineet came forward to shake his extended hand.

"God Bless You. So I hear you live nearby. Do you belong here?" He asked, gesturing him to sit down.

Srishti smiled to herself. Her Grandpa was going to grill him now.

"Well, I don't know where I belong to, but yeah, we have a home here in Block C. Dad's a Diplomat, right now posted in Wellington, Mr. Navneet Sharma," Vineet stated.

"So you are Navneet Sharma's son. Great. A very fine officer he is. I'd known him while he was a young officer and had a chance to interact with him when he was posted in Pakistan, quite a while back." Grandpa spoke and looked at his wife this time. "Remember. RR." And she nodded with a recollection.

"You do," Vineet asked, surprised.

"He was a wonderful and intelligent person as I recollect. I'm sure he still is. He's handled quite a lot of tricky situations back then in our troubled neighborhoods right from Pakistan to Afghanistan to the Middle East. In fact, he had escaped a few bids on his life while on the job in that period. I'm sure you didn't know any of those. You must have been very young back then." Grandpa spoke with a lot of empathy and pride.

"No, I don't. My parents never discussed these things." Vineet said, looking shocked.

"We Indian parents are very protective about our children, Son and very responsible towards our Nation. These kind of jobs come with a whole lot of risk and responsibility. I'm sure he had kept you out of harms way all that while." He asked.

"Yeah. I'd been in a boarding school from class sixth onwards." Vineet said with a newfound sense of respect and pride towards his father.

Grandpa took a deep breath and continued. "I'm sure you did. The biggest victims of our Nationalism are our children who grow up with the absentee parents either serving their duties or have lost their lives in avoidable battles, but that's what we sign up for when we join the services." He said partially clearing his throat and got up to have a gulp of water.

Srishti excused herself and rushed to the washroom. Her eyes had welled up with that statement and so were of her Granny's. She didn't want to break down right there. She was just as much of a victim of her orphaned existence. Vineet understood her pain and had wanted to run behind her to soothe her, but he couldn't. There was an ire silence in the room. Vineet kept sitting there thinking how wrong was he to unnecessarily blame his parents for his loneliness. All they'd wanted was his safety all the while.

The servant brought in soup meanwhile, and that was the necessary distraction they needed to dissolve the thickness of the room. Srishti joined back a while later.

"You are fine, Srishti. Are you?" Granny came and sat beside her.

"I'm good. Thanks, Granny." She said, leaning in to hug her sideways, and Granny just caressed her head and kissed her temple with love.

"I'm sorry if I upset you two," Grandpa said. "While in uniform, we don't get to act emotional, but we certainly are not oblivious to the pain, the families of the servicemen go through."

"I'm glad you spoke, Sir. I'd always blamed them for leaving me on my own at such a tender age, but now that I know why, I would have to make it up to them. Thanks. I certainly am more proud of my father now than I was half an hour ago. You did well." Vineet said.

"You've turned up good, Vineet. I'm sure, Navneet and your mother are just as proud of you. Tell your father that I remembered him and to meet me when he's around." Grandpa said.

"I will. And I'll take your leave now." Vineet said, keeping the soup bowl on the table.

"Not before you've had dinner, provided there're no other plans." He said.

"There're no plans, but I'm sure I'm intruding. You might like to spend some time with your Granddaughter." Vineet said.

"Don't worry. We old people are a sucker for company and with you young people around; it's always a delight. So tell me what you do and what you plan to do after you pass out of college?" Grandpa continued.

Both the men gelled well, and Srishti was amazed to see Vineet totally engrossed in conversation with him, not even bothering to look at her in between. She merely answered when she was asked about something and finally got up to help Granny in laying the table.

They settled down on the table and started having dinner, but Granny looked very distracted.

"What happened, Granny?" Srishti asked.

"Nothing. I was just thinking about time when I met your mother last. If I'm remember correctly, your mother's name is Rashmi, right. It's been a long time when we were together." She said, looking at Vineet's face.

"Yeah. It is. When did you meet my mother?" Vineet looked not too surprised this time.

A soft smile played on Granny's lips as she said. "Yeah. It was long back when Srishti was born."

That had everyone's attention.

Granny continued remembering fondly.

"Srishti was just a day old when your mother was rushed into RR in a terrible condition, with your father carrying you in his arms. You were probably two years old back then. She's had a miscarriage and had to undergo the hysterectomy. Incidentally, Naina.... I mean Neha, Srishti's mother had to share the room with her as there were no other rooms available. Your father was very anxious as he ought to be. I remember putting you to sleep in her bed while she battled for her life.

Rashmi was inconsolable that time having lost her six-month-old fetus, a daughter. After two days, she'd taken Srishti in her arms wishing that it was her own daughter in her arms and said, her daughter would have been this beautiful if she was born and had cried her heart out. I had no words to console her. I merely told her that she was lucky, she at least had a son, and she had to get better to take care of him. I can't believe, Vineet, life has taken one full circle. Do tell her about Srishti when you go back. She'll be happy to know how our Srishti has turned out to be."

She wiped her eyes and smiled between her tears and continued. "I don't know if I must say this, but you were quite a persistent boy back then. You had asked her if Srishti was your baby and had wanted to take her home. Your mother had to cajole you and placate you to leave her alone saying;

she would when Srishti was a little older. It's so ironical how you guys met in college and now, here for me to relive those memories. I'm sure Rashmi will be just as surprised to know about it."

Vineet smiled with misty eyes having gotten to know so much about his parents. He had come there for Srishti but seemed like it was an awakening for him too. Their destinies were etched together long back, and he was glad that he'd found her.

"Can I call you Granny as well?" He asked just as he was ready to leave.

"You sure can. God Bless You." Granny blessed him when he touched her feet.

"And if it's fine with you, can I invite Srishti for a party tomorrow. I've my school and college friends coming over for dinner. I'll drop her back before midnight." Vineet asked Grandpa.

"Do you want to go, Srishti?" Grandpa asked her.

"If that's fine with you Grandpa. I'm okay either way." She said.

"Okay. I hope you take good care of our Granddaughter and drop her back in time. It was good to meet you, Son. Good night. " Grandpa said with finality and left to go inside. Granny gestured her to see him off before she followed Grandpa, leaving them alone.

"Good night then." She said, walking towards the gate with him.

"It couldn't be better Srish. You were right. I never gave my parents the benefit of doubt. I've got a lot of making up to do. Anyways, I'll pick you up by seven in the evening." He said.

"Isn't that too early for the party." She asked.

"I wish I could pick you up at seven in the morning." He said, getting quirky.

"Some wishful thinking. Call me." She said, and came inside while he sped away.

"I will." He shouted as he waved at her from the rolled down windowpane of his ride.

She smiled to herself at his antics and turned to go inside the house where Granny waited for her in the living room.

Chapter 15

"Do you like him Srishti?" Granny shot as soon as she entered the house.

"What? Why do you ask?" She asked back.

"Tell me if you do." Granny came over to her and made her sit down on the couch.

"He's a friend, Granny, so of course I do like him, but we are not in a relationship if that's what you want to know." She lied.

"Oh. But I guess Vineet likes you more than a friend would. I could read his eyes. He looked so unsettled when you had rushed into your room, you know. It seemed like he would follow you right behind if he could." Granny said.

"I don't know." She said sheepishly with nothing to counter.

"It's not so bad, Srishti. He seems to be a nice guy and from a good family to top that. If you ever thought about him or if he ever proposed, count me in. I quite like the guy." Granny said, getting up to go.

"I'm still two and a half years away from my degree Granny, and Dadi and Dada Ji would be apprehensive if I... You know..." She tried telling her, but Granny was quick to rescue her.

"It's just between me and you, Child. I told you because I wanted you to be watchful. Keep your eyes and ears open when you are on your own, Srishti. And do tell me well in time when you would be leaving for his party. God Bless You." Granny said and left to go to her room but turned back thinking about something.

"I skipped saying something back then. That little boy had insisted on taking you in his arms, but he was just a baby. I held you out with him holding you when he had kissed you on the cheek. Today, I feel so funny thinking about those childish antics." She grinned, looking at her and closed the door to her room.

Srishti stood there, shell-shocked. Her Grandmother had an eye no less than a hawk, but she would stand by her at a time like this, Srishti had never thought. She left to go to her room.

As soon as she'd freshened up and changed into her pajamas, Vineet had called up.

She locked the door and drowned herself into the soft comforter to answer his call.

'*Hey there! Hope, your folks liked me.*' He asked.

'*Granny asked me if I liked you.*' She said.

'*Smart woman! What did you say?*' He asked again.

'*Denial was the best defense. But seems like, you've impressed Granny.*' She said.

'*Were we destined to meet, Srish? I can't believe what I heard today; about Dad, about Mom. I feel like a jerk holding a grudge against them for this long.*' He said.

'*Make the amends now. It's never too late Vin.*' She said.

'*You know, Mom calls me Vin. It sounds just as right now when you called me that. I'll never tire of saying I Love you*

Srish, no wait. I'd wanted to call you Sera for a very long time.' He said.

'You could call me anything, you know. Why did you wait? And yeah, Sera sounds so good, something no one else calls me with.' She whispered.

'You smelled different today.' He said.

'It was 'Crush by Victoria's Secret.' Naina Masi had sent for me. Reminds me, I've to talk to her too.' She said.

'What else did she send from VS?' He teased.

'She can't send everything you know. Someone else would need to take that responsibility.' She blushed but mustered up the courage to retort.

'Would you wear it if I bought that?' He asked.

'Vin. Stop it. Will you?' She said, feeling totally flushed.

'Tell me, Sera. Would you?' He asked.

'You know, I would.' She said.

'That'd be your gift from Wellington. But you would need to tell me the stats.' He said.

'Good night, Vin.' She said, cutting the conversation short, her heart beating dangerously in her chest.

'You're leaving me to make my guesses Sera. I'm gonna dream of you wildly tonight'. He said.

'I Love you, Vin. Sleep now.' She said, kissing the phone.

'I Love you too, babe. See you in my dreams.' He said and kissed her back.

She closed her eyes to contain the hormones that were threatening to spill out of her system. Vineet's proximity was doing her no good. He acted completely in control when he was with her physically but stirred her dormant desires when he spoke on the phone or texted her. It puzzled her at times, but she overlooked it. Right now, all she wanted was to think of him and think about him. She grabbed her Teddy and squeezed it in her arms, but it was no match for his muscular built, something she could disappear in.

She slept till very late and got up only after Granny had called her umpteen numbers of times.

“Are you well, Srishti? How come you got up so late?”

Granny asked, looking at the clock that struck eleven.

“It’s so cold here. I don’t feel like getting out of the bed.” She said peeking out to see the cloudy day as she came out and put her arms around Granny who sat at the dining table and kissed her. “Good morning.”

“Eat before its afternoon.” Granny pointed towards the warm Idlies and Sambhar, the cook had made for breakfast.

“It’s delicious. Thanks.” She said to the cook after taking a bite of her food, and he nodded happily.

“Do you want to come along for this event, I’ve to go to this afternoon, or if you want, I can skip that,” Granny asked sipping her tea.

She’d previously eaten with Grandpa who had already left to go somewhere.

“No and no. I can’t come with you because your events are very boring and you don’t have to miss them for me. I’ll be fine.” She said.

“Though the event would last for a couple of hours, the traveling would take another two. So I’ll be gone for a good four to five hours.” Granny said.

“That’s fine. I think I’ll sleep or maybe go to the nearby market for some window shopping.” She said shrugging.

“Do you want to go to some saloon? You’ve to go to Vineet’s party in the evening.” Granny asked.

"Oh come on Granny. I'm not going to get all decked up for an informal party. I'll just wear my jeans and a coat, and I'm done." She said.

"Why don't you wear that red dress tonight, the one we bought yesterday. Team it up with your black leather coat and boots." Granny said.

"It's so cold, Granny. I can't." Srishti shrieked.

"Then when are you going to wear your leather jacket? In the summers! Act like a grown-up woman now. Stop being a tomboy." Granny scolded.

"But dress. I don't even know what kind of people will be there." She said.

"I'm sure everyone will be overdressed. Don't worry." Granny said.

"Okay." She said resigning. There was not a way she could win the argument with Granny when it came to high-end parties, as she knew nothing about them. She could call up Vineet and ask him after Granny went out.

She showered and dressed up in her denim and a thick sweater when Granny was leaving around twelve. She said bye and ran back to her room to talk to Vineet.

He yawned on the phone as he spoke.

'*Are you still sleeping?*' She asked.

'*No. Just showered and had breakfast. But I'm feeling so lazy.*' He said.

'*I'm home alone.*' She said.

'*I'm always alone. What's the big deal?*' He said.

'*Nothing. Bye.*' She said, and cut the call.

He called back within minutes.

'*I'm so sorry, Sera. Get ready. I'm coming to pick you up.*' He shouted as soon as she picked the phone up.

'Good morning, finally.' She joked.

'I'll come. Right.' He asked.

'Around the bend! I'll walk till there.' She said.

'Start after five minutes! I'll wait.' He said, and she felt good at his protectiveness.

She looked at herself in the mirror. She brushed her hair again, fixed her lip-gloss, and sprayed another squirt of 'Crush' and smiled to herself, remembering the conversation from the last night. She then told the servant, she was going to the markct for a couple of hours and left for the place he was already waiting.

"Where do you want to go? Market or home." He asked, looking expectantly at her face.

"Don't you have some Circus running somewhere around? Take me there." She said bitterly.

He got the jibe and drove quietly towards home.

His house was huge and impressive. The lush green lawn looked manicured with rows of beautiful flowering plants. The guard opened the gate, and he parked the Fortuner on the patio and held her hand to take her inside straight to his room.

His room was still undone. The duvet lay there crumpled as if someone pushed it aside in a hurry. His clothes from last night were lying on the couch and his shoes lying somewhere. His travel bags were stacked in one corner and the shopping bags from the previous evening lying close to the closet. The empty cup of tea stood on the nightstand.

She looked around the room and then at him.

"What? You didn't give me enough time to clean up. And anyway, I'm leaving tomorrow." He said in his defense.

The next moment, he moved forward and took her in his arms. “You wanted to go to Circus. Consider this one.” He whispered in her ears.

“I Love this Circus.” She whispered back trying to squeeze him as much as she could.

He then suddenly left her and went out to lock the main door. She sat at the edge of his bed. He got back quickly, tossed his shoes out, and took out hers as well before pulling her into the covers.

Chapter 16

"I'd wanted to laze around in the bed today. Didn't know, it could get this good." He said, leaning on top of her as she lay there on her back, her hair spread across his pillow.

"Me neither." She said, cupping his face.

"I can't wait for the day when you'll belong here officially and when we would not have to sneak in like we do today." He said.

"Don't say things we can't do anything about right now. Do something to ease this pain, Vin." She said, closing her eyes.

He bent down to seize her lips, and they poured their heart and soul into the kiss. She arched her body against him.

"Don't do that, Sera. Don't test my resolve." He murmured, holding her head nibbling her ear, their hearts pounding against each other. She kissed his cheek, going down to his jawline and then his neck.

"This is not helping, Love. Let's get out of here." He said, finally holding her face in his hands.

"No Vin. Just let me hold you if not more." She said, coming to her senses.

Vineet wrapped his arms around her, and they lay there motionless, the only sound audible was of their raging breaths and their pounding hearts.

"Do you remember, Vin when was the first time, you kissed me?" She asked, cuddling him.

"Three days ago. Why do you ask?" He asked back.

"It wasn't. It happened a while back, long back. It happened twenty-one years ago." She said, sinking in deeper.

"No way. I marked you when you were a little baby. Gosh. Is that for real?" He asked, surprised.

"Yeah. Granny skipped telling that when you were there, you know. She told me later. Seems like, after your mother's miscarriage, you'd wanted to take me home, and your mother pacified you saying, she would bring me in when I was a little older." She said.

"You were destined to be mine, Sera. I brought you home finally, and one day, this will be here where you would belong." He said, taking a deep breath and keeping his chin on her head as she rubbed her nose against his neck.

"What time is the party if it's there at all?" She asked when they were a little sober.

"My friends would come by 8.30 or 9 may be." He said, tightening his grip on her.

"What should I wear? Granny wants me to wear a dress. I don't know what's the dress code for the party." She asked, kissing his shoulder.

"Wear whatever you are comfortable in, though the girls would mostly be in dresses. Your Granny knows the stuff around, I guess, but you are not competing with anyone. You, Sera are the best when you are yourself." He said, kissing her hair.

"How will you manage it all by yourself?" she asked.

"I've ordered food and drinks. The servants will be back by the evening. I just gave them a few hours off." He said, winking at her.

"Oh! So what did you think what will we be doing, for them not to be here?" She asked, running her index from his forehead down to his lips.

"Well, you don't have to do much to have people's imagination running wild. I just wanted to avoid that where you are concerned." He said, holding her hand and kissing it.

"Why are you so protective of me, Vin? I'm not a baby, not anymore." She asked.

"I seriously don't know why, but I want to be. Bear with me." He said.

"Let's go out and grab some lunch. It's three already." He said, leaving her and jumping out of bed.

"OK." She said, and got out as well.

He dropped her back a little later and promised to be there by seven to pick her up before his friends came over.

She looked stunning in her new red one-piece number that hugged her curves at right places and fell a little above her knees. Worn with the short black leather jacket, stockings and black boots with her hair done in soft curls, she looked no less a Diva as Granny had put it. He'd showed up at quarter to eight to pick her up when the guard had called her out since he was in a hurry. Granny had waved her off, giving her millions of instructions, she didn't remember. He was there to take care of her. She didn't need to do that by herself, she had thought.

The house looked party ready, with the bar set up at one end of the living room and a makeshift dance floor created with the music playing. The two of the house servants along with a couple of temps, were busy making sure that everything was in order. The terrace on the first floor looked softly lit though it was too cold to venture out. She felt nervous about being introduced to his old friends; she didn't know what color or form they came in.

"Do you want to see the house?" He asked.

"Yeah. We still have time until your friends come in." She said.

"Are you nervous?" He asked.

"Yes." She said, biting her lip as they climbed up the stairs.

"Hey. Don't do that. I'll be jobless otherwise." He said, pulling her into his arms as soon as they arrived at the landing and ran his thumb over her lower lip.

"You aren't meeting my parents. They are just friends." He pacified her.

"Would I fit in?" She finally asked.

"No. You wouldn't, but that's precisely the reason you are, where they aren't. No one is. You are meant to stand out and not fit in." He said.

"Then why did you invite me in? We had our little time together earlier. You could've done without me." She asked.

"But I didn't want to. You are where I am, Sera. I wanted you to know this side of me as well or whatever I was before I met you. Relax." He said.

"Do I look, okay?" She asked.

"Are you kidding me? You look stunning, and it's not the dress. You always do because of the attitude you wear. Don't just let that slip away." He said, tightening his grip on her and kissing her on the head.

She smiled.

Soon enough, his friends started piling up. The number was steadily increasing with the friends of friends and their friends as well, half the people Vineet didn't even know, but he didn't bat an eye. She could never understand the idea of going to a party uninvited, but he'd rightly said that she didn't fit in.

She simply tagged along as he introduced her to some of his friends. The house came alive with people constantly mingling with each other, the booze flowing, and the music getting louder.

Vineet was aware of her slight unease and kept a close watch on her while he rotated among different groups.

"Hot catch Bro. Thought you'd be out of your mettle at the dead place you went into. You still rock." Sid slapped his back while he was alone with the group of his school friends and everyone had laughed.

"She's a great girl Sid and I quite like her." He said gently to play it down.

"Wow. Like her! Since when did our Mr. Casanova start liking girls or for that matter, any one of us? Oh, she's not given it to you yet." Manav joked.

"Seems like he's losing the charm. Did that place do it to you? Tch Tch. Want us to try." Anuj added as they went on.

Vineet controlled his anger looking at Srishti and got up and went to where she stood with Alisha.

"Hey, Alisha. I hope you didn't let my girl get bored. Did ya?" He asked, putting an arm around Srishti.

"I guess not. I was only telling how far and how close we went at some point in time. You didn't tell her yet." Alisha asked, keeping her elbow on his shoulder. Srishti chose to look the other way.

"I think, you need another drink. Should I get you one?" He asked, lowering his shoulder to slip her arm away.

"Aww… Did I touch the raw nerve Vini boy?" She asked and then turned to Srishti. "Don't you want to know how and what your boyfriend likes Srishti?"

"As a matter of fact, I don't." Srishti's words surprised him all of a sudden. "I'll learn it my way in times to come," Srishti said, folding her arms and looking her straight in her eyes.

"Only, he doesn't waste too much of time with anyone, you know. You'd better learn it fast." Alisha drawled and winked at him shamelessly plucking a glass of Vodka from the server passing by.

"Didn't update her with your ways Vineet or better still, with your conquests." She now asked Vineet.

"Let's go Sera. She's out of her mind right now." Vineet caught her by her arm to take her away, but she held his hand.

"Let me." She said, looking at Vineet. A few of his friends had already started converging around them to witness the argument. Alisha's friends stood beside her.

"When a man doesn't kiss and tell Alisha, it means that he respects the woman with who, he had spent the private moments. I wouldn't trust him if he did. So yeah, he didn't tell me anything about the women he'd been with because I'll be feeling secure with him knowing, I wouldn't be discussed either if anything were to go wrong between us. He's done his part in showing you the respect. It's time, you respected yourself better." She said, and a sense of pride washed over Vineet's face.

"Some feisty girl you are," Alisha said, patting her back. "Good going, Vineet." She said, shrugging it off.

Vineet smiled, went and lowered the volume of the music and came back to stand beside Srishti.

"Hey, Guys. Listen up. Got an announcement to make." He said, looking at the puzzled faces of his friends.

"This is Srishti, my girl, my life and my everything and now if anyone utters a sleazy word about her, I'll punch his face, and if anyone has a problem with that, he or she knows where the exit door is. Enjoy the drinks, food, and music while you are here and the party gets over by eleven. We have got an early morning flight to catch." Vineet said firmly holding Srishti by the waist and kissed her on the head as he ended.

His friends were quick to apologize, and the party was back in motion. He saw to it for a while that everyone was thoroughly engaged before he held her hand and took her to the upper floor towards the terrace.

"Hey, Baby. I'm sorry for what happened there." He apologized.

"That's Okay, Vin. You could've avoided it by not inviting me in. You should've spent some time with your old friends instead of babysitting me like this." She said, smiling curtly.

"Look at them, Sera." He pointed out towards the hall from the mezzanine. "Do they look like, they care if I'm there or not? They aren't like your friends who care about each other. They are the ones with whom you can spend time but not form those lifelong bonds. Look at Alisha and the other girls. They are trying to woo every man in the room. Do you think that they care with whom they went home tonight?" He said.

"Then why did you invite them? Why extend these courtesies?" She asked, totally obfuscated.

"Because that was me before I met you. I was one of them. Did what they are doing right now. And I wanted you to see that before we went any further." He said.

She closed her eyes, leaning back against the wall and took a deep breath.

"Terrace. It's noisy in here." He asked, motioning her towards the terrace door. The ice-cold breeze welcomed them as they made their way towards the two-seater Caine couch laden with a furry blanket. Alongside was placed a fire pan, red hot with burning coals to keep the surroundings warm. She looked at him, confused.

"What? You don't like it here." He asked as she sat there, warming her hands not looking at him.

"Look, I'm sorry if it offended you but..." He said, but she was quick to butt in.

"But what Vineet. Why all this? You could've told me what you'd wanted to and I would've believed you. Why this drama? Why are you, in fact, doing it if you don't like it?" She asked, looking visibly pissed.

He sat beside her and put the blanket on their legs.

"I didn't know any other way to tell you, Sera. I'm not saying they are bad people. Each one of them has an issue or other. Some are angry with themselves, others with their parents, or some with the system. The worst are the ones who are doing it out of peer pressure. I'm hardly in a position to judge them, but that's how it is." He said.

"Then what changed for you?" She asked.

"You happened." He looked straight into her eyes, but this time, she averted her gaze. He continued.

"I got bored with this lifestyle a year before I graduated, so I put my complete efforts into cracking the IIM Bombay. I did get in Bombay but not for Finance that I badly wanted. I had to choose Indore, and I thought that I was marooned. That's why I waited until the last moment to join in. That's when we met. The player in me spotted you just as quickly, but there was something about you that made me step back. Something within me refrained me from messing with you. I watched you for a week. You were so full of life, always ready to help everyone, always fooling around with your friends. You looked too happy, something that I had always missed in my life. I was badly attracted to you, and after a week,

I couldn't stay away. I followed you to the Pi Store when we spoke. Before I knew it, I was opening my heart to you, something I had never done before and that moment I just knew, I'd irrevocably fallen in love with you. It happened just so instantly, or maybe I'd waited all along for that kind of emotion. Rest is history, and you know it."

She kept quiet for a while, not knowing what to say.

"Say something Sera." He said, holding her hand.

"Were you scared that you'll get over me if we had sex? Is that why you stayed away?" She asked.

"Noooo. I could never get over you, Sera. I love you, damn it. People get over relationships. You can't get over love." He said.

"Then?" She asked.

"I'd been there, done that and trust me, it never mattered so far, but with you it's different. I wanted to go slow. I wanted us to experience the romance, the little happiness that comes with it rather than jumping the gun. I wanted us to appreciate and enjoy the climb as we approached the peak because it is sure to plateau if not descend after that." He said, looking at her and continued. "That life, it's addictive."

"I thought, love was addictive. Our love is not addictive to you, Vin." She asked.

"It is. More than you know, but it is different. How do I tell you, Sera?" He said, trying to look for words before he spoke again.

"That life, those relationships are like the weed, like coke, that give you an instant high, a euphoria, and you forget about everything else, anyone around you. You only live for yourself and your half-baked happiness.

But this love we share is different. It's addictive like that morning brew of tea or coffee that brightens our day. It opens our eyes to the brightness of a new day, energizes us to take on the world and connects us to our own. You did that to me, Sera. I look at life differently. My perspective towards my life and that towards my parents changed after I met you. I'm not angry anymore. I want to feel the feelings; I deprived myself for a very long time. Is that wrong? Am I asking for too much?" He said.

"I guess not." She said, finally leaning into him keeping her head on his chest and he put his arms around her.

"I'm truly sorry to put you through it, but I'd wanted to come clean. Can you forgive me for all the crazy things I did before?" He asked.

"What you did before you met me doesn't concern me Vin but tell me one thing honestly." She looked into his eyes and asked. "Could you be this cool if it was me in your place?"

He smiled, shaking his head. She sure had put him in a spot, but he had to be honest.

"You know, I would've gulped it, though not very easily, I'm sure but I would've. Love makes us do the strangest of things, but honestly, I'm glad you were not there. Right now it's killing me to even think of you with anyone else. That's chauvinistic, but that's true." He said.

"Why such double standards?" she asked again.

"It's not double standards. It's insecurity. It's competitiveness. Guys are extremely insecure, Sera when it comes to their sexuality or their professional acumen. We don't like to be compared or judged by our skills or salary or professional shortcomings. We don't like to be measured in bed either. Who wants to live with his woman constantly comparing him to someone better than him at some point in time? Would you?" He asked.

"Won't you measure me up then by the same yardstick? Would I not be insecure?" She asked.

"No, you won't. Women are more self-assured than what we like to give them credit for. Women I guess are fast learners and they don't hesitate to learn or unlearn to get going in a relationship. Men don't. It hurts their pride to be told that they are not good enough." He said.

"But you did change, Vin." She said.

"I wasn't told to Sera. I wanted to. There's a difference." He said.

"Would you always love me, Vin?" She asked, snuggling up to him.

"That's hardly a choice. It's like asking if I could live without breathing. Never ever question that. Okay." He said, tightening his grip around her and rested his cheek on her head. They kept sitting there like that, and then she stirred.

"Let's go down. It's your.... I mean our party, Vin. Let's start the dinner. I gotta go too." She said, looking at her watch. It was half-past ten already.

"Yeah. Let's do that." He said, getting up and holding her hand to climb down the chair where she sat with her feet folded.

He dropped her home later ending the night on a positive note laying the foundation for a new beginning, a new dawn in their lives with no baggage that could shackle them in. Next morning, they went their separate ways promising to be back just as soon.

Chapter 17

The vacation at home was not what it used to be before. Though Srishti socialized with her old friends, her relatives, her second and distant cousins, she felt distracted. Dadi was quick to point out, but she dodged her.

"You know, I'm giving you the benefit of doubt Srishti, but I know there is something that's keeping you up at night. Don't hesitate to share whenever you want and better still don't keep to yourself if it is something that can put you in trouble." Dadi said, running her fingers through her hair when Srishti lay down, keeping her head on her lap.

"I will if there was anything. I'm just bothered about one of the exams that didn't go too well. I'll be apprehensive until the results came in." She lied, and Dadi only bent and kissed her head.

On the other side of Hemisphere, Vineet was pleasantly surprised to see his father, who had come along with his mother to pick him up. He was mostly very busy to extend such courtesies.

"Hey, Dad. How come? Did you resign?" He asked, coming closer and hugging him to his surprise.

"If I knew this is what you get from your son if you came to pick him up, damn, I would've done that years ago." He said, patting his back.

"Airport etiquettes, Dad," Vineet said, laughing as he let him go to hug his mother. He felt the warmth that he'd always shielded himself from, the content showing on his face. This time he had come home for real.

He felt relaxed talking to them. The happiness showed on their faces having their only son reciprocate their gestures of love in the longest of time.

On the dining table, his mother was quick to point it out to him.

"You look happy, Vin. You seem to have settled well in Indore, I guess." She asked, serving his favorite meal of minced chicken Burritos.

"I am, Mom. It's good. The course is well structured, and the place is beautiful. It's like living on a nice hill-lock in the midst of a city." He said enthusiastically.

"I met this old couple in Delhi, Dad; General Sood and his wife. He knew you and his wife remembered Mom from a long time back." Vineet broached the topic.

"Yeah. A very decorated officer and extremely nice people. They did help us in our time of need." He said, cutting it short.

"Why did you need him, Dad? I mean, you are so accomplished yourself. You always had means, then what happened?" Vineet persisted.

"Nothing too important, Son. They once helped us by sharing their hospital room when your Mom had taken ill. Mrs. Sood was quite a support when our own elders could not come." Navneet said.

"You mean when Mom had a miscarriage and had to get an emergency hysterectomy done," Vineet asked, looking stiffly at the shocked faces of both his parents.

"You didn't need to know that." His father said firmly holding his wife's hand to console her whose eyes had welled up listening to Vineet.

"Why, Dad? Why should not I? I'm not your little baby any more, not to ever know what you went through in your life. We are family and families share their happiness and grief alike. Why do you always want to not include me in?" He asked.

"Vineet...." His father said in a raised voice, but his mother held his hand, gesturing him to let her speak.

"It's not about not sharing, Vineet. You are our only son, and we don't want to burden you with information that could rattle you when you were a child, and later, it didn't matter. We had you, and that was enough for us." She said softly coming to a chair next to him and held his upper arm.

"It mattered to me, Mom. All those years, I lived a lonely life thinking, my parents didn't want me to come between their scheme of things. All those years I thought that I came into your life accidently and you weren't ready to have children, so you never planned another. I felt unloved and lonely." He said tears making a way out of his eyes.

Navneet and Rashmi were stunned by his revelations.

"That's not right, Son. We were forced to put you in boarding for your safety as I was constantly posted in troubled nations when you were growing up. We did not have a choice, and about the sibling, you already know." Navneet said, trying to control his emotions as his wife, Rashmi sobbed.

"That I know now. You should've told, Dad. I would've understood. I resented you and Mom for years, and now I feel awful." He said, taking his sobbing mother in his arms.

"I'm sorry, Vin. I'm just so sorry. In our efforts to protect you physically, we didn't see, we were hurting you more emotionally and psychologically. You don't have a reason to feel awful for our mistake. I can't rectify the past but going forward, we'll see to it that this doesn't happen." Rashmi said between her sobs while Navneet came to his side as well and hugged both of them from behind. Their tears cleared the clouds of mistrust that had shadowed their relationship for a very long time. He had his family back, and his parents had their life.

"Where did you meet Gen. Sood and Mrs. Sood, Vin?" Rashmi asked as they settled down in their living room for dessert after the emotional drama at the dinner table.

"Oh. They... they happen to be the grandparents of one of my friends. Srishti is the name." He said, trying not to look flustered. He had not thought that his Mom would ask him that.

"Their daughter's daughter, is it?" Rashmi asked excitedly remembering the little girl she'd held in her arms after having lost her own.

"Yeah. That's her." He said, keeping it short.

"You know, you'd wanted to bring her home. I'd been preparing you to accept the baby that I was to deliver, your sibling and then that accident happened. I lost the baby and the ability to have another child again. Mrs. Sood had consoled me saying, I was lucky that I had you. You were so fixated to bring the baby home; you had cried knowing that we were not getting one and then you'd wanted to bring her home. We kinda had a tough time trying to make you understand that she was too young and needed her mother. And you had agreed on the pretext that we would get her home later. You'd cried for days or probably a couple of months before you came to terms with it and forgot about her." She recollected fondly.

"Maybe I didn't forget Mom. I just let it pass, and you never fulfilled your promise." He said, smiling now.

"What do you mean, Vin?" Rashmi asked, looking surprised.

"I mean, I'm going to do that someday, something that you forgot to do. I'm going to bring Srishti home and then never let her go." He said, a naughty smile playing on his lips.

"You mean...what I think it is?" Rashmi asked, her eyes shining with excitement.

"Yes, Mom. You think, right. I'm in love. I'm madly in love with Srishti." He said excitedly. "I hope you don't have an issue with that."

"Are you kidding me? It's the best news we've heard in a million years. We're happy if you are. Isn't it Navneet?" She said enthusiastically.

"Yes, we are. If it's her who has done this you, there isn't any other girl for you. I'm sure you chose right. God bless you." Navneet came and hugged him back.

"Show us her picture." Rashmi cried.

Vineet took out his phone and scrolled through the album. Rashmi took the phone in her hand feeling her face softly with her fingertips, her heart blessing the little girl who'd given her the taste of having her own daughter and now her son was hers again because of her.

"I love her, Vin. I loved her back then when she was merely two days old, and I love her more now knowing that she has tamed my wild son." She said, pulling him closer and kissing his temple.

"But she must be junior to you. Isn't she?" Navneet asked.

"Yeah. Srishti will be completing her MBA a year after I do, Dad and that's the toughest part. She still has two and a half years to complete her studies, and she won't tell her family about us before that. By the way, she lost her parents when she was three. Her paternal grandparents have raised her." Vineet said, sitting back reclining against the headrest of the couch.

"Oh! I see." Navneet exclaimed somberly and Rashmi took over and continued, "That changes nothing, Vineet. A few years of courtship is good. You both are too young to think about it right now. Enjoy the time you have together now. We'll formalize the relationship when the time comes." Rashmi said.

"Yeah. You are right, Mom. And thanks for understanding. I never told you guys, but I love you, I love both of you very much." He said, putting his arms around both of them who sat on his either side.

"We didn't need words to know if you loved us or not Vin. We knew you did. We have resentment with people we've expectations from. There could be differences in the family, but love never goes out. Now, let's put all that behind us. It's time for celebration. Our son is in love after all." Rashmi chirped.

Her family was complete and happy. There was nothing more she could wish for.

Vineet got up; kissing his parents goodnight went to his room. He was tired after a 22-hour long journey, but he'd to call up Srishti to tell her the good news. He'd already texted her about his arrival as soon as the plane had touched down. He calculated India time to make her the call.

Chapter 18

Srishti's phone rang while she was lazing in the afternoon sun after the sumptuous lunch Dadi had gotten made. She still lay with her head in Dadi's lap. She got up quickly to pick the phone from the coffee table and looked at the international number.

"I'll just take it, Dadi." She said and ran towards her room with her phone in hand and closed the room door. Her heart was thudding heavily in her chest. She picked the phone.

'Hey. What took you forever to get the call?' Vineet asked impatiently.

'And what I may ask took you so long to call? You landed four hours ago.' She complained.

'So we're playing games now. Aren't we?' He asked.

'No. I was outside with Dadi. Came running in to get the call.' She justified.

'And I was creasing out the differences with my parents. It's all good now. I told them about you.' He said.

'No way Vin! It's too early. How could you?' She said.

'Relax Sera. They aren't coming to your house to ask for your hand any time soon. I told them, and they were ecstatic about it. You should've seen the expression on their faces. It was priceless.' He said.

'Okay, if you say so. What are you doing now?' She asked.

'Besides missing you, I'm totally drained out and am going to hit the bed just as I finish the call or rather, I might fall asleep while talking to you. Please disconnect the call if that happened. It's ISD, you know.' He mumbled.

'No Sir, you do that yourself and call me the first thing in the morning which happens to be my midnight. Till then, keep missing me.' She retorted.

He cut the call and fell into a deep sleep shortly. Srishti kept the phone close to her chest and closed her eyes, taking a deep breath. The next two and a half years felt never-ending, but she knew that at the end of it, her future awaited her with open arms.

His day began with a call to her, and her day ended with his. They had found their pattern in their long-distance romance. He made her happy with his stories, got her emotional with his love quips, and made her blush with his romantic references.

A week later, Naina had called.

'Hey there! What's cooking? I can smell the fish.' Naina had asked.

'Why do you think like that?' Srishti asked.

'Well, I don't know. You tell me. Mom just spoke about a very young and handsome man. I thought you won't bring just about anyone home.' Naina asked.

'He happened to have dropped us home.' Srishti said.

'You sure, it's nothing?' Naina asked, getting serious.

'Actually, it is, but I wanted to keep it under the wraps until I completed my degree. Granny said that it was between two of us. She broke the code.' Srishti said, complaining.

'No, she didn't. She just mentioned about him from the time she'd known his parents. I was simply pulling your leg.

You seem to have ceded to my tactics. So tell me all about it.' Naina said.

'You know that amounts to cheating.' Srishti asked.

'Cheating or whatever, tell me about him.' Naina said.

'Well, he's a senior; an eco grad from IIT Kanpur and studying Finance 1st Year. What else you wanna know.' She asked.

'Those are stats dearie. I wanna know how much are you into him.' Naina asked again.

'Quite much.' She said.

'I hope you know all about protection.' Naina asked.

'Hey. That's not what I meant Masi. We're taking it slow. We are in no hurry.' She cried.

'You sure?' Naina asked again.

'100%.' Srishti reassured her.

'Do you love him, Srish?' Naina asked on a serious note.

'Yeah, I do, and so does he. Put your doubts aside and feel happy for me.' She chirped.

'Oh! I'm happy for you sweetie but stay cautioned always. More you trust, bigger hit you take if it crashes.' Naina warned.

'I'm aware, but you don't worry. Our relationship is founded on a firm basis like the 'till death do us apart' kinds.' She boasted.

'Watch what you say, Srish. Death doesn't just do people apart. It rips them apart. It shreds the one who's left behind, and even if you put those pieces together, you aren't the same person anymore. All your life, you are just stitching the gaping wounds that keep opening from one place or another.' Naina shouted into the phone.

' I...I...I'm sorry Masi. I really am.' She stammered.

Naina inhaled heavily enough for her to hear that. Srishti had evidently scratched the old wounds.

'No. I'm sorry, but you and I are both the victims of it, the death of our loved ones, Srish. Don't use it so loosely.' Naina said.

'I'll take care of it from now on. And you take care of yourself. I'm sorry once again. I hope I didn't spoil your day.' She apologized.

'Talking to you could never do that to me but yeah, keep me posted. Good night sweetheart.' Naina said and cut the call. Srishti had opened her old wounds today, the kind of wounds that you believed have healed with the passage of time, but they bled just the same even with effortless grazing, a mere touch sometimes.

Shivesh was out on tour and children had already left for school. She called in sick at the office and went back to her room. She needed to let her steam out today in a very long time, and she was glad that Shivesh wasn't around. Srishti's admission of having fallen in love had her mind reeling back to the time when she stood in her shoes, only it ended in a raw deal. Srishti had thought her reaction to being out of her loss, the loss of her twin, but she had other reasons just as well buried in her heart.

When the tears had dried, and her heart had felt empty, she leaned back closing her eyes peeping into a complete blankness. She wanted that blankness, the nothingness for a change to help her dissolve the unspoken and forgotten flickers of her life that came to haunt her time and again, tugging her heart, dragging her back to the barren lands, she'd run away from. But it eluded her just as always. Those flashes never ceased to leave her, accusing her of the betrayal. For all the years of her now married life, she'd been trying to negotiate her way through life so as not to face the acridity of own conscience, she'd unknowingly held herself captive of.

'A sliver of light came piercing through her darkness, and there he was with all the charisma that still had the power to pull her towards him. She stood her ground as she wanted to, reminding herself that it wasn't where she belonged now, but her insides revolted against her own resolve. He was a part of her being. She stood back, her face marred with jaded emotions while he extended his hand, his eyes a whirlpool of unfulfilled desires. She closed her eyes, and in a matter of moments, she was in his arms, a sense of tranquility washing over her soul. Nothing else existed, just their souls soaked in the elixir of the unadulterated love, they had once felt for each other, transporting her back to the time that defined their relationship going forward.

She was her mischievous self, and he was the one with restraint, but on that rainy evening, it washed away all the control, all the inhibitions that they ever knew.

She wound up her play at the college and was ready to leave for home with him, on his Enfield. He insisted that she changed into her denim and shirt, but she refused. It only felt surreal to have him watch her get wet in the sky blue chiffon sari that she wore for the play. She was feeling just filmy, acting on her instincts while he wore a worried look, but there was little he could do to make her change her mind. He only took out his denim jacket and put it on her shoulders before they drove back. She kept teasing him, tantalizing him from the rear seat before they got inside their residential complex and it was only then she realized as to what explanation would she give to her mother for not changing her clothes. She insisted that they go to his place so that she could get into her denim. He abided by her wishes. She wanted to stand in the open and sing and dance in the rain only if it wasn't the army residential complex where everyone knew everyone. They entered his small, under-furnished quarter. She had been there before, but it felt energized that day. She took off his jacket; her curvaceous form visible through the now transparent Sari sticking to her like a second skin. He looked away, his own chiseled body peeping through his now wet white shirt. He wiped his face with his hands lifting them to his head to smoothen his ruffled hair; his expressions not visible to her. She felt a sting in her heart, her hands itching to feel those taut muscles under her palms. Her feet took her to him, and as she snaked her arms around his trunk from behind his back, she heard a gasp with an intake of his deep breath that matched hers. His body tensed, and she felt the tremor rising in his body that vibrated her insides as well.

"Not now, sweetheart." He murmured.

"Ummm..." was all she could manage.

He turned towards her in a rush and took her in his arms, her veil landing on the floor, leaving her semi-naked bosom to his view. He didn't pay attention and held her tightly in his arms lest his control gave up, but she wanted more. She kissed his neck frantically going up to his very defined jawline. He tried not to before he could bear no more and captured her lips in his, pushing his full form against her pinning her against the wall. She undid the buttons of his shirt to feel the pulsating rigidity against her almost bare skin, and he tugged her, his erection pressing hard against her pelvis, their raging hormones treading along the point of no return.

"Don't test my patience, baby. I'm only human." He gurgled.

"Don't then. Give me what's mine. All of it and now." She pleaded.

That had him. He lifted her up like she was a rag doll and took her to his room. They were in a daze. When they lost their clothes, they didn't know, merging their bodies and their souls with a salvo over-riding their bridled desires; the salvation of their sanity and a pristine spectacle of the celebration of love in the purest of forms. The time stood still as they rode the high tide of human emotions where nothing else mattered.

There on, they floated hand-in-hand across the clouds, and they wandered around the woods in a sheer state of tranquility. She stood in his sturdy arms, secure and protected just when she felt his loosening grip and a splash of red fluid soaking her Sari. He lay limp, his majestic body falling on the ground, lifeless. She stood there soaked in his love; the most beautiful color of red that coursed through his body once. She was shocked. She wanted to lie down on top of him to stop the invisible hands, which were trying to pry him away. She felt those hands on herself, restricting her and peeling her Sari, the last of his insignias printed on it in the form of his blood. She wanted it back, her garment, and his blood that he'd left for her, his last signature of their undying love. They washed her as they tried washing every remnant of his being from her body even before his pyre had gotten cold. She stretched her hands to take away the last of her possessions, her Sari that lay there, but she was pulled away. She didn't have the energy left to resist. She walked away, leaving everything behind, only to fall into the arms of Shivesh, her savior.'

She opened her eyes with a start with her entire body soaked in perspiration. This dream, a stark reminder of her first love, her first act of lovemaking was muddled with the images of her repressed psychosis and had been haunting her for years. She knew that it didn't end the way she always saw it in her dreams, the beautiful vision of her proximity to him that always ended into a nightmare.

She was so in love with him, but for him, she stood at a distant second. His first love was his uniform and the Tricolor that he got to adorn when his bullet-ridden glorious body was laid out to receive the guard of honor along with four others of his unit. She'd lost him to destiny, and it tore her beyond repair. In her own grief, she was so stoned that she couldn't see what happened around her. She couldn't see a little Srishti wailing in the arms of her grandmother, who was just as inconsolable on the loss of her own son, her only son. She saw Neha disintegrating right in front of her eyes, and she did nothing to rescue her while she could. She was as guiltier of betrayal to Srishti, as to herself. She had no courage to face that orphaned little girl so much so that she didn't come to India for ten years hence.

She got lucky that Shivesh's unfathomed love had held her together, but today Srishti's words had disturbed her She wanted to tell her so much, share with her what she felt in her heart, wished to know how was Srishti handling her relationship and had wanted to be a part of her happiness but she couldn't. She felt deprived of her right on her. She had abandoned her totally for years out of compulsions first and then out of guilt. She couldn't reverse the time and make amends now. The thought of Srishti, knowing that she had the blood of her mother on her hands, was killing her from within. She had cheated the very people who had loved her unconditionally, and she stood guilty if not charged. She didn't know if she was capable of making up to Srishti for whatever wrong she'd done to her or for that matter to Shivesh for keeping the most significant truth of her life from him. It had been eighteen years, and though she'd moved on in her life with Shivesh and her sons, Srishti stood as a stark reminder of her misdoings that muzzled her heart time and again, something she was incapable of redeeming in this life.

Chapter 19

Srishti had never felt happier going back to the college after her break like she felt this time. Vineet was getting back after a couple of days. He'd called her up a few days before she left.

'Hey there! Ready to go back.' He asked.

'Like never before. When are you reaching?' She asked.

'A couple of days, after the classes start! Stopping over in Singapore for a few days with Mom and Dad.' He said.

'I'll miss you.' She said.

'So would I. I'm still to shop for you Sera. I still don't have your stats.' He asked.

'I don't want any Vin. I'm not gonna say anything.' She had turned crimson on his insinuation.

'Please. I'm going out shopping today, and I'm excited about it.' He said.

'No and what's the point if you are never going to get to see what you bought.' She said cheekily.

'Please. Never-say-never! We'll see about that. Meanwhile, you can text it to me if you want. I'll be waiting.' He said.

'Okay.' She said, giving in.

'I Love You.' He said.

'I Love you more.' She said, and cut the call.

She looked at the phone and kissed it as if it was he it would be getting wired to but what the hell, she thought.

For a fleeting moment, Naina Masi's words resonated in her ears, but then she shrugged and opened the message box. She wrote the smallest message of her life. *'34B/M'* and pressed send and hit her forehead with the phone thinking of what she just did. Vineet was right. These gestures of romance were priceless, and now she wanted to live them to the fullest before she gave in to her desires.

The life on campus got busier by the day, but they snatched their moments of love one way or another. Sometimes their desperation increased, but their resolve to stay put was stronger, and they made it up for the other when one got weaker. A year and a half passed, and it was already the time for Vineet to leave. He'd landed a plum job with an Investment Banking Giant with their base in New York, and he was required to join their Delhi office. His father had helped him get the interview call, and he'd made him proud by acing it.

Vineet was happy about it, and so was Srishti, but in their hearts, they knew what troubled them. It was a period of separation they both knew would come and were prepared to go through it, but when the time came, it made it no less easy. He had taken her on a four-day trip to a nearby Resort before they left for Delhi. He was leaving for good, and she had her vacations after the completion of one year of PGP. Few of their common friends had gone along.

Meanwhile, she did her internship with a company in Delhi till the next term began and they spent their evenings together. Their dependence on each other increased. Her Granny now knew about their relationship, but she neither confronted her for the same nor approved of it. In her heart, she was dreading to witness the conflict that came along with

Srishti's relationship to Vineet, but she knew better to be a silent spectator till the lid blew. She genuinely liked Vineet.

Srishti had felt empty when she'd gotten back to the campus for the first time with Vineet not there, after they were together for two years. Naina had consoled her, saying that their generation was lucky that they had the advantage of technology on their side. They could easily call or video call, and they had aerial connectivity with regular flights between their respective cities. Vineet had promised to visit at least once in a month. She'd felt lost, but her friends had proved to be handy and the time sailed. Vineet had kept his promise and had come as often as his job permitted.

She was actually enjoying the space between them, which came with the occasional perks in the form of his emotional urgency. The tug she felt in her heart that made her realize what he meant to her. She couldn't envision her life without him, and she could barely wait for her, waiting to be over and for the time when she went and told her grandparents about Vineet. She was so sure about their positive reaction towards her happiness that not for a moment, she stopped to think of a situation if they disapproved.

Vineet was the kind of a guy, parents wanted their daughters to wed, she had thought, but how it worked with her Dada Ji, she never thought otherwise.

Srishti had landed a plum job with an e-retailer firm during the campus selection and had to join their Delhi office on request. She got what she had wanted and shared it with Vineet. He almost danced with joy at the great news. Their destiny seemed all set to roll out the next phase of their shared life, the time they'd waited for long. Surprisingly enough, Dada Ji had not sounded too happy when she'd told him about the campus selection. He'd merely said on the phone.

'You write the exams of your final term, and we'll see about that.'

Dadi brushed it off, saying that they were happy for her and she should first focus on her last term. She felt disconnected with them for the very first time in her life, but she let it pass.

Her Pre-convocation happened in March, and that was the time she along with her friends realized, it was the time to go back to their respective folds making tall promises to stay in touch. Vineet had come to attend the ceremony, and she was overjoyed to have him there to share her happiness with. She hadn't spoken about her job offer to her grandparents ever again till her end of term exams were over, and they had also not broached the topic. It was a teary farewell to her friends as well as for the institution that was her home for the last five years. After that, they would be the Alumina of the Institution they held in very high esteem.

Vineet had come to pick her up at the Delhi airport after she'd wound up things at Indore. She was staying at Granny's for a few days before she flew down to Jammu. Dada Ji wanted to welcome her back early, but she insisted, she stayed back for a few days. It was then she'd openly spoken to Granny and Grandpa about her decision to get married to Vineet.

They blessed her with their permission but had insisted that it was a decision her other set of Grandparents had to be ready for since they were the ones who had brought her up. Her optimism had surprised Granny though knowing fairly well what conflict lay ahead. Only she didn't want to kill her enthusiasm until the time she was there. After four days of stay at Delhi, she'd left for Jammu promising Vineet; the next time they met would be for finalizing their nuptials.

Srishti was in for a surprise when she came to know that Dada Ji had thrown a big celebratory party on the same night as she reached to celebrate her homecoming. She had felt so happy at their gesture.

The evening was great as her old friends, distant cousins, and the family friends joined in her celebration. Dada Ji was always up for parties, and she always enjoyed this easy and fun side of him. Maybe he'd seen the death from such close quarters and knew the uncertainty the life came with, he lived every moment to the fullest. Dadi was introducing her to some of their new friends.

They were so exhausted by the time the party got over that conversation was the last thing on their mind. Srishti slept off texting to Vineet, her inability to talk that night.

She'd slept till late and had gotten up when Dadi had called her for breakfast. They were busy discussing something when Srishti joined them on the breakfast table. She went to them to kiss them Good Morning.

"You look Happy. Am I missing something?" She said, looking at them pulling the chair to sit.

"Why isn't it enough that you are back and a management graduate to top that?" Dada Ji said.

"Yeah, but what difference does that make? I'll be going to join the job in a couple of months much like I did during college." She said, taking a bite of her toast.

"And who said that we are letting you go this time?" He asked, looking squarely at her face.

"What? Stop joking. You wouldn't do that and plus I'll be nearer. I can come home pretty often, at least once in a month." She said, sipping her chocolate shake.

"I'm not joking Srishti. Please understand. We want you to stay here. We'll start something on our own. We are getting old now, and we would want you to settle down. There are a lot of marriage proposals that have come for you. Please meet the guys, and we'll see how it goes. After all, your professional choices would depend heavily on the man you marry." Dada Ji said on a serious note and got up to go, running his hand over her head.

If Srishti was shocked, it was an understatement.

She looked at Dadi, the expressions on whose face looked torn between the unanimous decision of her husband and the shock written all over Srishti's face. Dadi's lips moved to form some words to console her, but it was her helplessness that spoke through her eyes.

Srishti wanted to say so much, rather scream at the top of her lungs but her vocal cords wouldn't help her. She got up briskly and ran to go back to her room. Her head was spinning, and the skies seemed to have come down crashing upon her. She'd just landed and had landed herself in trouble. Her individuality was at risk, and so was her love, and she hadn't even spoken to them about him yet.

Chapter 20

The year 2017

She looked at her room, a room that stood witness to her carefree days did not look like her own. Who was she? Was she the same Srishti who enjoyed an unequivocal love and adoration of her grandparents? They were the only family she'd known for as long as she was alive. The other people had filled in as she grew up, but they were her anchors and today they rocked the same boat they had taught how to sail in rough waters.

Who was that person who spoke to her the way he did today imposing his decisions thoughtlessly? It could not be her beloved Dada Ji who knew what she wanted even before she spelled it. It could definitely not be her Dada Ji who had loved her unconditionally, gave in to all her tantrums, her demands, and encouraged her to be the confident self that she was today. It could not be him because he was the one who had taught her to look beyond the paucities of her life, beyond the disparities that plagued the gender-centric mindset of our society and helped her evolve as an individual. She was shocked to see this face of him. He was the one who had helped her develop the ability to choose between right and wrong and had taught her to fight when she was right. But today he stood right across from her shoving all those ideal notions and preaching under the carpet telling her that she was nothing but a responsibility for him and her worth depended upon the man she married. He did not even wait for a day for her to indulge in their warmth that she'd missed for years living away from them. He didn't also wish to ask anything about her opinion as to how she wanted to lead her life. She sat on her bed thinking what should she tell Vineet about what just happened. She knew, he would stand by her side whatever came her way and would not hesitate to fight any battle to have her in his life, but she didn't want it. She didn't want to stand across from her family if the battle lines were drawn, but she wasn't ready to give in without a fight for the man, she so loved.

She wiped her tears. It was not the time to back down. She could debate with them; tell them about Vineet and maybe, what all she was thinking right now was an over-exaggeration of her own thoughts. Maybe when they knew about Vineet and knew that he lived in Delhi, they wouldn't mind her joining the job. Perhaps they were scared of her living on her own. College campuses are always safer places, but maybe, the apprehensions they had were derived out of the fear that she would be living all by herself in a big city. Why was she simply being negative? They loved her, and they would be happy in her happiness only if they knew, she was safe. The conflicts within her own mind were killing her already, but this thought brought a smile on her face. She would have to tell them about Vineet and fast. Maybe, things would crease out eventually.

With these thoughts, she turned on the music and left to take a shower, thinking that later she would sit them down and talk to them about her life plans. She was sure they would consider it if not be too enthusiastic about it.

Her hands trembled as she opened her suitcase to unpack her stuff, but she chided herself for thinking like that about her family and about her home. Later, she opened the door of her room to go to Dadi's, but from across the living room, she saw their door half open, and the heated voices of her grandparents hit her ears. Dadi was trying to tell him something while he was repeatedly running her down. She'd never seen them or heard them arguing the way they did today. It was not the time for a conversation and definitely not for a confrontation. She got into her room and closed the door.

It was around the lunchtime that Dadi called out for her. She shook herself out of her negativity and called back saying; she was coming. She would not let the morning incident shake her confidence in them.

She took her seat on the dining table without any fuss registering the gaze of both of them who were gauging her mood. She smiled at them, letting Dadi serve her the food and started eating. There was no discussion on the table today, unlike all the other times when they dined together. Many a time Dadi had to scold her to eat her food properly, but today, no one interrupted. They settled on the living room couch after the meal. It was her best shot, she thought.

She cleared her throat but didn't know how to start her conversation.

"I...I wanted to talk about the job offer I've accepted already." She mustered up the courage to speak.

"What about that? I told you, I don't want you to take it." Dada Ji said firmly.

"Yes. You did but understand that it is my first job, a selection through the campus and I've already signed the bond. They've offered me the NCR office, especially on demand and I'm obliged not to go back on it since it would reflect poorly on my CV as well as on the reputation of my institution." She said calmly.

"Listen Srishti, I'm sure there is some way out. There always is because I'm not comfortable to send you away and to be on your own any longer. I didn't stop you when you went to college though I was not very comfortable with that either. This would have to stop now. We would have to think about other things about your future." He justified.

"This is future Dada Ji, this very job is my first step towards a future, an independent future. This is exactly what you let me go for in the first place, to make an identity for myself. I don't understand why do you stop me now?" She kept her cool.

"No. I let you go because that was what you wanted to do then. I'd always let you do what you'd wanted to do but this time hear me out and try doing what I'm telling you to do. It can't be that bad." He said, trying to make her understand.

"So you say that I've consumed my lifetime quota of 'I want to do this.' That was what I was eligible for in this lifetime. Is it?" She asked.

"Look, what you don't understand is that we'll be worried if you lived alone in the NCR." He said.

"I can live at Granny's. I don't think anything could get any safer than that." She asked.

"Also, we want you to settle down, and before that happened, we want you to spend some more time here, with us." He said, twisting the conversation.

"And how do you suppose people settle down without accepting a job offer. To settle down, you've to be able to be financially independent, to be able to pay your bills and be in a position to make decisions. Your insinuations are not making any of those happen." She said.

"By settling down, I meant, get married. You are twenty-three already, and I crossed eighty, last year. I'm not getting any younger. I want to discharge this one last duty before the heavens come calling for me." He said in a resigning tone.

Srishti breathed deeply and came over to his side. Putting her arms around his neck, she said. "You are not going away anytime soon Dada Ji. Why do you worry so much? You have done a great job of raising me and making me self-sufficient. What makes you think that I can't take care of myself?"

"I'm not saying that Srishti. You can move heaven and earth if you so wanted but understand that I'm responsible for your wellbeing. I want to make sure you are well taken care of." He said.

"What am I then, a three-year-old who did not know how to take care of herself when my parents died? You did take care of me then and did a fine job, but I'm a big girl now who doesn't need to get married so that she was taken care of. That I can do for myself. If I wanted to get married and I do, it has to be out of love. I'm not and will not be a burden on a man or his family for my survival. I'll meet him on an equal footing, and you know I can." Srishti said as Dada Ji looked on squarely at her face.

"Do you like someone?" Dadi asked this time.

"Yes, I do. His name is Vineet, my senior at IIM. He's working in Delhi as an investment banker with a Multi-national firm." She finally said. There was shock written all over their faces.

Suddenly Dada Ji got up and went to his room. Dadi looked at her with a mixed emotion of sympathy and helplessness. She had always appeared to be a strong lady, or so she thought. She'd never been witness to any kind of conflict between them, or that conflict was never there because Dadi could never stand the ground in front of him. She did what he expected her to do. The arrangement suited them fine, but for her, it was a bitter truth to swallow.

Srishti got up quietly and went to her room as well. She would have to give them some time to absorb the newfound information, something they were totally not ready for. She would have taken some time and then would have told Dadi before she went all throttle with Dada Ji.

According to his beliefs, she might have impinged upon the territory he held, the duty, he thought was his and the undisputed right he felt on her to make the decision of her marriage, but she could not care. Three decades back, her parents had made the very decision by themselves, and if her grandparents had accepted it that long back, they would do so now, only if she persisted and did not lose faith in herself. Now she knew, it was a battle from here on; the battle that she would lose whichever way it went if she had to choose between Vineet or them and it was wiser to turn them on her turf rather than to go on an all-out war.

Vineet's love was precious, but so was theirs. She hated the idea of choosing between the two. She composed and promised herself, she would not raise her voice and would try to debate with him for as long as it took him to understand her. She was a soldier's daughter and giving up on what she believed in was not a route she could ever think of choosing.

She started arranging her closet with her stuff that she'd gotten from the boarding. She was there to stay for quite some time, and she did better get going starting from making herself comfortable in her own house.

The thought put a smile on her face, and she patted her back saying.

'Welcome, Home Srishti! The Battle Begins...'

Chapter 21

Srishti hadn't seen Dada Ji the whole day after lunch. He had to go somewhere for a couple of days, and this time, he didn't even meet her before he left. Dadi remained non-committal, rather evasive the whole time trying not to broach the topic of Vineet with her. She felt offended; somewhat hurt at their behavior but swallowed her pride and acted as normal as she could.

Later in the evening, she finally asked Dadi where had he gone.

"He's gone to Srinagar for some secretarial work. He'll be back in two days." Dadi said.

"Really. Dada Ji could have taken us along as well. I haven't been there for so many years now." She said cheerfully.

"Things are not very smooth in there. He wouldn't have." Dadi said, sipping her tea.

"Are you angry with me, Dadi?" Srishti asked.

"Well, what can I say? You should have at least told me earlier. Your Dada Ji was not expecting it nor was I. So, maybe a little disappointed." She said.

"I'm sorry for that but please, meet Vineet. You will definitely like him." Srishti pleaded.

"That's one decision which is for your Dada Ji to make, Srishti. I'll go with whatever he thought was right for you. I would have to." Dadi said in a resigning tone.

Srishti nodded and kept quiet. There was no reason to argue any further if Dadi couldn't even take a stand for her. It would have to be a one-on-one now with Dada Ji, and though she didn't like the thought of it, she barely had a choice. She would have to wait for him.

She got up and went in to call her school friends and decided to meet them the next day. She needed to recharge herself before she went on an all-out war with the man she'd always looked up to.

After two days, she heard Dada Ji's over-the-top laughter from the living room as she was entering the house having spent her day with her friends. He was sitting in the living room sipping his tea with a bunch of his friends from the army. Srishti went in and greeted them.

"Here! See my beautiful and intelligent granddaughter, Srishti. She's back after her MBA." He introduced her to them.

"That's wonderful. Where are you joining Srishti?" Asked Col. Pradeep.

"I..." Dada Ji unceremoniously interrupted Srishti even before she uttered a word.

"Oh! She has an offer from a very big company, but I'm telling her to stay around for a while. I want to take her for a trip around the state that we live in. You must know where you belong before you step out to explore the world." He said in a very decisive tone, and Srishti had no choice but to nod in affirmation.

She excused herself in a while and went to her room. She had no clue as to what Dada Ji meant by what he said, but all she could do was to wait. He sure had something on his mind, which meant, he wasn't giving up anytime soon.

Was he buying time to see if she would be able to get over Vineet, something she knew she wouldn't? She changed into her pajamas and plunked on her bed. She texted a quick message to Vineet and slept. He was on an official trip to New York for a fortnight, and she didn't want to bother him with the situation at hand. That was her mess, and she would have to clear it all by herself. Dadi had later come to call her for dinner but on seeing her in a deep sleep thought not to disturb her.

Srishti opened her eyes to a new day. The morning rays of the sun were filtering through the sheer curtains of her room. She looked at the clock. It was a little past five. She got up and thought of going for a jog like she always did when she was at home. Dada Ji had been a tough taskmaster when it came to maintaining a healthy and sporty lifestyle. Even at eighty, he still went on regular walks. She changed into her tracks and hit the road that led to the nearby park where she'd spent every morning of her childhood running and working out at the huge jungle gym that Dada Ji had contributed to building for the children of their area. The warmth of the mid-summer dawn made her realize how much she'd missed being here. Back at the Institute, she preferred to work out in the gym or play squash or basketball to keep her fit but the feeling of the early morning run was something, she always loved.

She was through with a good three-kilometer run when she stopped to catch her breath. She moved out from the track to the middle of the ground for some stretches and there he was. Dada Ji was looking at her lovingly as he completed his yoga lessons along with his friends. She waved at him and completed her own work out before heading towards him.

"So, you still jog. I thought you must have taken to the newer ways of exercise in college." He asked as she reached closer.

"I don't mind either. Air is a lot cleaner here to enjoy the jog." She said, wiping her face with her face towel.

"What's the plan for today?" He asked as they started towards their home.

"Nothing much. You tell me." She said casually.

"I'm going towards one of the forward posts today, closer to the Border. Want to come along?" He asked.

"Yeah. I'd like to but what for?" She asked.

"The ceasefire violations are on a high, and the villagers are terrified as well as agitated. Forces are doing their bit, but they had asked if I could go over there and comfort the people in their language, they would really appreciate. I agreed." He said.

"Is it safe to go there?" She asked hesitatingly.

"It's never safe where an army man is called in. We make it safe; make the people feel safe. But you don't have to be scared of it. I won't let anything harm you." He said, putting an arm on her shoulder and she knew that he wouldn't.

They freshened up and had a sumptuous breakfast before they left for their adventure closer to the Border, the area that was usually out of bounds for the civilians. She'd never been to this side of their town. The perimeter of the Border was fully fenced with electric poles with halogen lights. In that very region, BSF guarded the International Border between India and Pakistan. Closer to the Border, there were some homes of the villagers that resided almost at the line of fire. A few of the houses bore the marks of destruction caused by the mortar shelling, but in all, life was going on as usual. They drove all the way towards Suchetgarh that led to the gate towards Pakistan and stopped over at the pillar number 919, the crossroad that separated two warring nations.

The sound of guns had fallen silent, but the desperate cries for help could be heard and felt in the depilated homes and desolate farms around the region. Srishti had never been privy to this side of devastation that was taking place so close to her home. It was indeed a chilling realization of the fact;

how safe she'd always felt inside her home like millions of others in our country whereas these people bore the brunt of the enemy's aggression down generations and still held on.

One of the officers was narrating Dada Ji about the issues of the villagers and the excesses caused by the mortar shelling from across the Border. They then moved towards the school where the villagers had gathered along with the local politician. Dada Ji tried quelling their fears, told them how to recognize the live shells, and inform the nearby BSF posts to help diffuse them among other motivational stuff.

Srishti stood at a distance watching the whole thing. The people were scared, but they were just as helpless. The villagers had no other place to go to. The shadow of death loomed large over their heads. The future of their children looked bleak, and the only source of their earning was the paddy fields that kept them alive. And off lately, those very fields bore the craters formed by the mortar shells from across the Border, and the fear of having live shells in there kept the villagers away from working in their land holdings. The government authorities made rounds of the place, promising them compensations, but the promises were forgotten just as soon as they left those places. At times like this, such congregations with the locals who could placate them and take their voice forward were brought in, and that was the reason for Dada Ji to be there. He had been on both sides; his tryst with the armed forces as well as at the receiving end of the civilian disquiet. His farms that were closer to the Border and were looked after by the tilling help bore a similar look.

There were some food supplies, which were distributed to the people, and the assurance to repair their houses was made. She was astonished to see the involvement of the armed forces in looking after the interest of the villagers when the guns were down, and these would be the very men deflecting the wrath of the enemy when the guns came out blazing.

For a moment, she'd forgotten her own worries, and she wondered if that was what Dada Ji intended to do when he'd asked her to come along. But whatever it was, she felt glad; she came there. Instances like such make us aware of the amenities of life we so take for granted.

She interacted with some village women and heard their stories, each one distressing than the other. She really wondered why were these people still holding on to that region, but she didn't have the heart to ask that out loud. She didn't want to rub salt in their already bleeding wounds, but she did decide to ask Dada Ji about it sometime later.

She met Radha whose husband had suffered a shrapnel injury on his leg while working in his field. He kept bleeding unknown to anyone till the firing between the two sides subsided, and the extent of damage was beyond repair. The time lapsed between the injury and till the time he reached the hospital. His leg had to be amputated little below his knee and in the process; the only breadwinner of the family was incapacitated to earn his living. The compensation came in terms of monetary benefit but psychologically; the man lost his confidence to do good by his family and thus became alcoholic. Radha now worked in the farms with some help from the villagers and looked after her home, her three young children and aged parents-in-law.

There were other stories about the loss of lives and loss of livelihood due to the existing conditions; no one had a clue how best to avoid it.

By the evening, Srishti's head was spinning listening to their woes and having looked at their conditions. She simply got back to her room, freshened up and after nibbling at some small snack, put on her headphones, as she lay listless on her bed. Dadi had wanted to know as to what transpired, but Dada Ji stopped her. He felt it was better to leave her alone for a while, and so they did.

The heavy beats of AC DC drummed against her head, but they were not enough to drown out the desperate voices of the villagers from her system. She felt restless and just as helpless. She stormed out of her room to go to Dada Ji who was sitting on the veranda, talking to someone on the phone. She held her anger folding her arms against her chest and waited till he finished his conversation.

"What happened Srishti? Why are you looking so agitated?" Dadi came from behind and asked in a hushed tone. Just then, Dada Ji got off on the phone.

She first looked at Dadi and then at Dada Ji and asked angrily.

"Why are those people still living there, Dada Ji? Why doesn't the government shift them somewhere safe?"

Dada Ji looked at her with the mixed feelings of tenderness and pride and said. "Don't be in a hurry to get all the answers. You will learn and understand when you see more of it. We are going to some other villages tomorrow. See them, meet more people, and if you want, you can ask them what you are asking me."

"But why do you want to take her along? It's beside me. Let her relax. She has just gotten back from college after five years." Dadi revolted.

"No. Srishti can't. She's been relaxing for all these years. She's a soldier's daughter. She has to know what is it like to be one and what is it that they fight and sacrifice their lives for. She has to know what her father has given up his life for. These are life lessons that she should learn and remember before she starts the new phase of her life." Dada Ji said with determination and left while both Srishti and Dadi kept looking at his retreating back in astonishment.

Chapter 22

The next day, Srishti woke up early as usual and accompanied her grandparents to the nearby park where they walked, and she jogged. This was going to be her routine for days to come. She had put the topic of her job on the back burner right now. There was still time for her results to be out, and the job would start only after two and a half, maybe three months. Right now, she wanted to concentrate on what Dada Ji was up to and what was actually cooking in his mind.

His words from last evening reverberated in her head umpteen number of times since then. Was it about his father? Was there something happening on the Borders that reminded Dada Ji of how he'd lost his only son or did he simply want her to feel proud of what her father had done, the circumstances in which his martyrdom had come? She was clueless, but she planned to let him take charge for a while. Even she was curious now as to what was going on around her.

They left home after the breakfast to go to the adjoining village called Arnia, a name she'd heard just a couple of days back in relation to mortar shelling. The condition of the forward post and the adjoining homes and farms were no different. The people had been told to move out till the BSF sanitized the area. They had apprehended two armed infiltrators and gunned down another in a gun battle a day earlier. The atmosphere looked grim.

This time she lent a hand in distributing food packets to the villagers who had taken shelter in a banquet hall nearby. The injured ones had been admitted to the hospital, and some others with minor injuries were given first aid at the Primary Health Center.

While she attended to one of the women, Asha who was struggling to contain her wailing toddler, she asked her in frustration. “Why don’t you move somewhere safer? For how long can you live in fear like this?” That got her the attention of a few others as well.

For a few moments, there was stunned silence, no answer, not that she expected any. There was helplessness and worry written lit large on their faces like she had witnessed the previous day. Then, there was another woman; she didn’t remember her name; mustered up the courage and spoke. “Do you know Bibi Ji, what are the people who get displaced from their homes are called? They are called Refugees, and no one likes refugees. They are a burden on the resources of the community that they are forced upon. This place might be in trouble right now, but this is home. We are among our people who stand up for us. We stand beside each other when needed. We are interdependent on each other but being dependent is something we are not ready to be.” Her words were heavy, the feeling–strong.

Srishti felt sheepish at her proposed suggestion and apologized. “I’m sorry. I didn’t mean it that way?”

Another woman who had gotten the voice now spoke this time. “It’s okay Bibi Ji. We know, you have our best interest in your heart but have you ever been to a Refugee Camp?”

“No. I haven’t.” Srishti said.

“They are mainly temporary shelters, sometimes tents and otherwise some old building that houses ten times the number of people, it can accommodate. Here, we have our farms and our homes, which might not be very big but they protect us from the harshness of the weather. These escalations at the Border only happen once in a while, but if we leave our homes, we would be fighting much more than what we do now." She said.

"I don't understand," Srishti said.

"Living the life of slum dwellers is much harder than what it is now. Here we can grow our own food at the least, have a roof over our heads and a cooperating society. In the camps, people fight a never-ending battle with chilling cold in winters, scorching heat in summers and the rainy season is the worst. The unhygienic spaces giving rise to diseases are another cause for worry. Meanwhile, the authorities would think that they have already done their duty by moving us to a safer place, and there would be no help. That is one reason, we stick around. We are happy the way we are. At least, there are armed forces and authorities attending to us when we need it." A middle-aged woman said.

Then another one spoke. "These BSF men are here from all over India to protect us, Bibi Ji. It would be disrespect to their efforts and a win for the enemy's efforts if we got displaced. The only way we, civilians, can help them is by standing behind them and reporting any suspicious activity in our vicinity."

Srishti didn't realize, she had spent close to two hours in conversation with the women. The clarity of the thoughts of the assumingly illiterate village women amazed her, and their strong will fill her heart with pride. A whole lot of so-called educated people had a lot to learn from them, she thought.

A young girl from the crowd came forward and sat next to her before she spoke.

"It is a frightful feeling when someone is addressed as Refugee in a place that is supposed to be their home. I have lived that feeling ever since I understood what it is, and before me, the two generations of my family did."

"But you don't look like if you do not belong here. Where do you belong?" Srishti asked with utter confusion.

"If you ask me, this is the only home I have known since I was born, but the state government calls us 'West Pakistan Refugees.' We are not the citizens of this state." She said.

"What's West Pakistan Refugees? Did your family migrate recently from Pakistan?" Srishti asked.

"No. My Great-grandfather and my grandfather shifted during partition. While in other parts of India, the people like us have been granted citizenship, the case in point of that of our previous Prime Minister Dr. Manmohan Singh and Mr. Inder Kumar Gujral, but in this state of Jammu and Kashmir, we are not the State Subject holders, the permanent residents of the State. Recently, we have been given the status of citizens of India by the Central Government, but we are still called the refugees in a country we thought that we would be accepted with open arms according to the Doctrine of Partition. We are still trying to find our feet." She said, looking far away.

"I don't know what to say. It must be an awful feeling." Srishti said.

"It's much more than that. We can't buy property here. We can't study in Professional colleges for want of domicile status. We can't get government jobs or can't even participate in the voting process in the state. There are about 25,000 families of West Pakistan Refugees in the state, but no one cares because we are not a sizable population and are thus not responsible for their fate in the elections. Very recently, the Central Government has decided to issue ID certificates to our community so that we are eligible to the Central Govt. schemes and jobs and can also participate in the General Elections. That's the best that can happen, I guess in the current situation." She said.

Srishti simply nodded. For as long as she remembered, she had known her state to be faring well on the social indices. She'd not seen people sleeping on the pavements or has known them living without food. But these revelations were eye-opening. People around her lived in so much of plight, and most of the youngsters didn't even know what was happening around them. She was one of them who was aspiring to clinch the best, the life had to offer, knowing little that there were few, who were fighting for their basic rights; the right to live with dignity and had subsequently forgotten to dream.

Just then, someone came to call her as Dada Ji was done with his meetings, and they had to leave. She said bye to the women assuring them that she will come again sometime to meet them.

On their way back, she was reticent. Dada Ji asked what was the matter with her and what was it that she was so engrossed with when he had called.

"There's so much going on here. Isn't it?" She asked him, and before he could say anything, she narrated him the worries of the young refugee girl.

Dada Ji smiled as he looked at her and then said. "West Pakistan Refugees are the ones who migrated to India from Pakistan during partition and even after that. Back then; Pakistan had two territories. Pakistan of now was called West Pakistan, and East Pakistan is Bangladesh now. Most of the refugees who had migrated then have been considered the citizens of India except for the people who migrated to Jammu and Kashmir because of the dual citizenship status in the state. Only the residents who lived here from before the partition are considered to be the natives, and there is no provision to include the outsiders. Nonetheless, they are now being issued the ID certificates as the citizens of India amidst a lot of resentment from some quarters."

"Isn't it awful? How can that be? Are the provisions penned down in the Constitution so rigid that the human cries of despair can't change them or rewrite them?" She asked.

"That's one battle that's been going on for years now, but I guess, no one is ready to bite the bullet yet. Protectionism was at an all-time high when the accession of the state happened to the Indian Union, and it's worse now." He said, shaking his head in despair.

"There are so many stories, so many versions associated with the accession of Jammu and Kashmir. Why don't you explain it to me in detail." She asked, looking hopefully at his face.

"You really want to know. Most young people are not interested in it as it doesn't affect their today and when it does, they have very little to make amends." He asked.

"I do. I seriously want Dada Ji. Maybe, I wasn't, to begin with, but now that I have started seeing things differently, I want to know where it stemmed out of." She said decisively.

"Well, for now, this was all. We've reached home. Go freshen up and relax for the evening. We are going to Poonch tomorrow. It's a long journey. I'll tell you about it on the way." He said.

"Why are we going there?" She asked, surprised.

"It's your father's 20th death anniversary in two days since he was martyred. I go there every year to salute my son and all the others who have relentlessly given their life for keeping our Borders secure. I want you to come along this time. His soul will be so happy to see the woman you have become." He said, averting his eyes before he got down from his SUV as the driver halted the vehicle on their porch. She looked stunned, almost unable to move. So that was the reason, Dada Ji had been so proactive in doing what he was doing, and his enthusiasm peaked around this time around. She suddenly heard him calling her name and getting out of her thoughts, she made way to her home.

Chapter 23

Srishti was distracted for the large part of the evening. Dadi had enquired about it, but she simply brushed it aside saying, it was nothing. Her intermittent gaze was getting stuck at the picture of her father that hung in their living room, and for once, her heart swelled with the conflicting emotions of pride and deprivation. How she wished, she had known him a little more and had made some memories with him if she was a little older when he died.

Dadi noticed her unease and took her hand in hers. She looked up at the reassuring face of Dadi as if the older woman was implying; she understood her disquiet.

"Did he tell you about your father?" Dadi asked to which she nodded.

"Do you want me to talk about him?" Dadi asked again.

"I do. I want to know about Dad, the person that he was when he was not in his uniform. You and Dada Ji always talk about how gallant he was, but I want to know the real him. How was he as a father, as a son or as a husband to Mom." Her inquisitiveness poured out along with a trickle of tears from her eyes. Dadi wiped her tears and smiled.

"Okay. I'll tell you all about my son and your father today. It's just that it is easier to bear the pain when we think of him as a soldier. Otherwise, it would have been even difficult to breathe if we kept thinking of him as the wonderful son and the person, he was. A mother is nonetheless a mother whatever her children might be, and their loss is just as painful. You just have to brave it out." Dadi said, as her own eyes turned misty.

"Am I making you sad?" Srishti asked.

"It's sometimes good to go down the memory lane, Srishti. It's been long since I talked about him." Dadi said lovingly caressing her cheek, trying to relive the affection she once shared with her only child.

'It was the best day of my life when I held him in my arms. He was a beautiful little boy. Your Dada Ji wasn't there. He was posted on the front during the Indo-Pak war of 1965, 10th of August. As the date of delivery neared, I wanted that war to never start. No one wants the war to take place, but as the family of a soldier, I dreaded the war, especially at a time when I was expecting his child. Those were difficult times. The communication was slow. All we did was to pray for our men to come back alive after the war. Jassi was already two months old when your Dada Ji could come back home.

He was very close to me since I was the one who was always with him when your Dada Ji was away for his Border postings. He grew up fine amidst the joint family that we had, growing up along with his cousins, your Dada Ji's brother's children. I joined the army school back as a PG teacher and was later promoted as a Principal of the school. We went to school together, and I indulged him in all sorts of things to keep him occupied, be it sports or other extra-curricular activities. He was exceptionally good at Basket Ball and playing chess. I didn't want him to join the army. It's a very lonely and unpredictable life for the wives and the families of army men, and I wanted a perfect life for him. But unknown to me, he idolized his father. He was fascinated by his uniform and would insist on him to tell the stories of his brave encounters with the enemy whenever your Dada Ji was home. More I tried distracting him from going for armed forces, his resolve to get in there got stronger. He followed the disciplined life that his father wanted him to. He practiced yoga regularly and learned Marshal Arts very diligently. I thought he wanted to be a sportsman, but he had other plans. As a mother and as the Principal of the school, I was incredibly proud when he represented our school and later our state for different sporting events.

He was very loving and respectful and won anyone's heart easily. He was very popular among his friends, just like you. This house used to echo with their laughter when his friends used to come over so much so that his grandmother would shout at them for making so much of noise. With seven children of the similar age group in the house itself and their friends, it always felt as if there was some party going on here. I loved that laughter. The house was so alive with them there and I along with both my co-sisters would be busy making snacks for them. They were a good lot, very respectful, and extremely helpful. Maybe because they were my students as well, but they had been quite a support system when Jassi was away on duty and even when he left us. They still look out for us whenever there's a need, and you have met them over the years. You know how they are. Don't you?'

Srishti smiled and nodded in affirmation. She sure had seen all that. Their extended family, her grandfather's both brothers along with their families, lived just next door and her uncles and aunts as in her father's cousins were more than a family to her. She had grown up with them and their children and never felt as if she didn't have siblings. Her father's friends came over once in a while and had never forgotten to invite their family over whenever the occasions arrived. Yeah, she just never realized, it was all because of the goodwill that her father had generated around him. Dadi was right. He must have been just like her, or maybe she was just like him, the friend of friends, a sports person and the life of every party, she went in. It felt good to know this side of her father and to be able to relate to him.

"What happened? Where are you lost?" Dadi suddenly asked.

"Nothing. Kinda trying to imagine how it must have been. It feels good to know this side of Dad." She said, brimming with happiness.

"It feels good to talk about him this way too. I wish we had spoken about him like this, more often." Dadi said, taking her hand in hers and planting a lingering kiss on it as if she was reliving the memory of doing it to her son.

"Then what happened Dadi? How did Dad decide to join the army?" Srishti asked again, and Dadi continued.

'Unknown to me, he'd filled up the forms for NDA though he had applied for various Engineering colleges as well. Then what! He appeared and cleared the exam with flying colors. He was thrilled and though, I was a little reluctant in sending him to forces, I was happy in his happiness. His father was super-elated. Jassi was one of the best cadets, and before we knew it, my young boy was a man, an army man, and a man of honor. His first posting was in Arunachal Pradesh along the Indo-China Border. He did well and climbed the seniority chart sooner than his peers. After three years he was posted in New Delhi as a cool-off posting where he met your Mom.'

Dadi paused for a while to gauge her reaction when she spelled out her mother's name. Srishti's eyes shone with brightness, and her enthusiasm raged. Dadi smiled and continued.

'She was the daughter of his superior, so he did try restraint, but your mother was a very smart girl, a typical metropolitan. She knew, he liked her but might not have the courage to ask her out, her being the Brigadier's daughter. She chased him, and finally, he gave in too. They loved each other and dated for about two years until she completed her MBA. Her parents liked him also as a person, but they had thought that she would marry someone in her profession. Her life was more of a city girl, and they weren't sure if she could manage both her profession as well as her marriage if each one of it pulled her in the opposite direction. They weren't wrong, and it did become

an issue for a while. They married nonetheless. A few months later, Jassi was posted in Kashmir when the insurgency was at its peak before being transferred to Poonch. Both the stations were not conducive to taking the family along. She stayed back in Delhi doing her job, and then you happened. You were born in RR, Delhi. That year, your Dada Ji took retirement as well. We saw you when you were one week old. We were on cloud nine. I'd always wanted a daughter, and you just were an answer to my prayers. Those were happy times. Jassi had taken a few days off and had come too. Neha was on six months leave so we brought you both here. Jassi would come down from Poonch every now and then. My house felt complete after a very long time.

Neha was an adorable girl. She not once complained about anything while she was here though I knew that the life here was a lot slower than what she was used to in Delhi.

She extended her maternity leave for another three months so that you were a little more manageable before she joined office, but the time to go back came a lot sooner than we imagined. She left with you in tow and joined the office. Those days, she lived in the apartment your Dada Ji had gifted them as the wedding present while they were in Delhi. He had wanted them to have their own house instead of them living with her parents. She felt guilty to leave you with the nanny while she worked before she tried putting you in the crèche. She asked your Granny for help, but your Granny was a busy woman back then. So finally, after struggling for three months or so, Neha decided to give up her job. It's not easy to look after a small baby if one has to do it single-handedly that too while working. That was the time I went there. I stayed with you and Neha for a couple of months during my summer vacations. We bonded well, but I could not live there endlessly. I had to come back. So I finally decided to bring you along. It was a tough decision, both for Neha and me as well, but I insisted that she did not give up her job. The life of the wife of an army officer is very lonely if she did not engage herself in something of some worth. She had to be self-reliant in case of an eventuality. She gave in and you, my dear came to Jammu along with me. Your Dada Ji looked after you when I went to school.

Neha came over on most of the weekends and whenever she could. Though she felt guilty about leaving you here, she was satisfied that you were looked after well when she went to work. Parent's love is not always about keeping their children closer. Sometimes, the children's wellbeing overweighs the proximity, and it's no less a sacrifice. Jassi also came over whenever he could, or we visited him with you along when he could not. In all, everything was going well for another couple of years. Jassi was due for his cool off posting, and Neha had planned to take a transfer in whichever city he went, and they would have eventually taken you along. We were happy about it, but that was never to happen.

Jassi was leading his troops while he exfoliated an infiltration bid by the terrorists from across the Border. Militancy-related activities in Rajouri-Poonch district had increased many folds those days. His team succeeded in the mission and had gunned down all the terrorists, but Jassi along with four of his men got hit while trying to save some civilians. It would be twenty years to that fateful day, day after tomorrow.

You were too young to understand anything but Neha couldn't survive it. Her dreams were smashed, and her life turned upside down. I didn't know what to grieve of more, the loss of my children or to see you become an orphan. You looked like a scared kitten with so many people crying all around, and all I did was to hold you tight around my chest and consoled you or instead consoled myself that everything will be all right. I could not even cry because that baffled you. For you, I was your mother, and that day I became one. Our life started revolving around you, and it still does. Your Dada Ji busied himself in the welfare of the families of martyrs as well as the people affected by militancy and those living a fearful life along the Border. It was his way to get over his grief. But not for a day in all these years, he has forgotten to visit the place where Jassi attained martyrdom. This time, he wants to take you along, I guess.'

Dadi looked at the changing expressions on her face and cupped her wet cheeks and said. "We can't change the destiny, my dear, and even though I sometimes wish; I should have insisted that Jassi didn't join the army, it changes nothing. He only had come with that much of life for himself, and if that is what it had to be, I'm glad that he went the way he did. He was a good man, and he has given his life to save the lives of some very unsuspecting families who were caught in the cross-fire between the army and the terrorists."

Srishti was too overwhelmed with emotions and hugged her Grandmother. She felt a lot closer to her today, sharing the same grief and the same pain about a man who bonded them together for eternity.

She then took control of herself and said. "Now I really want to go with Dada Ji and pay my respects to Dad. Would you also come along Dadi?"

"No. I won't. I never did. That place recreates the scene of Jassi's bullet-ridden body falling there in pain, and howsoever I try, I can't bear that in my heart." Dadi said wiping her own eyes and Srishti didn't console her. She needed to vent it out for the longest of time, and Srishti let her.

Now she knew why her grandfather was so possessive about her and didn't want to let her go away too far from him, but that was the topic of another discussion. Before that, she needed to get to the root of their insecurities, and she sure was making inroads in there.

Chapter 24

The next day, they started early before the dawn broke from their home. She'd packed a bag for a few days stay in Poonch.

Srishti was lost in her thoughts when Dada Ji asked. "So, you made my wife cry yesterday."

"Oh! Did I? She did need to cry it out. Besides, she's my Dadi also. You don't have a copyright on her." She retaliated.

"Hey. Who taught you that? That used to be your father's dialogue whenever I asked him anything about his Mother." Dada Ji said, getting surprised.

"Really. Was it? I simply said." She said.

"You know, you are so much like him. Always ready to strike back but that's what I liked about him, and that's what I like in you. It's good to know that my genes are passed on and exhibit dominance." Dada Ji said, laughing.

"Are you praising me or Dad or yourself? I'm totally confused." Srishti said, shaking her head in disbelief and Dada Ji laughed out loud.

She had too many questions in her head about the existing conditions there, but that would have to wait. She totally wanted to look around and feel the essence of her father's presence in those winds. She inhaled the cold air and closed her eyes in an attempt to feel him in. It felt soothing.

She opened her eyes when their SUV halted at a check post in Rajouri. She'd dozed off for a good four hours. She rubbed her eyes, adjusting to the bright summer's daylight and wiped her face.

"Have we reached?" She asked.

"A couple of hours or so. You did sleep well." Dada Ji said.

"Yeah. I did. Where are we now?" She asked.

"This is Rajouri. Do you want to freshen up? We can have something to eat." He asked, and she nodded, getting down behind him. They went to a nearby restaurant to grab a cup of tea.

It was around lunchtime when they arrived at their destination. The weather up there in the hilly terrain of Poonch was much cooler than the scorching heat of May back home.

"The weather is so good here. Why is this not a famous hill station?" She asked, looking at the plush looking Government Dak Bungalow, the guesthouse.

"You will have to first understand the politics of J&K before you could understand the situations on the ground. Right now, you go freshen up and then we can have our lunch." Dada Ji said.

During the time of their journey from Rajouri towards Poonch, his demeanor had turned very solemn. He was much quieter, and only then Srishti realized what they were there for. She simply nodded and went to her room while Dada Ji settled in his.

In the evening, an army jeep was parked on the porch of the guesthouse when she went out looking for him after she'd taken a nap post lunch. He was sitting in the lawns with a couple of middle-aged army officers who had come to meet him. She greeted them from a distance and went to the boundary wall to look outside at the valley. It felt very peaceful, but she knew that it wasn't. There was news of cease-fire violations coming in every other day. There was a case of two men each from the army and that of BSF who had been killed and their bodies mutilated earlier that month. She really wondered what was it that instigated the people to turn so ruthless so as not to spare someone in their death as well. The questions she had, had no answers to. Amidst the tense atmosphere around the Border, the locals had learned to live a normal life, she realized.

The army men left after a while after giving Dada Ji a pass to visit their forward position. Dada Ji turned down their offer of sending them the army vehicle since it was safer to go around town on their own, especially since she was with him. Official vehicles draw unnecessary attention, he'd said.

They spent the evening strolling around the nearby meadows and retired for the day early. The next day began with him taking her to the Nangali Sahib Gurudwara for prayers before they left for the Army front post. Though the town appeared relatively calm, there were the telltale signs of devastation visible in the villages closer to the LOC. The patchwork on the walls of the village houses told a story she'd been privy to closer to her home. The high density of the forest with a challenging terrain was sure to pose a lot of problems to the security forces to keep a tight vigil, but still, they did what they could to keep the surroundings safe.

Soon they reached the army camp in one of the posts. The officers posted there welcomed them in their temporary hutments. She was astonished to see the living conditions of those brave men. Comforts were a very long shot there. Even the basic amenities of life were hard to get but what tugged her heart was the fact that not a trace of unhappiness reflected from their faces. The men in uniform were full of life, always ready to strike back at the least of provocations. The basket of homemade snacks and sweets was enough to bring a smile on those faces that probably hadn't seen their homes and families in the longest of the time. Some of them happily shared their stories of triumph over tea that was served. An atmosphere of bonhomie existed among the superiors and the sub-ordinates unlike that of what is there in the barracks.

Having interacted with them for a while and taking stock of the prevailing conditions, they proceeded towards the spot that her father had taken his last breath on after making sure that he had neutralized the last of the men who had dared threaten the sovereignty of his nation where he stood guard at.

It was a little groove in the jungle adjoining the nearest village where villagers often went to collect wood and twigs for burning. Their livelihood depended on the forest where they collected honey from the beehives, some natural and the others artificially planted in the woods. Some were hired by the Forest Department to collect raisin from the rubber trees. On the way, she learned from the officer who was traveling with them was that differentiating between the locals and the intruders was the most difficult task for the forces as the latter looked and spoke just like the ones on their side. If they weren't carrying guns or ammunition, they could just pass off as the inhabitants. It was the locals who reported them a lot of times, which was quite unlike of what happened in the other part of LOC that fell in Kashmir. At least in the larger parts of this belt, the local support for the terrorists was not there, which made the task of the forces much more efficient.

They reached the spot, which didn't look any different from the rest. There was no structure raised in her father's memory, nor was there any mention of his brave act. She felt disappointed. She had imagined that some small memorial might have been built in his memory since her grandfather came there so religiously every year to pay his respects and donated generously to the cause. She couldn't stop herself from asking him this time.

"There's nothing here Dada Ji. Don't you think, they should've or probably you should have contributed to raising a memorial for him here?" She asked.

Dada Ji sensed her displeasure, came around her, and held her by her shoulders.

"No. I didn't. It does not fit in this context." He said.

"Why not? He gave away his life for the nation. He did deserve it. Didn't he?" She asked again, her eyes misty with unshed moisture.

Dada Ji moved aside looking in the other direction and said. "There's 'Amar Jawan Jyoti' at 'India Gate' that pays homage to all the martyrs this country has seen, Srishti and now we hear that the construction of National War Memorial is underway too, in the memories of our martyrs. Your father was no different. I come here because I want to remember him on this day. It keeps me motivated to live another day. If memorials were to be built for every martyr, this land would fall short. There are so many men and women who have given their blood to make this nation live for so long. The ones who still live on; have given the best days of their youth to nurture this land. No ones sacrifice is any less. A soldier doesn't want memorials. He does it because he loves his motherland and puts his own life before it. All he wants in return is the love, trust, and respect of his countrymen and a promise that his family would be looked after well after he's gone. We were fortunate that we were well provided for, but a lot of them are not. Those are the people I work for. A life of dignity is everyone's right, Srishti. There are dead, disabled, and retired among the forces. They need their fair share of dignified allowances. You must have heard about the army men's struggle for OROP that had taken forever to be realized. Sometimes, it's not about the money alone. The parity of allowances in relation to the services provided is more about the recognition of their contribution to the nation building or rather survival of the nation in such hostile conditions."

He wiped his eyes this time and said again. " Don't for a moment think what your father did was any less, but there had been many before him, and there had been many after him who have knowingly joined the forces and sacrificed their lives. He's just one of the proud sons of this nation, and that's how it has to be. We, as his family, can do whatever we want to do to make him live in our memories, but that's how far it can go."

He then moved away as the driver got him the holy water that he had brought along from the Gurudwara; they had visited earlier in the day. He went to the tall tree, which had probably shielded his son while he shot at his enemies. There was a short plantation of Marigold around the tree, unlike the other trees in the area. The flowery plants which might have been huge if the sun could touch the base often, she thought. Dada Ji watered the base of the tree and offered flowers, the Marigold. He looked at her, and soon she joined him in his annual ritual. It felt soothing. She felt connected to her father suddenly as if he was blessing her in person. She leaned against the tree and ran her hand along its trunk to feel his touch and Dada Ji moved away, trying to keep his own emotions in check. As the age was catching up, the realization of the absence of his son from their lives had started coming to him with full force.

She hugged the tree and stood there for a while, mouthing a quick 'I Love You, Dad'.

Dada Ji came over and patted her on her back, gesturing that they had to go back. She nodded and wiping her eyes smiled faintly and followed him towards the car. It was an emotional moment for Dada Ji and her, and it was time to go back. As they headed back, there was some movement of troops around the corner. Gunshots were getting fired somewhere in the vicinity. The army officer who had come along got on the wireless and directed the driver to take the safer route to the Guest House. On the way back, she saw people around the area rushing back home from wherever they were, and the houses were bolted. Her heart thudded erratically in her chest, and she held both her hands tightly against her stomach.

They reached back safely, and the sound of gunshots receded as they neared their destination. Dada Ji was quiet but reassuring on the way back and soon went to his room asking if she needed anything and if she was feeling fine. She nodded and went to her own room. Srishti quickly closed the door and plunked on her bed, leaning back at the high pillow. She'd felt so scared, rather terrified at the sound of gunshots as if each one of them were aiming at her. Till then she had not thought, she loved life so much like all others who were squirming with fear and were trying to reach the nearest place of safety. She wondered what it felt like to be going towards the danger knowing fully well what it could land you into and what was it that drove the men in uniform like her father to be able to face that. It was beyond her, and right then her head bent down to pray for the safety of those men who were fighting the enemy right now while their families waited for the news of their well-being back home. She prayed that on that very fateful day, no other Srishti lost her father as a stream of tears made way through her eyes. She stayed there motionless for a while till her bursting bladder could take no more. She went to the washroom, and finally washing her face collected herself. Whatever had happened had happened many years ago. She couldn't afford to feel weak right now. She was the daughter of a brave man, and it was the time she had to stand in support of her aging grandparents. Thinking this, she looked at the clock. It was two-thirty in the afternoon. She left for Dada Ji's room to call him for lunch.

"When do we leave for Jammu, Dada Ji?" She asked over lunch.

"Tomorrow. We'll leave early in the morning. Do you want to go out somewhere if the situation got better? There are a few places worth sight-seeing." He asked.

"I think not. We'll just walk around the adjacent area in the evening. It's quite pleasant here, unlike the scorching heat back home." She said, and Dada Ji nodded.

Then they simply spoke about random things. He told her as to how they used to come over to this place when she was a mere one and a half-year-old to meet her father, and she would be running around the place in excitement. She loved the tales of her childhood that involved the presence of her father and mother, even though she didn't remember a thing. It was quite a departure from the kind of conversations she used to have with her grandparents, who were always guarded about talking too much about her parents. Maybe they didn't want her to grow up thinking about what she'd missed. Now, she was big enough to handle emotions, she thought.

In all, it was a fulfilling experience, and she was glad, for whatever reasons her grandfather deemed it fit; she was a part of the journey, he started years ago.

Chapter 25

For the last week since she was home, she hadn't gotten much time to talk to Vineet as well. Being in two different time zones made it utterly tricky. Besides, she didn't want to startle him with the cold shoulder that Dada Ji had given to even a mention of him. She saw the message regarding his missed call while her phone was out of reach when she was in the army camp. She texted him about her current location and assured him that she would call as soon as she was back home.

Srishti was a bundle of nerves since morning; from the time she visited the site of her father's martyrdom and later was a witness to the State of war-like conditions in the area. At a ripe age of twenty-three years, she was so taken aback by what went around. Her heart had dropped to the pit of her stomach, listening to the sounds of gunshots. It had felt so scary to be caught in the crossfire, and her father was only twenty-two years old when he was commissioned into the army. The four years in the Academy that he spent along with the others must have been instrumental in shaping them into the selfless warriors they became. At an age when most of the young men are still boys trying to find their feet, enjoying the life at various college campuses and dreaming big to be a part of some high-end corporate houses, there are those cadets who are learning how to defend the dreams of their countrymen at the cost of their own. At this juncture, she wasn't able to understand as to what compelled them to put the lives of others before their own. She must ask Dada Ji that, as he would know. He had been a part of the similar grind.

Her chain of thoughts broke when Dada Ji called her from behind. She had inadvertently walked right till the edge of the parapet when she was texting Vineet and was later immersed in her thoughts.

"Coming." Srishti shouted back.

"Stay alert. Where are you lost?" He asked.

"Nothing. Just that the events of the morning were playing on my mind. I was completely terrified today. How did you get over these fears when you joined the army, Dada Ji, and how did Dad cope up?" She asked.

"It's the motivation Beta. If you are motivated enough to do something, it will come. And then there's training. You learn to build your confidence, learn to endure pain and hardships, and learn to believe that no force, however intimidating; can take over your motherland as long as you stand guard. You are another person when you are in your uniform. It gives a high that matches to none. The pride you feel when you stand tall wearing the uniform saluting your national flag is by far the most intoxicating feeling I've felt, and I'm sure all my brethren in the forces feel the same." Dada Ji said, his pride dripping from his words.

"Yeah. I'm sure it does. Your expressions justify it." She said, hugging him dearly.

"Why is this conflict there, Dada Ji? What do we achieve out of these animosities, living in the neighborhood?" She asked again looking at the horizon as far as her line of vision took her.

"Nothing. There's always everything there to lose in conflicts. The damage is collateral whether you want to be a part of it or you are forced to join it. Sometimes, the nations want to prove their supremacy over the other, at other times to fan their inflated egos and in this case, there is the vested interest. Militancy as it started out to be and the terrorism it has shaped as is a business in this region. It keeps the politics of some running, and the people pay the price of it, both in terms of their life as well as in economic slowdown. There are people on either side who have stakes in it. They thrive on public sentiments and their fanatic tendencies by invoking the fear." He said.

"When did it all start?" She asked.

"It dates back to the time of accession or probably even before, down to 1931. The voices of decent started in Kashmir stating repression by the kingdom as Kashmir was predominantly, a Muslim region ruled by a Hindu king. It was a call for the end of Monarchy in favor of self-government. The thought behind the agitation was the need of the hour but the sentiment behind it was guided by the principles of theocracy, much on the lines of Muslim League. It was a Muslim rebellion and it was believed to have been instigated by the British who were become wary of the Maharaja's stand on Nationalism. Fear mongering among the Muslims of the state was done purposely against the Hindu-raj so that Maharaja Hari Singh yielded to pressure of letting British forces take control of Gilgit Agency. Maharaja had no choice but to give in. The agitation was suppressed, and the process of establishing a Legislative Assembly called Praja Sabha was brought in. Though Praja Sabha was a toothless body with poor representation of all sections of society, it was the beginning of a democratic set up; probably a shift from the Monarchy mindset. Change isn't easy especially if it takes away the absolute power of a ruler, which was an accepted norm back then. Nonetheless, Maharaja Hari Singh tried to bring in the change. The Maharaja accepted the recommendations of Praja Sabha, but the implementation of the legislation was delayed till 1934 when it actually came into being after several protests.

Between 1934 and 1940, there were realignments in the political parties with one faction supporting the Indian National Congress and the other Muslim League. That was the time when the attempts to partition India were being made. The leaders of both the factions; The Indian National Congress as well as Muslim League were making attempts to accede Kashmir to their respective Dominions as Jammu and Kashmir was one of the princely states and had a choice to join either of the Dominions. The letter 'K' in Pakistan stands for Kashmir.

There were several attempts made to oust Maharaja by the Muslim leaders of the valley who wanted to decide the fate of Kashmir.

In 1944 when Sheikh Abdulla proposed 'Naya Kashmir' to Maharaja to end the constitutional monarchy, his plea was rejected. So in 1946, he started a 'Quit Kashmir' movement against Maharaja. The attempt was foiled, and he along with other Kashmiri leaders was put in jail for carrying out an act of sedition. Pundit Nehru wanted to go to plead his case as his party, 'National Conference' supported 'Indian National Congress' but he was stopped by the State and was sent back. That soared the relationship of Maharaja with Nehru, which became the cause for Maharaja's reluctance to join any of the dominions. He didn't want to align with Pakistan knowing fully well that his Hindu and Sikh subjects would be subjected to immense hardships as was happening in Punjab. And he wasn't sure if he and his State would get a fair deal if he acceded to India since Nehru was to be sworn in as the Prime Minister. Nehru though wanted Jammu and Kashmir to accede to India but was constantly insisting that Maharaja transferred the power to Sheikh Abdulla before that instead of signing the instrument of accession directly in India's favor. The treachery and the intent of the two politicians, one in Delhi and the other simmering disquiet in the State was evident in their conduct, very visible to those who knew what power play felt like." Dada Ji paused to look at the confused as well as the curious face of Srishti and smiled before he continued.

"Sometimes, the personal equations of the rulers or leaders play a vital role in the way the states are ruled. The conflict of Kashmir is unique in history. The leaders of Pakistan wanted it as it was Muslim majority State and India wanted it as a Hindu king ruled it. And since it was the prerogative of the king to decide upon the accession of his Kingdom according to the British terms, one would believe that the leaders of the two warring factions, Indian National Congress and Muslim League would've tried to convince Maharaja Hari Singh to join their respective dominion. Mohammad Ali Jinnah and the first Prime Minister of Pakistan did try convincing Maharaja to join their Dominion assuring him that his Hindu subjects would be protected and his legacy would remain intact. Well, Maharaja wasn't convinced. On the other hand, the representatives of the Indian Dominion tried forcing the transfer of power to Sheikh Abdulla instead of taking the great king into confidence. Maharaja wasn't convinced to do that either. He knew; he was stuck. He needed time to make that all-important decision and the time that he didn't have. There were external pressures from the two dominions and there was an internal unrest that was being fuelled by the likes of Sheikh Abdulla and others in the Muslim dominated regions. The proximity of Nehru to Sheikh Abdulla was the bone of contention between the two, and that's what has landed us where we are today."

"Did Maharaja really need that much of time to decide, Dada Ji, when the threat was looming large? Shouldn't the Maharaja have transferred the powers before it came to an inevitable war back then? Was his decision to dilly-dally on the fate of his people governed by his compulsion to hold onto power for as long as he did?" Srishti asked impulsively.

Dada Ji laughed. "Quite judgmental; aren't you dear? But yes; this had been a question that had haunted a lot many people because the perception created around the accession of Jammu and Kashmir had always demonized the mighty king. He most definitely wasn't the power hungry feudal that his image was concocted to be. Rather he was the most unfortunate victim of the conspiracy that was woven around him, to oust him of the state, he nurtured and modernized."

Srishti looked confused and Dada ji ran a loving hand on her head before he continued his narration.

"Political decisions sometimes are hard to take in the wake of prevailing circumstances, amidst negotiations that the common people aren't privy to. Accession of Jammu and Kashmir was one of them. For people sitting in Delhi and in Islamabad, it was just another state; some viewed it through the barometer of religion and the others from the point of view of its ancestry. But Jammu and Kashmir wasn't a state then. It was a kingdom with smaller feudal regions, which were different from each other like chalk and cheese. The three major regions of Jammu, Kashmir and Ladakh had Hindu and Sikh, Muslim and Buddhist populations respectively, differed from each other not just in Religion but in terms of Geography, Language as well as Cultural preference too. But even within these regions was diversity, people of ethnicities that were divided in their opinions about going to either of the Dominions. If the decision to accede was taken abruptly along the lines of the partition of India, Jammu and Kashmir might have seen a bloodbath bigger than what happened in Punjab.

Strategically, Jammu and Kashmir shared its Borders with Afghanistan, USSR on one side and with China and Tibet on the other. Imagine the valor of the state forces that had extended the Dogra regime in the most difficult terrain in the entire world and that too at a time when resources were skewed. They had a long history of guarding their forts against the Afghan Tribal Forces and the Czars of Russia. China was silent back then fighting for its own independence. How could the Maharaja let it all go without making sure, he'd secured his Borders? On the other side, the kingdom was better connected by road to Rawalpindi and other regions going to Pakistan than the ones in India. If the entire region of Gurdaspur in Punjab as it was stipulated to go to Pakistan had gone that way, Maharaja would've had no choice but to accede to Pakistan. So he had to wait till the final proposal of Partition was out in the open. The only road that connected Jammu to Punjab was via Pathankot that too was a mere *pagdandi,* a narrow muddy trail. His options were limited, the pressure mounting. The tug-of-war between the two Dominions was choking him and then there were Sheikh Abdulla of National Conference and Chaudhary Ghulam Abbas of Muslim Conference in constant bargaining with the two regions to ascertain their personal benefits. The accession of Jammu and Kashmir was more about the personal advantages of the leaders of the political outfits involved than about the political righteousness. Maharaja for all his efforts was still treated just as sacrificial goat. All he'd wanted was to keep his territories intact. So, no, he was wiser in not acceding at the time of partition."

Dada Ji cleared his throat and took a gulp of water. Talking about older times and thinking about what the condition of his state has become is mentally draining for any son of the soil. Before Srishti could ask another question, he gestured her to wait before he could resume his narration. He was kind of enjoying telling his very inquisitive Granddaughter about the dusty pages of history, the history many historians hadn't done justice to. He and the many among the aging population of keepers of the truth believed that the true account of the history of Jammu and Kashmir had to go down the generations even if it was just through the word of mouth; only way to beat the history created by false propaganda. He glanced at his little girl obliquely and was amused to feel the restlessness in her demeanor wanting to know as much as she could and as soon as she could. He took a deep breath and continued.

"When Maharaja Hari Singh decided to delay the process of accession, he had sent a Standstill Agreement to both Indian Union and that of Pakistan. For all we fault Pakistan for and it's politicians, they responded with alacrity and signed the document but the Indian Union dragged its feet on it. Instead of signing the agreement to respect the will of the Monarch to at least decide thoughtfully about the future of his subjects, Delhi still tried to arm-twist him for submission and that too through the route of Kashmiri leaders, mainly Sheikh Abdulla. The Kingdom was denied delivery of essential goods and defense support till the King yielded to their pressures. These pressure tactics from Delhi probably created a sense of insecurity and increased alertness in Islamabad that started influencing the Muslims of the regions of state Bordering Punjab. The state forces split in the Poonch Region on the basis of religion and a near carnage took place on the lines of what happened in Punjab back then, Maharaja so feared. Maharaja asked for help from Delhi to blow up the bridges connecting his kingdom with the state of Punjab in Pakistan but got a ludicrous response. Later, the invaders from Pakistan breached the Poonch Borders, the Muslims of the State army in cahoots with them massacred their fellow brethren from JAK-4 and a huge chunk of that region is still under the control of Pakistan, a part of POK (Pakistan Occupied Kashmir). If the ruler's plea was heeded to well in time by the greats like Sardar Patel and V.P. Menon, the rebellion within the army as well as the outside invasion from Pakistan could've been avoided. Delhi knew that Maharaja would finally accede to India. They just wanted him to do that on their terms, by transferring the power to Sheikh Abdulla. Nonetheless, Maharaja after not getting much support from Delhi got the road built between Jammu and Pathankot on a war footing when the three districts of Gurdaspur were awarded in India's favor, the only link Jammu and Kashmir had with Punjab of India. These signs should've assured the Central Government in Delhi about the King's intent but being the head of Indian Union, Nehru wanted to play by his rules; by crippling the ruler who had dared stop his entry to the state a year ago. In an effort to nurse his bruised ego, Nehru forgot that the lives of millions of people of the state were at the peril of extinction."

"So Jammu and Kashmir was not in India when partition happened?" Srishti asked with surprise.

"No. It wasn't. It happened a little later when the forces of Pakistan invaded Kashmir in connivance with the Muslim Conference, and Maharaja was forced to ask for India's help to fight Pakistan. It was on 26th of October 1947 that The State of Jammu and Kashmir acceded to India. For whatever it was, accession would have been complete if it was not for the clause of plebiscite put forth by Pt. Nehru. Accession was the prerogative of Maharaja, and he quite did it in his earnest wisdom sending the instrument of accession to Pt. Nehru. But after getting a cold shoulder from the Prime Minister's office, he sent the Instrument of Accession to Lord Mountbatten adding the clause of self-determination. In a separate letter to Mountbatten, Sheikh Abdulla also put forth his willingness on behalf of the people of Kashmir to join Indian Dominion but Pt. Nehru in a streak of overenthusiasm and on the advice of Lord Mountbatten put forth the clause of plebiscite or referendum, the people's verdict for the accession of the state to either of the Dominion and thus complicated the Kashmir issue. Jinnah had rejected the offer of plebiscite earlier when states of Junagarh and Hyderabad were to be annexed. There was no need to push it in terms of Kashmir. Besides, when the Indian forces were fighting hard to get back the lost territories, Nehru's unanimous decision in consultations with the British advisors and against his own Home Minister and Cabinet to go to UN for help cost the country a good 40% of the area of J&K that is still held by Pakistan. The regions that had the enormous strategic advantage, the Bordering regions of Afghanistan and Russia on the Northwest are still in the occupation of Pakistan and the ones on the Eastern side had been gifted away to China. It was shabby and an avoidable handling unlike the accession of other Princely states or so is the sentiment among the people of the region. Besides, a huge chunk of Indian territory on the north-eastern side of Ladakh was gradually occupied by China and the Central Government in Delhi or the State Government had no clue or inclination to safeguard the region, which was won and guarded bravely by the Dogra warriors for nearly a century." He explained.

"Then what happened to the king?" She asked.

"The monarchy had to go anyways, but the way it happened was very disgraceful. Maharaja was made into a powerless head of the state with Sheikh Abdulla heading the Government. But the new Prime Minister of the state was still not satisfied. He feared that the popular sentiment might prevail and Maharaja might destabilize him, so he forced the abdication of the last ruler through his well-wishers in Delhi.

Maharaja was ousted unceremoniously who lived in exile for the rest of his life, and his son was made 'Sadar-e-Riyasat,' an equivalent of President and the government headed by Sheikh Abdulla was sworn into office in 1952. A lot has happened since. There had been two major wars in 1965 and 1971 and then in Kargil in 1999. But ever since, the condition along the Border and LOC is terrible. Initially, it used to be between the armies but now; they have started targeting the locals around the area. They do it either through direct firing or shelling to distract the forces and facilitate the infiltration of terrorists and other times via their trained terrorists what you heard today." He said with sadness.

"Would this problem ever solve?" She asked.

Dada Ji laughed and said humorously. "It could occur sometime in future if there are more free-thinking youth like you on either side of the Border or someone with an **Iron-fist** at the Center. Till then, this battle continues..."

Chapter 26

The next morning, they left to go back home. Srishti rolled the windows down to feel the gush of cool mountain breeze on her face. This luxury was missing in the busy lanes of urban traffic, which often smelt of automobile emissions barring the few rainy days during the monsoons.

"You know Dada Ji, this area is so beautiful. Why hasn't it been developed into Tourist spots? There's so much potential here for tourism." She asked.

"These are political decisions girl. The politics in J&K has always been dominated by the Kashmiri politicians post-accession. Jammu is still fighting to end the discrimination in the region. Any development here would end Kashmir's monopoly over tourism besides that of Mata Vaishno Devi in Jammu." He said lazily.

"But that's awful. Any increase in tourism will enhance the State's economy, create jobs, and end its dependence on Center. It is bound to help the entire State. Isn't this protectionist mindset a very myopic view of the administration?" She asked in surprise.

"I like this ring of an economist in your voice. Sending you to IIM was definitely not a bad decision." He said laughing, his eyes still shut while he leaned back in his seat. The driver gave throaty laughter at his words.

"Very funny." She said and leaned back herself. She wondered as to how ignorant she had been, regarding the state of affairs in her own State, probably like many others. Her generation was in so much of a hurry to go out and succeed in their professions that they had forgotten to form a connection with their very roots, the very history that defined their existence.

"I want to see where the refugees live." She said suddenly.

Dada Ji now opened his eyes in disbelief.

"What refugees?" He asked.

"I don't know. One of the women in the village we went to, I guess Arnia it was, said that I should go and see, under what conditions the refugees live, so as to know their plight. Are there any refugee camps around?" She insisted.

"Well. There are some in Jammu. They are for the displaced Kashmiri Pundits who were massacred, brutalized and then thrown out of the Valley. It's been nearly thirty years that those people are still suffering. There hadn't been conclusive attempts made to rehabilitate them rightfully, just the piecemeal stuff." He stated.

"But thirty years is an enormous time, enough for a generation shift." She said, shock evident in her voice.

"It indeed is. Rehabilitation is a long and slow process. There's always a hope that they could go back. So little efforts were made to provide them with permanent home replacements. The affluent families made their ways and moved out. A lot of them settled outside of the State. Since the entire class of Kashmiri Pundit society was a very literate and hard-working society, most of the middle-class could sustain themselves with jobs. A few states offered seats for their children in professional colleges. It is the lower class; the people who had no means or the ones who were left with nothing, are the ones still under the weather. They had been tossed from one refugee camp to another. Living conditions there are quite not up to the mark. Relief materials in terms of food and medicines sent to them are often substandard. It is a very sorry state of matters." He said.

"Why's that? Why there's no rebellion against this mistreatment?" She asked again.

"There is a handful of people there, nearly 4,200 families. There are old people and young children along with a few of the people of working age. They would be skeptical that their rebellion against the government and the bureaucracy might cost them their monthly allowances and the relief that keeps them fed at least They were a literary class and had always stayed away from aggression. It's pitiful to think back at the times when they formed the skeleton of the administration of Jammu and Kashmir, down to the times of monarchy. They were the thinkers and policymakers from that time until very recently in the late eighties." He said.

"They were. It's hard to believe." She asked, surprised.

"It's a saying in Urdu '*Lamhe ne khata ki thi, sadiyon ne saza pai,*' meaning that a small mistake done in the matter of a moment is capable enough to punish you for the eons that follow. It is very heartbreaking to know that way back in 1927, the Kashmiri Pundits, being the think tanks in Maharaja's court felt threatened that the climatic conditions in Kashmir might attract the British to acquire land there as they were used to that kind of weather. It was argued that the beauty of Kashmir was a magnet to anyone who had enough money to acquire land in Kashmir and settle down there. They had launched a movement called 'Kashmir for Kashmiris.' Maharaja had given in to their demands, and the law of 'Hereditary State Subject' was passed. It meant that only the people who were born in the State were eligible for buying property in the State and also could avail the other state benefits. Just see, how it had only come to bite the very people who fought for the supremacy of Kashmir over the other regions of the State. Today they are everywhere but in Kashmir. This acute sense of protectionism and a quest to prove yourself better than the rest can sometimes come to haunt you in times to come." He said sighing.

"You think that their alienation is their own doing?" She asked curiously.

"No. I didn't mean it that way. No one can possibly predict things like that. Those were different times and Kashmir being a hotbed for invaders at different times in the history of India, we can't fault them for observing caution. After all, their community had been a victim of the aggression and brutality 400 years prior to it. A huge population of Pundits was forcibly converted to Islam or made to flee in the late 14th century. It was much later, somewhere in the 15th century, with the newer generations of Muslim rulers that their dignity was restored, their places of worship reconstructed and they were made to come back. That was when they were given their due respect for their intelligence, and their literary services were used to conduct the administrative operations. But between all these upheavals, their numbers had drastically dropped.

During the rule of Maharaja Hari Singh who himself was a forward-thinking ruler, they were pivotal in bringing the social reforms in the State. Social justice, banning of sati, widow remarriage, equal opportunities for the education of girls, entry of schedule casts to the temples in the State are some of the reforms for which the residents of Jammu and Kashmir did not have to struggle. They were adopted by Maharaja's administration with the Pundits being at the forefront of his advisers. Even during the ongoing talks of accession, it was a Kashmiri Pundit Prime Minister, Ram Chandra Kak, who was at the helm of affairs in J and K. That's a different story that blames him for favoring Accession of the State to Pakistan than to India and the breakdown of talks between Maharaja and the leaders of Indian National Congress, even to the likes of Mahatma Gandhi and Sardar Patel." Dada Ji explained.

"Was he going behind Maharaja's back while doing so." Srishti asked surprised.

"It was widely understood that he was offered better prospects by Jinnah than Delhi could provide him but at the same time, Maharaja was reluctant to join Pakistan. It was then, he proposed a years delay in taking a call on accession. His words were, 'If Kashmir would not accede to Pakistan, It could not accede to India.' And that was when the Standstill Agreement was brought in. Pakistan had signed the agreement with Jinnah reportedly saying 'he did not mind the State not acceding to Pakistan if It did not accede to India'. Later, both 'The Tribune' and 'The British Resident' in Kashmir had reported that Prime Minister Kak had facilitated the entry of Pakistan 'crusaders' in Kashmir to establish an operational base for Muslim League to propagate their theory of Pakistan among the Kashmiri population. Later, Maharaja had ousted him but a substantial damage was done." Dada Ji said.

"Did the administration of Jammu and Kashmir hold it against the community after the independence?" Srishti asked.

"No. It didn't. Such acts are always undertaken more in a personal capacity than charging the entire community for it. Kashmiri Pundit Community was still the backbone of administration and bureaucracy in the State." Dada Ji said.

"Then why this sudden downfall Dada Ji? Isn't it a shame, this kind of exodus was allowed to take place in a country that swears by democratic principles in modern times?" Srishti asked.

"It is. That was an awful time. The militancy was at its peak. The irony of the very situation is that the tormentors were the very successors of the people who were once brutalized, their women raped and converted to Islam just about 400 years back. They were fighting their own DNA blinded by a religious belief that actually never belonged to them and was forced upon their ancestors. But that is the ground reality of our times." He said.

"How do you know so much about history? We never studied all this while in school." She asked that made Dada Ji laugh.

"You know, what we study in school is mostly meant to pass exams and not to learn. Learning begins after school when you confront real-life situations. Reading is a good habit, Srishti. You must always find reasons to read. History might seem to be a boring subject in school; it has a fascinating capability to construct a narrative for life going forward. It helps us to deconstruct a society's behavioral pattern and thus provides us with a point of view to look at things differently. You will always view a person differently if you knew where he's coming from and will always respect his narrative how much so ever different it might be from yours. It makes you a lot tolerant of others in the sphere of faith, habits, and preferences." He said.

"There's one thing that I don't understand. When J & K acceded, what was the role that was played by the Kashmiri Pundit community? Were they not significant in the administration?" She asked.

"Oh, they were everywhere. They were in government jobs, policymaking positions, advisory boards, and every position of importance in the government. Like I said, theirs had been a literary class that laid complete emphasis on education. I haven't seen an uneducated Kashmiri Pundit so far. I don't have the data, but their literacy rate might have been 100% even back then. But why do you ask?" He asked.

"Then, why didn't they do anything to build harmony within the State if they were so accomplished. Didn't they see it coming?" She asked again.

"You know, you are grilling me like some shrewd journalist, but I'll tell you. Post-accession, the power center shifted from Jammu, from the hands of Dogra Monarchs to

Kashmir based politicians. At that time, the division between both the regions was more along the lines of linguistic basis with the religion at the back seat. The interactions and relationship between the people of both regions were cordial. But at the political level, fault-lines existed. Pundits stood with Kashmir, with Kashmiri politicians. All the policies made were Kashmir-centric with little or no significance to Jammu and Ladakh. The literacy rate among the Muslims in Kashmir and the people of Jammu were less, so it was Kashmiri Pundits that formed a formidable number in state government jobs. The sense of supremacy sometimes is perilous. It creates more enemies than friends. The divide between both the regions grew wider when they were the ones who could have worked as adhesive to bridge the gap. They enjoyed the perks of their proximity to the rulers and thus alienated themselves from the people of Jammu.

Kashmir thrived solely on Tourism along with its handicraft industry while as the people of Jammu were left to fend for themselves. The only bright spot was the Tourism to Mata Vaishno Devi shrine and the agricultural produce. The business growth in the private sector was mainly in the trading sector rather than industrial growth. Being the only region with the working conditions throughout the year, Jammu could have been made a business hub, but it just remained a transit junction that catered to the tourists going to Kashmir and Katra. The hilly regions under Jammu province were neglected. That was the undoing of the administration. A perception was created that development in Kashmir was favored, but if you look at it, there's not much development anywhere in the State. The policies were made merely to placate people and sustain power fanning their sentiments. Kashmir might not have been what it is today if there was a holistic approach to the uniform development in the State, including all the regions." He paused and looked at her face; curiosity dipping through it.

"Then, what happened? When did it all change?" She asked him to go on without interruption.

He smiled at her enthusiasm and continued.

"As time passed and somewhere after the war of 1971, things started to change. Pakistan's energy shifted completely from East Pakistan, which was now Bangladesh, towards efforts to destabilize India via Kashmir. Meanwhile, with an increase in literacy rates among the Kashmiri Muslims, a shift in administration started taking shape, and the influence of the Pundits started diminishing in the policymaking roles. The religious sentiments started taking precedence in Kashmir beyond the threshold of administrative tolerance, but the authorities kept ignoring the warning signals. Lack of private sector growth, joblessness owing to the season based tourism, the fanatic influences of Pakistan, which took the softer approach to divide Kashmir after having lost the third war in 1971, the signs of unrest brewing were always there. And became more evident in the eighties. Then a slow exodus started from Kashmir with families, both Hindu, and Muslim, who had resources to settle down in the large cities of India and abroad. It is always the middle class or the lower class that bears the brunt of any escalation of hostility. It was later, in1990; a mass exodus of the Pundits happened that has shaken the very basis of our democratic and sovereign principles." He said sighing.

"It must have been a challenging time, both in terms of human emotions as well as political stability." She commented.

"It was. The people who are suffering are the most unsuspecting people who had not an iota of the political know-how. They turned homeless and jobless overnight, the refugees in their own State, their own Country. The people in prime positions had already secured their resources. Though the entire world sympathized with them, there was nothing much done on the ground to make it any better. The sentiment among the people of Jammu though was not very conducive at that time owing to the high- handed attitude of some people of the Pundit community in the earlier years, but the human cries of distress and helplessness can melt the most rigid hearts.

The local help poured shortly, but that is not enough to sustain all those lives. The sustainability comes with provisions for livelihood, which is still missing. A society that had always been regarded for its intellect has now become a mere adjective of misery in public discourse and discussions about Nationalism.

I think the buck lies with all the policymakers who had systematically destroyed the framework of inclusive growth and parity in all the regions of the State, be they be Kashmiri Muslims, Pundits or even Hindus from Jammu. When people are in power positions, their religious or ethnic allegiance is overtaken by their personal interests.

Anyway, Farooq Abdulha, the then Chief-Minister fled to London after the carnage leaving the administration in the doldrums. So, the State government was dissolved, and the President's rule was put in place with the Governor in charge. Though the condition had put the State behind by many years, it turned out to be a blessing in disguise for Jammu. The then Governor put the speed of infrastructure growth in Jammu and some parts of Kashmir on acceleration. The flyovers that you see today were built during that time. He ended the monopoly of priests on The Mata Vaishno Devi Shrine and constituted a Shrine Board. A considerable impetus was given to upgrade the facilities at Katra, and the infrastructure that catered to the Shrine and finally the donations at the Shrine were used rightfully. Now, a University runs with the money from the Shrine. He ran an extremely honest administration with the entire government machinery working very cohesively, totally on their toes." Dada Ji elaborated.

Srishti looked too much in awe. That was a hell lot of information to take in. Dada Ji smiled, looking at the face of a speechless Srishti.

"Well. Don't blame me. You asked for it. History is not a multiple-choice paper, unlike science. It is an elaborate subject." He joked.

"It sure is but so much has happened. Is it normal?" She asked.

"Civilizations don't build in a matter of days. A lot of struggle goes into it. A whole lot of events, both pleasant and unpleasant, take place. The different point of views clash, each justifying itself in the realm of their origin as well as their veracity. You can't fault one from the other. The issues resolve only when effective or corrective solutions are put forth." He said.

"Would there ever be a solution to this problem?" She asked again.

"That's the toughest question you are asking for the second time. I don't know what to say." He said.

"Oh! Come on Dada Ji. You always know what to say." She said, cajoling him.

"I can only say this, beta that there is no problem in the world that does not have a solution. It only depends on how much of a keen observer are you to recognize that solution. There is another rule for finding solutions, and that is to recognize the problem, to deconstruct it and understand it in totality. But when people make it a battle between Nationalism and Anti-nationalism, sentiments get involved. The objectivity of issues is always clouded by sentiments. Most of the great surgeons don't treat their loved ones for the same reason." He said.

"You mean to say that our politicians and administrators lack objectivity?" She asked.

"No. They might not, but these are politicians, the public representatives who are captive of public perception. They have constituencies to cater to, and in the troubled region that we live in, the antagonism between the two provinces is so high or has been created so, that even a constructive effort in one region provokes the other. Thankfully, people of Jammu are quite tolerant and believe in democratic ways to take their leaders to task and do not react until pushed against the wall.

Even, the majority of people in Kashmir also want peace; it is a notorious few who create a disturbance. The peace-loving population of Kashmir is held hostage to the nefarious designs of select few, and they, themselves are the biggest victims of this long period of insurgency. After all, who wants to live in the shadow of death day in and day out? When the children take to guns rather than a pen, the biggest causality is parents. A gun doesn't kill only the opponent. It kills a part of your human ethos within you. A soldier can conciliate himself for the reason that he's done it to safeguard humanity, but it does haunt him from time to time and eats his conscious. Just imagine the psychological drain out of those who try finding reasons to justify it. They know it too well that there would be one bullet coming their way anytime in the future. The plight of a mother, rather the parents who lose their children, is just alike, be it a soldier or a terrorist or the ones who are caught in the crossfire. A celebration of death in either of the cases is totally unwarranted, and as a society, we should refrain from it."

Meanwhile, the driver announced that they had reached near Akhnoor.

"You did keep us busy, Srishti. We have covered a major stretch. Let's break the journey and have something to eat." He said.

"You wanted me to know about my State. Why are you complaining now?" She said as they made way towards a small restaurant and Dada Ji smiled.

He loved this new bonding between the two, he wasn't sure as of how best to sustain it to influence Srishti's decisions when it came to it.

Chapter 27

They rested for about half an hour over tea and snacks.

"Can we go towards the banks of Chenab before we leave?" Srishti asked cheerfully.

"I'm an old man girl. Where all do you want to take me?" Dada Ji said, laughing at her suggestion.

"All this trip was your idea. I'm just asking to take a detour, a very refreshing detour in this sweltering heat." She pleaded, wiping her sweat with her hand towel.

"Okay. Do you want to go and see the Fort as well?" He asked.

"No, the riverfront is good-enough." She said.

"It is just old banks, barely a riverfront. I wish the local administration had done something along those lines." He said, his dejection very evident in his words.

It was a cool breeze at the banks of river Chenab that made its way from the mountains of Himachal Pradesh and entered the province of Jammu in the Kishtwar region before hitting the plains at Akhnoor, finally flowing into Punjab of Pakistan. The icy cold water flowing from the upper ranges of Pir Panchal imparted the air it's coolness even on a hot summer day. Srishti and Dada Ji walked around for a little while before proceeding further towards their home.

"Sir, do you want me to stop at Mishriwala or Muthi camp on the way. Srishti baby wanted to go there." The driver asked as they neared that area. Seems like, he was listening to their earlier conversation very keenly.

"No.." "Yes."

Both Dada Ji and Srishti said almost simultaneously.

"Please. I won't go inside. I'll see from afar. "Srishti pleaded again.

"Look Srishti. It's demeaning to go to see people's condition when they are already in misery if you can't do anything for them. It's not a Zoo." Dada Ji reprimanded her sternly.

"But..." He interjected even before she spoke.

"If you must, I'll send you along with one of our Organization members who bring them some relief materials from time to time. People are sensitive when they are vulnerable. Don't ever treat them as a project if it doesn't fetch them any substantial benefits." He said decisively and instructed the driver to carry on towards their home.

Srishti sat back, absorbing Dada Ji's words. He was right. She certainly won't want to disrespect someone. She took out her phone and surfed for it instead.

"OMG. You are right Dada Ji, and so were the women in that village. Their condition seems so pathetic. How could people live like that and raise a generation in those tents." She spooked and cried, looking at the images.

"They are just images taken on good days. They are unable to tell you as to how is it in hot summers, chilling winters and worst still, during the rainy season." He said sighing and put his head back against the headrest.

She kept quiet for a while, trying to make sense of things around her. Dada Ji was right. Before she started out to explore the world, exposure to what was happening around her home was very important. Like many youngsters, she never bothered to sit through the documentaries and discussions that kept coming on TV regarding the social issues. TV and the Internet had always been there for entertainment. Her focus had always been on enhancing her own skills and this aspect of knowledge; she never bothered to acquire.

Suddenly Dada Ji spoke.

"Education is not only about reading textbooks, Srishti. That is just literacy. Education is about keeping your eyes and ears open and to observe things keenly. Education is about trying to find the appropriate questions before you look for answers, and about finding the etiology if a situation arises before you go out and address it."

"I guess you are right. I'll keep it in mind. And while we are on this, I want to know what this Hereditary State Subject means and how significant it is in this time and age. I remember you taking the impression of my fingers on a green paper, a few years back, before I went to college." She reminded.

He closed his eyes. He so wanted to tell his beloved granddaughter, his sole heiress all about it but he knew that a colossal confrontation awaited him when Srishti understood the clauses of the Act. For him, it was not just a piece of paper. It was a double-edged sword that was threatening to rip the threads of the relationship that existed between him and his only Grandchild, just because she was a girl. On the other hand, he would be the one responsible for breaking her heart to push her into a loveless marriage; even he didn't subscribe to, a good fifty-four years ago when he got married to his wife. He won't have bothered if it was his Grandson instead like he let his son take the call when he got married to Neha. Whoever said that the rights of the girls and boys were equal, had probably never factored in the prevailing conditions in Jammu and Kashmir, a century after, the Act came into place. Maybe, the women of the state needed to fight an equivalent of the 'Suffragette Movement' to sustain their birthright. He thought.

"What happened Dada Ji? Why are you in such deep thoughts?" She asked.

"I think I'm exhausted now. Let's discuss it another day. It is one crucial issue about our state that you must know and understand. But now is not the time." He said deflecting the topic. Srishti agreed. Anyways, they would be home, in another fifteen minutes. Dadi had been anxiously waiting and had already called a couple of times to know as to where had they reached.

Dadi was eagerly waiting for them when they got back. The yummy smell of Mutton Roganjosh and Yakhni hit their nostrils right as they entered the living room.

"Umm..." She moaned in delight. "It's been so long Dadi that I haven't eaten that food. I didn't know that I was craving it this much. Love you, Dadi." She said, running up to her and hugged her.

"Easy girl. I'm drenched in sweat." Dadi said though she hugged her back.

"Who cares? Now we both will smell of Roganjosh." She said joking and separated out. Dada Ji went straight to his room, taking the glass of Lemonade that Dadi had gotten for them.

"How was the trip?" Dadi asked just before she realized that she might unsettle Srishti remembering what she had gone to Poonch for. But to her surprise, Srishti wasn't unnerved.

"It was good. I'm glad I went there, Dadi. I felt closer to Dad somehow but more important is that I have come back much wiser having spent some very informative time with Dada Ji. I never knew, he knew so much about the socio-political stuff." She responded.

"I'm glad you did. Now go and freshen up. I'll also take a shower before Lunch. I've been in the kitchen for so long today. This new cook doesn't know how to cook Kashmiri dishes." Shc said, complaining.

"No one can make this food better than you, anyways. Good, you made it yourself." Srishti said to make her feel good.

"Stop buttering me now and go and freshen up. Next time, I want you to learn to cook, now that you want to live independently."

"I will someday but definitely not in summers. And before you start another of your lectures, I'll go." She said and dashed towards her room.

Dadi kept looking at her lovingly and smiled at her carefree antics. She wished her little girl stayed just as happy always. Her happiness brightened their hearts and their home alike.

Half an hour later, the house was echoing with her anecdotes about the trip. She described as to how pleasant the weather was there to the time they almost got close to the gun battle that took place between the armed forces and the insurgents. Thankfully, the troops had overpowered all the three mercenaries, neutralized the two and captured one. One of the army officers had sustained minor injuries but was safe. She had thanked God for listening to her prayers. Dada Ji was a little quiet, but she assumed, he was tired after a long and an emotional journey.

She retired to her room after Lunch for a nap. It was 3.35 pm. She badly wanted to talk to Vineet, but it was a bit early for him in New York. After tossing and turning for about twenty minutes, she finally gave up. She had to hear his voice. She called him nonetheless.

"*Good Morning.*" She chirped on the phone as soon as he picked it up.

"*Good Morning.*" He said lazily stifling a yawn.

"*Did I wake you up too early?*" She asked almost regretting it.

"*Are you kidding me? I've been so dying to talk to you for days. And anyway, I was about to get up. It's almost 6.30 am.*" He said, having gulped some water to moisten his mouth.

"*I missed you.*" She spoke with a drawl.

"*I missed you more. And tell me what you had been up to? Your phone had been constantly out of reach all along. So much for 'Digital India.'*" He asked, complaining.

"*Aww... You really missed me more. And stop blaming 'Digital India.' I'd been going along the Border areas in the last few days. Signals are purposely weaker there.*" She said justifying.

"*Don't tell me, you are planning to join the Army. Are you?*" He suddenly became alert and sat down upright on the bed.

Srishti laughed hard at his words.

"*Stop it, woman. What is there to laugh so much? Knowing what you told me about your Dada Ji, I wouldn't be surprised that when I see you next, you'll be in army uniform. Actually, do they have women cadets in the Army?*" He asked.

"*Don't let your imagination run wild, Mister. Nothing of the sort is happening. And about women being in the Army, let me ask Dada Ji about it. I'm learning a lot of stuff nowadays.*" She said.

"*You know, on second thoughts, you'll look a hell lot sexy in uniform. I can just imagine you wearing one with a revolver in your hand and trust me; it's doing no good right now. I'm ready to surrender.*" He said, almost sighing.

"*Yeah! You do. Now that you sound so desperate, I won't mind giving you a very personal dress rehearsal, the next time we meet. Remind me to buy one.*" She said in a very sultry voice.

"*I can't wait for it, baby. But meanwhile, I need a shower to cool myself now, a very-very cold shower.*" He said sluggishly.

"*Call me at night.*" She said.

"*That'll be your early morning.*" He said.

"*Yeah. I go jogging at around 5 am. Call me before you sleep. I'll wait.*" She said.

"*I will. Love you.*" He said.

"*Love you too,*" Srishti said and cut the call.

Keeping the phone right on top of her chest, she dived deep into another space where just the two of them existed. For last few days, she'd been so occupied with the distressing stories around her that she'd even skipped thinking about Vineet. Today, she didn't want to think about anything but him. Everything else could wait.

Chapter 28

By the evening, her friends had called, and she became busy for the next few days visiting one friend or the other. They went for shopping and movies. It really felt great to be catching up with old pals after a long time. They had planned to go to Mata Vaishno Devi Shrine after three days. Ironically, Dada Ji gave permission when he knew that some of the boys among her group of friends were accompanying the girls. Vanya had also called up and both the friends talked for hours. She felt so strange that till about a few days back, the people she'd lived with, the day in and day out were so far away and the ones she had left behind were getting closer back. Life really plays us up in strangest of ways, she thought.

Things at home were casual since no one picked up the topic of her job or that of her marriage. It had been a fortnight since she got back from Poonch. It had started bothering her now. She wanted to talk to them about Vineet, but Dada Ji had been extremely busy with something or the other. In between, he had to go to Srinagar twice to meet the Director Relief, on behalf of his Organization. Srishti had tried talking him into taking her along, but he'd categorically rejected her request on the pretext that the army crackdown on the terrorists was on an all-time high and he wouldn't want to knowingly put her in the harm's way. She had no choice but to listen to him, like always. On the subject of safety, she'd learned that it was futile to go against the wishes of your family. They definitely are better and more objective judges of the situation at hand than what we might not be able to comprehend in our enthusiasm.

Granny called up every two to three days to ask of her. It was Naina Masi, she hadn't spoken to in quite some time, and she was missing it now. Naina Masi was away to Europe for three weeks for a family holiday. She called up as soon as she got back.

"*I guess, the vacation was too engaging. You almost forgot about me.*" Srishti complained as soon as she picked up Naina's call.

"*It indeed was but your bro.... I mean cousins are quite a handful, you know. They kept me on my toes.*" Naina said.

"*You know Masi, you can call them my bothers. It doesn't matter. They are the closest to siblings that I have.*" Srishti said in a low voice.

"*I'm sorry, Srish. I unnecessarily made you sad. I'll take care. Okay! Now cheer up. Don't you want to know what all we did there? How I wish you were with us as well.*" Naina said excitedly.

"*Then you should've waited till my exams got over. But we can do that some other time. Can't we?*" Srishti said.

"*We sure can. Why don't you come over to California for a few days before you join the office? You are sure to get too busy once you join in.*" Naina suggested.

"*There are battles to fight before that. Dada Ji is pretty reluctant to send me to Delhi for the job. He wants me to settle down, as in get married.*" She said.

"*Then tell him about Vineet. It's the right time now. In that case, you can join the job as well.*" Naina suggested, her heart already constricting thinking about how Dada Ji would react to the proposal.

"Like I already didn't mention. Dada Ji simply didn't listen and left. I'd been trying to find the right occasion to talk about him. Anyway, Vineet is due back from New York in two days. I'll talk once he's in Delhi so that if needed, I can call him over to meet them or they go over to Delhi to do the same." She responded rather lethargically.

"Oh! I understand. Tell me if you need any help. Do you want me to talk to him, though I won't stand a chance in front of him. He's just too domineering." Naina said.

"I know. But that is who he is. I'll do it myself. He might not like it if someone else spoke for me. He has the copyright on me, you know." Srishti laughed.

"Tell me about it. If it's up to your Dada Ji, he won't let you disappear from his line of vision for a moment. I'm sure he's looking for a 'Ghar-Jamai' (live-in-son-in-law) for you." She said, pulling her leg.

"Stop it, Masi. Now you are frightening me." Srishti cried.

"No, I'm not. You are a courageous girl, Srish. I know our Srishti can fight her own battles." Naina said.

"That's the thing, Masi. I don't want it to escalate it to the level of a war between him and me. I've everything to lose. I can neither lose Vineet nor them, and wars always end up in one side winning and the other losing. I'm right in the middle." She said.

"I understand, child. I know it's not easy and it's not everyone's cup of tea either but remember one thing, the trick is in winning a war without fighting. It spares the bloodbath. Discuss, debate, negotiate, and do whatever you can but don't give up on your happiness. God Bless You." Naina said, her voice getting heavy.

"I will and thanks, Masi. It means a lot. Please keep calling more often. You give me strength." Srishti said.

"I will. Bye for now." Naina said and disconnected the call.

Naina's eyes had welled up while talking to Srishti, but she tried to control herself. She gave up trying and started crying as soon as the call disconnected. The images from twenty years ago started dancing in front of her. It was the same time of the year when Jassi was martyred. The entire house was quiet, and when it was time for everyone to leave, it was Neha who was caught in the tug-of-war. Her husband of five years and her love of seven years were gone. Her three years old daughter clung to her Dadi more than she came to her. She was too torn between the two. She could not stay there nor could Srishti go with her. Her Grandfather wouldn't let her even if she tried. She was all they were left with; like Srishti had jokingly said today, *'he had a copyright on her.'* He didn't fail to exercise it either. Her own mother too supported his decision so that Neha could get to live her own life. Only Neha couldn't.

Naina was inconsolable today. Only if she'd stepped up the offensive, only if she had been strong enough to fight for Neha, Srishti could've known her mother and lived with her. Neha needn't die. Jassi could've lived through Neha and Srishti. She sat there mourning Jassi's death as well as love of his life, Neha's demise today after many-many years. She tried reviving that part of her being which had died that day, but it lay there within her like a lifeless piece of flesh, decaying and fermenting; a constant reminder of her meaningless limitations.

And soon enough, she had gotten over it all to start her life with Shivesh moving over to California. The distance did help mask the pain and the guilt, but it surfaced time and again to gnaw on her senses. She had mastered the art of not letting it disturb the peace of mind of her family, but today, all her wounds got bare and bled ruefully in the longest of time. She let them. She needed that release to get her sanity back. She knew, Srishti needed someone with her more than ever before, but her hands were tied. She could never stand her ground in front of her Grandfather, no one could.

Back there, Srishti was in no better condition. Having spoken to Naina Masi today, she did find a lot of moral support, but at the same time, she felt a little void. She felt as if Naina Masi was holding back something, trying to get some message across without out-rightly speaking about it. She was after all her mother's twin. She was sure to be privy to some information about what happened after her father's death and as to why her mother couldn't survive. Being the daughter of an army officer and having consciously married another, Neha sure couldn't be a chicken-hearted person, but to Srishti's loss, no one spoke about it in both her families. She promised herself, she would get to the bottom of it once her own issues got sorted. She could ask Naina Masi once she met her face-to-face. These kinds of things were better not discussed on the phone.

Srishti looked at the calendar. The month of June had already started. Yesterday's ambush on the military convoy on the Jammu-Srinagar National Highway was baffling knowing that Dada Ji was around that region at some time. He'd called up later to inform that he was fine. She, along with Dadi, had breathed easy. It was then she broached the topic of Vineet with Dadi.

"I want to talk about Vineet, Dadi. You will definitely like him once you meet him." She said.

"If you like him Srishti, I'm sure he must be nice. But trust me, your Dada Ji would never agree for you to get married to him. Try forgetting him. We'll find a nice guy for you." Dadi said.

"How can you reject someone without even meeting him Dadi? He belongs to a very good family, has a well-paying job and more than anything, I love him." Srishti said.

"Look Beta, if we could, we wouldn't need to be told twice. If he belonged to Jammu, we would not have given it another thought and gone with your words, but he doesn't belong here. He could never belong here and if you did get married to him, nor would you. You don't understand." Dadi tried to make a point.

"I seriously don't understand, Dadi. You and Dada Ji had a love marriage 54 years ago. Mom and Dad also had a love marriage, and Mom never belonged to this place, then what has changed now." She asked.

"It's your gender. The gender has changed this time." Dadi said in a shallow voice.

"I...I don't get it. Come again." Srishti asked in a state of utter confusion, but Dadi kept quiet for a while.

"Speak up Dadi. Tell me where the problem is." She asked in desperation.

"Listen Srishti, please have this conversation with your Dada Ji once he's back. All I can tell you is that our hands are tied. You are our sole heiress, and you get to lose what we have if you got married to a non-state subject holder. Damn this article 370." She cursed bitterly in her breath, got up, and left.

Srishti stood there, stunned. Not in her wildest dreams, Srishti had thought that an Act of Constitution would come in the way of her exercising her birthright, her right to marry the man of her choice. Every religion in the world, every constitution across the globe gave this right to its followers. Who was the state, any state to strip its residents of the very basic human right? She stood there appalled; her breath caught in her throat.

Chapter 29

Srishti came back to her room with a very heavy heart. She'd heard about the families, which objected to their children marrying by choice for the reasons of faith, caste or social status but some damned Act, this was a first. She needed to know what it was. She took out her laptop and tried finding it on the net. She did better look into it before Dada Ji got back so that she could be ready with some counter-narrative to defend her case.

She punched in *'Hereditary State Subject'* as soon as Google appeared on the web page. A smile crept up on her previously sullen face thinking about how Vineet was cursing 'Digital India' when his call was not getting connected. The very 'Digital India' was serving her a great deal wondering how petty we become at times when things don't work in our favor, not understanding the circumstances around it. She closed her eyes to cool off her agitated nerves before she dived deep into decoding the reason of her Dada Ji's reluctance to let her live her life, the way she wanted.

Several web pages showed in the scroll down menu starting from the history to the cases of recent times. Dada Ji had briefly told her about it as to how the Act came into power, way back in 1927 on the insistence of the Kashmiri Pundit elites through their movement called 'Kashmir for Kashmiris.'

What she wanted to know was its relevance in today's time and age. On surfing further, she came across an article of **'The Hindu.'** She specifically went down to the issue of Gender Bias, which read.

"Gender bias?

Fifth, is Article 370 a source of gender bias in disqualifying women from the State of property rights? Article 370 itself is gender neutral, but the definition of Permanent Residents in the State Constitution — based on the notifications issued in April 1927 and June 1932 during the Maharajah's rule — was thought to be discriminatory. The 1927 notification included an explanatory note which said: "The wife or a widow of the State Subject ... shall acquire the status of her Husband as State Subject of the same Class as her Husband, so long as she resides in the State and does not leave the State for Permanent Residence outside the State." This was widely interpreted as also suggesting that a woman from the State who marries outside the State would lose her status as a State subject. However, in a landmark judgement, in October 2002, the full bench of J&K High Court, with one judge dissenting, held that the daughter of a permanent resident of the State will not lose her Permanent Resident status on marrying a person who is not a Permanent Resident, and will enjoy all rights, including property rights."

She read it again, and again. Where was the problem? It did state that the High Court judgment had come in favor of the women of the State. Was Dada Ji unaware of it? That was not possible. A man of his intellect can't possibly omit this critical piece of information. She thought of digging deeper and tried finding other articles with a similar reference.

She looked into another article from **Tehelka,** which cleared the air about the status quo. It read,

"The state government, then led by the PDP-Congress coalition, appealed against the order in the Supreme Court, claiming that it undermined the State's special status under

Article 370. It later withdrew the petition fearing that the SC might endorse the HC order and instead sought to settle the issue in the State Legislature.

A Bill titled J&K Women's Permanent Resident (Disqualification) Bill was moved in the J&K legislature in March 2004. A part of the Bill read: "Notwithstanding anything contrary contained in any law... a female permanent resident on her marriage with a person who is not a Permanent Resident shall with effect from the date of such marriage cease to be a Permanent Resident."

The Bill was passed in the Lower House with a voice vote and was headed to become a law with its passage in the Upper House when it attracted controversy.

While both the Congress and the BJP opposed the Bill at the national level, women's groups too plunged into the fray. Consequently, a Bill that was endorsed by the two major parties in the State, the Jammu and Kashmir People's Democratic Party, and the National Conference, didn't go through the Upper House. The Legislative Council Chairman Abdur Rashid Dar adjourned the session sine die without permitting a vote.

Since then, there has been another attempt to pass the Bill — in 2010 — but in vain. Regardless, the J&K HC's 2004 order that allows women from J&K to retain their Permanent Resident status, even after they marry non-state subjects stands."

She still wondered. This article again endorsed the previous one. Where was the problem? Would she have to file a petition in the court to sustain her 'Resident Status' if she married Vineet? That was not very difficult, though. She could always do that, and she was sure that Dada Ji couldn't be worried because of it. Was there something more than what was so apparent, Srishti didn't get it? She could try finding still. On second thoughts, she wondered as to how vital her Resident status was anyway. She barely had any future in Jammu. She had a job that needed her to be in Delhi and so was of Vineet's. The only place they could go was beyond Delhi, to some Metropolitan city or to some other countries like the UK, or US where they would have a better chance of growing in their professions. Yes, Dada Ji held a substantial spread of immovable assets there, but she possibly couldn't get tied to them and let go of life, she had so dreamed of making with Vineet. She could take care of them wherever she lived if that was his concern.

It was then, on further search, she found the reference of a couple of cases filed in the year 2013, where the Kashmiri Muslim woman had married a Bihari Muslim and had been residing in the State for years. The Husband and children were not passed down the same rights as they are given to the wives and children of the male Residents. So, that was the bone of contention, which was making Dada Ji jittery about her possible alliance to Vineet. She still wondered as to why did she need all that crap. She was better off the place that gave little or no rights to its women in this age. When the whole world was opening up globally, this protectionist policy had only done damage to her State.

The feminist within her felt outraged by this patriarchal law, which should have outlived its life in the Twenty-first Century at least. It's so ironical that while she searched answers for the legitimacy of a Law, a woman Chief Minister, a daughter of the State, ruled it. How could it be that her own blood never boiled at the supposed second-class citizenship offered to the women of the State that remained instated only until her father or her Husband held the Resident Key?

Looking at the profile of the other Dynast in the Electoral fray from Kashmir and reading his statement about the still in force Resident status of his sister; she wondered if his views would've been just as same if he was the father of two girls instead of two boys. What if the girls who lived all their life away from the State and someday married the non-residents ending the power-play with the third generation itself. She laughed at her own insinuations thinking about how the politics worked, over-riding the social security of half of its population. She could not let that happen to her. The only question remained as for how to bring Dada Ji to the level of her thought process, only time would tell. The wait was far from over, and the time was ticking. She better hurried up just as soon as Dada Ji got back.

Chapter 30

Three days later, Dada Ji was back home by the afternoon.

"You are back early. Did you start yesterday?" Srishti asked as she met him at the dinning table for Lunch.

"We started very early plus this new tunnel is state of the art. It has cut down the travel time by a third." He said, pulling his chair.

"Yeah. I read about it. It was inaugurated about two months back. Isn't it?" She asked.

"Yes. On the 2nd of April, this year! I'll take you till there someday. We'll just go from the one and come back from the other. You'll love it." He said.

"I love a few other things as well." She said, almost inaudibly.

"Did you say something?" He asked.

"Oh! Nothing. Nothing of importance." She said, looking at Dadi's sudden expression of perplexity relaxing as she averted the confrontation.

"Good. So what did you do on all these days? You should start to learn cooking or some other household work." He said very casually.

"Did Dad know how to cook or as for how to manage the house?" She asked in the same tone.

"Never. Jassi ran miles away from it." He said laughingly but stopped with a sudden reflex understanding what Srishti meant when she asked him the same. He looked at Dadi's pleading face that requested him to eat his food in peace and let her do that too.

Dadi was aware of Srishti's intent and didn't want her husband to open another front even before the one at hand wasn't tackled. They finished their food and left to go to their own rooms for a nap. She let go of discussing it with him in the evening as well since he looked too tired.

She logged on to her Facebook account and looked into their pictures taken before. She realized how quickly her Grandparents had aged over the last couple of years. Does age do that to people, she wondered?

She sat down to watch a movie till late at night and got up late the next morning. Dada Ji was sitting in the living room reading the newspaper while Dadi was seated next to him.

"Good Morning." She greeted them sluggishly and plunked on the couch next to them, keeping her head on Dadi's shoulder. Dadi ran a loving hand over her head.

"Are you feeling fine, Beta? You are looking like you didn't sleep well last night." Dadi asked.

"Yeah. I was watching a movie, and then the lights went off. It was so hot. I couldn't sleep." She complained.

"There was a power failure. It would get restored by afternoon, maybe." Dada Ji informed.

"There are so many hydroelectric plants in the state. Why do we not have enough electricity?" She cringed.

"They cater to a lot of other states via the Northern Grid. We are not the only beneficiaries." Dada Ji enlightened her.

"Stop complaining early in the morning. Freshen up, and I'll give you breakfast." Dadi said, patting her on the back.

She left to go to her room. As soon as she closed the door, she heard Dada Ji reprimanding Dadi.

"You know, you are spoiling her. She's big enough to handle herself now. Stop treating her like a baby and teach her how to run a house." He scolded.

"You can't do that in a matter of days. It will take time. Srishti will eventually learn it. But before that, talk to her. You can't simply bulldoze your will on her. Like you just said, she's not a little baby anymore." Dadi retorted back and left to go to the kitchen.

She had stopped near her door when she'd heard Dada Ji speak. It felt good to have Dadi take her side. She happily went to the washroom to take a shower, realizing that the power was finally restored. Maybe, it was a sign that the things were falling into place. Even Vineet was due back last night. He must be back and be sleeping. She just thought of giving him time to rest before he called her up. Meanwhile, she should talk to Dada Ji.

They were back for breakfast and settled down in the living room after that. This time Dada Ji brought up the topic of her marriage. She kind of, felt happy since it broke the deadlock.

"I want you to meet Mr. Manhas's son, Madhur. He's a nice guy, an MBA from Bombay. He works for Citibank." He said without looking into her eyes.

"I also want you to meet Vineet. He's an IIT Kanpur Graduate in Economics and MBA Finance from IIM Indore. He works for 'Cognizant Business Consulting' in Gurgaon. Professionally, he's better placed."

"Look Srishti. Stop being stubborn. We know these people for years. Mr. Manhas is a Director in one of the Government departments here, and they like you also." Dada Ji said.

"Vineet's Dad is a Diplomat Dada Ji. Regarding, you knowing them, how could you be so sure of his son's conduct? Have you seen him in college? I guess he might be a nice guy, but regarding Vineet, I'm sure. Please meet him before you rule him out." Srishti requested.

"Look, he's ruled out because he is a non-Resident of J&K. Is that enough to tell you why I can't consider him for you?" Dada Ji said, his voice a little loud this time.

"He's not applying for a job for you to consider him. I love him, and I want to marry him. Is that not enough?" She said decisively.

"You know what that would mean. You would get disinherited of my assets." He said with concern.

"No. I wouldn't. I looked into the Act." She said calmly.

"But your children would not be inheriting it. You are my sole heiress Srishti. Why do you want to leave us in the lurch and go?" He pleaded this time.

"The guy that you are talking about must also be working outside of the state. Doesn't he? What changes?" She revolted.

"He can come back whenever you both want. He belongs here. Later, you can start something on your own here." He suggested.

"Why do you think that I would want to come back Dada Ji? Why do you want me to commit professional suicide? There are no jobs here. There's no industry. Government jobs are given off to people with influence. What is there for the people of Jammu? Why should I be stuck here like thousands of those who have nowhere else to go? I have an opportunity, and you are chopping my wings. That's not fair." She shouted as a trail of tears made way from her eyes.

"You can go wherever you want. Do you hear me? Go the hell wherever you want to go but don't shield yourself behind those whom you think can't. Those are the people who love their place of birth. They are there because they want to be. They are not quitters like a lot of you educated people. The men on the Borders are not giving their lives to simply secure the boundaries. They are there to help people live in peace. Your father didn't die to secure a piece of land. He died to safeguard people, the people who have lived in this land for generations. This slow migration of Pundits from Kashmir began early in the twentieth century. Look what has happened to them today. It is happening to Jammu now. A constant brain drain and a slow exodus of the minority is happening, tilting the demography of the place in favor of the majority community that would not think twice before repeating what it did in Kashmir three decades back. It's just a matter of time. Each one of those who leaves is going to be answerable one day, for the misery of those left behind. Do you understand?" He shouted on top of his voice.

Srishti was stunned. This was the first time, she'd heard Dada Ji raise his voice to that level. So much so, his younger brothers and their sons came running from their houses, adjacent to theirs.

She looked at him, terrified. Dada Ji's face was flushed with part anger and part disgust. His eyes were red. He looked ferocious, downright intimidating but she gulped her fear and asked in a very calm and composed voice.

"Did you tell all this to my Mom too, when Dad died? Is it why she died as well because you wanted to tie her here just like you are trying to do to me?" She asked.

"Srishti. Don't go that far." Dadi shouted this time and looked painstakingly at her husband's troubled face.

Suddenly, the color drained from Dada Ji's face. He did not expect this. His nose twitched as his hand went up to clench his chest. Next moment, he was on the floor, unconscious.

Chapter 31

The guilt weighed her down as she sat in front of the Cardiac Care Unit of the hospital. Srishti had never expected this to happen. Dada Ji indeed was a tough man. Dadi was very quiet. She simply sat there with one of her co-sisters while her uncles stood along. She was so thankful that her extended family was there and was quick enough to shift him to the hospital. She kept crying as one of her second cousins consoled her.

Vineet called in the afternoon to ask of her, but she was not in a state of mind to talk to him. She simply kept crying, and he knew what it meant to her, to be the reason for her Dada Ji's condition. He immediately booked the early morning flight to be with her. She needed him more than ever now, he thought.

By the evening also, Dada Ji was not responding. He still was critical.

Vineet reached her in the morning. She had not gone back home since the time they had come to the hospital. She ran up to him, and he took her in his arms. Dadi looked up but didn't say a thing. Vineet greeted all of her extended family that was there, and they simply nodded. It was not the time to get offended or be outraged. The primary concern was Dada Ji's health, which showed no signs of improvement even 20 hours after the attack. Her uncle impressed upon

Vineet to take her home. He convinced both her and Dadi to come along.

They freshened up and rested for about four hours when Srishti was ready to go back again. The doctor had prescribed an anti-anxiety pill for Dadi. She was still sleeping with one of her aunts watching over her. Both Srishti and Vineet left for the hospital.

She peeped inside the CCU. He was still on life support, his vitals very feeble. She asked her uncles to go home so that they could take turns to keep a watch on Dada Ji. They left with just one of her second cousins staying there. In case they needed anything, he would know where to get it. Naina Masi had called, and Srishti told her all about what happened the day before and how guilty she felt about the entire incident. Naina was totally taken aback by the turn of events. Her words stuck in her throat as she tried consoling Srishti. Srishti called her repeatedly to know as to what happened, but she cut the call.

Srishti suddenly became attentive hearing a man asking the duty nurse about her Grandfather. She looked at the phone once again to ascertain that the call was disconnected and went in the direction of the man. He introduced himself as one of her father's old friends from his army unit. He was currently posted in Udhampur army base camp and had come over to see Dada Ji.

Back in California, Naina stood still after disconnecting the call. She could not believe what happened. Shivesh came from behind and caught her before she fell down.

"What happened Naina? Who was on the phone? Are Mom and Dad, alright?" He asked in quick succession.

"It...It was Sri...Srishti, Shiv." She stammered.

"What happened to her? Is she well?" He asked with increased concern.

"Yeah. She is. Her Dada Ji, he had a heart attack just after Srishti told him, she wanted to marry Vineet. I told her to hold her ground, but I didn't know that it would lead to this. I feel so awful. She's miserable and thinks that all this is her doing." Naina said while sobbing.

"You should go there, Naina. You should be with her at this hour of need. I'll get your tickets booked." Shivesh said hurriedly.

"What will I do Shiv? What can I do?" Naina asked helplessly.

Shivesh got up, a little agitated this time and spoke, his pitch a little higher for his own comprehension.

"Stop it Naina, just stop being this helpless you. Stand up for her, now at least or else your conscious will never let you live in peace." He shouted.

"But, how can I, Shiv?" She asked between her sobs.

He held her by her shoulders and shook her to jolt her out of her stupor.

"How? You ask how. Just how a lioness fights for her cubs. For how much longer are you going to live in denial, damn it! For how many more years are you going to stifle your emotions and suppress your conscious. Stand up for her; for your First-born." He shouted and turned his face in the other direction, keeping his right hand upon the adjoining wall.

"Shiv. How ...how...when... God!" Naina stood shell-shocked at Shivesh's words.

He mellowed down and looked at her face.

"I'm your husband, Naina. How did you think I would never know? When Shreyansh was born, it became apparent that it was not your Primary. Still, I never thought you might have lied to me. I thought you might have had a miscarriage or a stillbirth in your previous relationship and I let it be. It was years later that I met one of your old colleagues from Delhi office. I came to know, there was no Neha. It was Srishti's father who used to call you by that name. I felt defeated, not because it mattered to me that you had a child from your earlier marriage. I felt that way because you didn't trust me enough to confide in me about your past and also because you left your little child to fend for herself. I couldn't do a thing because I loved you; still, do. I thought that someday, maybe someday, you might find me capable enough of sharing the most guarded secret of your life, but it never happened. But this time I'm telling you to go and rescue your daughter from drowning in the guilt that you once did. Please go. She needs you now, more than ever." Shivesh said, cupping her face in his hands.

"I'm so sorry, Shiv, I really am. I didn't want to, but I had no choice. I'd promised her Dada Ji that Neha would not live another day so that Srishti could be with them. I did it for her. I feel terrible, always felt even when I left my little baby, but I kept on reassuring myself that I was doing it for her greater good so that I could live in peace. I'm so sorry." She cried inconsolably while he took her in his arms. He let her. She needed to let it out.

Meanwhile, at the Hospital, Srishti welcomed the unexpected guest.

"You are Srishti. I can't believe, I'm seeing that little girl who used to hop around when you came to meet your father. I'm Brigadier Sushant Menon. Anyway, what happened to Colonel?" He asked.

"'A Cardiac Event' is what doctors are telling. I don't know what to make of their statement." She said, almost crying.

"It's OK. Don't worry. Uncle will be fine. But you would have to be strong for him and your Grandmother. Where is she?" He asked.

"She's at home. The doctor has given her an anti-anxiety pill so that she could rest." Srishti informed.

"Oh, I see. When did you come and where is Naina? She hasn't come with you?" He asked again.

"I completed my MBA this year. I came back just last month." She said, a little puzzled by his quizzing.

"Came back means. You don't live with your Mother. Have you been living with your Grandparents all these years?" He asked again with a dash of curiosity.

"Oh! You know my Mother also." She asked excitedly forgetting where she stood.

"I certainly do. Jassi and I were together in Delhi and then in Poonch. I've seen Jassi and Naina fall in love, get married, and then you were born. I think we have spent celebrating all the important events of our life together more than we got the chance to celebrate with our families. His death had come at a very wrong time. We were getting posted to Bangalore after two weeks. He was finally planning to live a happy family time with Naina and you. You were too small to comprehend, but Naina was baffled. She loved him too much, and so did he." He said, reminiscing the old days.

"Are you sure you are talking about my Mother? Her name was Neha." She asked.

"Yeah. Jassi used to call her that. Naina was a very naughty girl back then. She teased him so much that he almost ran away from her. When he didn't reciprocate her advances, she posed as Naina's more sober twin by the name of Neha. They finally fell in love, and it was then Naina told him about the entire incidence. But Jassi being Jassi, he held on to it. He never called her Naina. He called her Neha, the woman he had fallen in love with." He explained. Just then realizing if he'd made a mistake telling Srishti all that, he asked, "I'm sorry if I've said too much. I guess you never knew about it."

"No...no, I knew. I just didn't know the story behind. She doesn't look as naughty as you say about her. Just a little confusion! Besides, she lives in California, works in a Media House there. She had married again and lives with her husband and sons, my half-brothers." She said, controlling the tremor in her voice. Vineet came and stood by her side, wishing for this torment to get over as quickly as possible.

"That is good to know. Naina was always a very career-oriented woman, so much so that she had left you to live with your Grandparents for close to two years before that mishap happened. It's good that she is still doing what she loved to do. Anyway, this is my card. Call me when Colonel gets better. I'll keep coming. Tell aunty, I wish he got well soon." He said and left, leaving behind a million questions that were erupting like a volcano in Srishti's head.

She looked at his retreating back. He suddenly halted to talk to someone and then turned to his left, bringing Dadi in her line of vision. The guilt on Dadi's face showed that she had heard every word the man had said. Both the women looked at each other, neither knowing how best to react. It was the most unexpected news at the most awkward place, she'd gotten.

Questions were plenty, and the answers were muddled with a concoction of unfavorable circumstances, unfulfilled desires, and bereft emotions, notwithstanding the honesty of confessions and vile suppositions.

She sat down on the adjoining bench with a thud, her mind numb and unresponsive, and her eyes cold and devoid of any emotion.

Chapter 32

"Get your bags packed, Naina. Your flight leaves in four hours for Delhi. There's a connecting flight for Jammu in the next two hours." Shivesh came back to the room after making her bookings.

"Won't you come, Shiv?" She could only muster up the courage to ask that much.

"I will but not today. Look, Naina, you need to be there as soon as you can, and you can use those twenty plus hours in the flight to think and be with yourself. You would have to collect yourself before you go and meet your daughter as one. First, you have to remind yourself, she is your daughter before you make her believe it and that won't happen if I'm with you." He said.

"Shiv..."

"No Naina. No more confusion. Running away from the truth doesn't change it; it only complicates it and ties it in tangled knots. Take this time to untangle those knots. I'll come ASAP after arranging things at the office and dropping children to Siddhi's place for a few days. They will be happy to spend a few days at their Bua's place." Shivesh said, and Naina agreed.

She hurriedly packed her suitcase, not forgetting to pack in all the stuff she'd gotten for Srishti. Maybe, it wasn't the time for gifts, but she could try. She boarded the flight without an iota of knowhow as how to redeem herself in her daughter's eyes, a daughter she had abandoned earlier to pursue her career and then to chase a new life for herself which she believed or was made to believe left no room for Srishti in it. How wrong was she in assuming those things and not confiding in her Husband. Only if she'd known that Shivesh was so forgiving like he came across today, she surely would have, but you would never know till it happened. The consequences of 'what if' is so unpredictable in our lives that we keep delaying things holding on to the status quo until the issues don't touch their pinnacle. She was lucky; she got off with her dignity intact. She closed her eyes to catch some sleep, but her mind kept wandering around. She tried shushing it like she did it ages ago to put her hyperactive little girl to sleep and it hopped off to another direction; the direction that was lit with the glow of the full moon. There he was, Jassi, her Jassi, and her first love. Her lips broke out in a childish smile as she traveled back in time.

'Hi, Major Jasvinder! How are you?' Naina asked spotting one of the new officers reporting to her Dad.

'Hi Ma'am.' He had only replied categorically waiting for his boss who had called him to get some confidential papers.

All the while that he was there, she'd tried seducing him, but he appeared detached. She was his senior's daughter, and he did rather not get into trouble right in the first week of his posting in Delhi. She spotted him on and off in the Officers' Housing Colony. She was one go-getter and if she set her eyes on something she never gave up until and unless she got it.

Jasvinder's reluctant attitude angered her initially, but as time passed, she started falling in love with him, but he remained unaffected. Her image from her initial quirkiness had turned him cautious, and she knew that if she needed him to see the other side of her, she would have to make a 180-degree turn in her behavior or be a new person. The notorious streak in her got the better of her, and she crossed his path posing as Neha, Naina's more sober twin, without even looking at him.

It took Naina a lot of courage to do that, but over a couple of months, she had won Jasvinder's heart. He asked her out and she, very reluctantly agreed to it, though in her heart, she was on cloud nine. Soon, they started dating, but the guilt of lying to him troubled her constantly.

And then, after dating for four months, he proposed to her. She was so lost for words that day, so much so that she broke down. It was then she told him about the whole mess that she'd dragged both of them into and she was not the person, he fell in love with. Jassi, as she now called him, was stunned but after realizing the extent of her love for him and her ability to go as far as she could to get him to fall in love with her, he gave in.

They had laughed over the entire episode for days later, but Jassi had vowed, he would always call her Neha, the girl he fell in love with. She had tried coaxing him to call her by her real name, but he had not budged saying, it was one punishment that she would have to endure for life. Only he didn't know that Neha's life would cut short just as soon as he left her and went away. The next year and a half went in quickly, and as soon as, she completed her MBA, they got married. Another eight months and Jassi was posted to Kashmir and then to his last posting at Poonch. She could hardly live her married life with him. In between, Srishti happened. She was ecstatic and went to live with her in-laws after her birth for a good six months of her maternity leave.

Those were good days. Jassi came over as often as he could. She extended her leave but eventually had to join the office. Raising Srishti all by herself wasn't working out, so she thought of quitting her job and staying with her in-laws. Her mother-in-law came to her rescue and spent the two months of her summer vacations with her. She was the one who advised her not to leave the job and then it was decided that Srishti would live with them till she started school or till Jassi was posted at some Residential Station.

Those were tough days. Naina flew down to Jammu every Saturday morning and got back by the first flight on Monday mornings. It did work well for a few months and then the visits reduced to two in a month or sometimes, just one owing to the increasing workload. She now regretted that. Only if her own mother had lent a helping hand when Srishti was a toddler, she would've been with her today. Destiny has a funny way to play things out, and she was the one here who got the shorter end of the stick. Only, she didn't realize it till now.

Jassi was her first love, and though she loved her current husband Shivesh, she could never feel the same rush of emotions for him like she felt for Jassi. For many years now, she'd blocked the memories of Jassi so as not to let them haunt her in her private moments. She, herself had killed Neha to the extent that her sub-conscious had started believing in the existence of Neha in her past. She was not her. Naina was not Neha anymore. Neha was another person, a shadow of her distant persona who disappeared in Jassi's hallow as soon as he joined the stars but what she did to Srishti was unpardonable if she looked at it today.

She saw him, coming out of the bright light again along with his magnificence, his lips curved into his reassuring smile and he blinked. He blinked in her dreams like he always did when she was unsure of something so as to convey her the message that everything will turn out well if she tried, and he would always be with her. He always did it, before her every singing performance in the college from backstage. And again when she sat amidst his huge clan of family and friends when she entered his house for the first time after their wedding and even when she shared the news of her pregnancy with him, telling him that she wasn't sure about it. His eyes spoke volumes when words were few and too loud to convey personally. He gestured and brought her attention to something behind him.

And then she saw that sari, her blood-soaked sari with his blood on it, like she always saw in her dreams. She didn't know what it signified. She was never with him when he died.

She extended her hand to feel it, to feel a part of him, but it disappeared, taking the shape of a little girl, her little girl. It was Srishti, a part of him, his blood that he had left for her to keep, and he kept reminding her in her dreams, only she couldn't decipher the meaning of it. She had failed him, failed her baby. She moved forward to reach her, to take her in her arms but Srishti looked at her with skepticism, her eyes a myriad of emotions ranging from disbelief to rage to abhorrence, just not love that Naina wanted to see. Srishti took a step back away from the mother that Naina never was, her hand hanging in the air, empty and her heart bereft of adoration she sought twenty years too late.

She got up with a start. All the while, she was reliving what was long forgotten. Shivesh was right. She had to go down the memory lane to recreate the connection she so conveniently lost over the years. The journey was long and agonizing, but she had found the right tool to live through it. She thought of all the moments that she'd spent with Jassi and Srishti back then and relived the happy times gathering the courage to construct a narrative to make Srishti believe that she loved her just as much as any other mother would. This time, she would tell her who she was and plead and request and beg if needed for her to forgive her mother.

Her anxiety rose with every passing moment as the plane neared her destination. She finally washed up a generous amount of the House Wine and surrendered to sleep. After an excruciatingly long journey of over 26 hours and a change of plane at IGI Delhi, she reached Jammu. It felt surreal to touchdown on a land that was once her home, her Jassi's home.

She would've stayed there even after Jassi as well, only if it was not for his father-in-law's insecurities. She was young. She could live there, or keep the connection but she possibly could not marry someone there like he'd asked of her, not just because it could save her Resident status intact. She wasn't ready to even think on those lines before she'd come to terms with her loss. Why did Jassi die? He shouldn't have, she thought as her eyes prickled with unshed tears.

She took the cab and reached their place. She had no courage to call Srishti to inform her about her arrival. One of Jassi's older cousins and his wife was at their house. She greeted them, and they explained as to what happened. They left to go to the hospital immediately since everyone was there, and the condition of her father-in-law was deteriorating. She prayed to God that he got better or else Srishti would always blame herself for what she did to him. Only if someone up there was listening.

Chapter 33

The scene at the hospital was extremely depressing. Everyone from the family was almost huddled around the room while doctors were examining Dada Ji. It didn't look good, and Naina was getting the same old vibes, the vibes she felt when she touched down Jammu the last time. She was told that Jassi was critical, but her heart had felt like sinking as she neared his place. Her heart was sinking just the same as she approached the CCU. Srishti looked in her direction briefly and then went back, trying to peep through the small glass hole. But realizing what she just saw, she turned her head towards her side with a jerk. She didn't probably believe if it was Naina there for real. Naina smiled at her weakly, but Srishti averted her gaze. This time, her Dadi and the others looked in her direction. Before she could reach there, the doctors came out of the CCU.

"I think you should go in and meet him. He doesn't have much time." One of the doctors suggested.

"We tried Ma'am, but he's not responding. His heart is fragile, and his organs are shutting down fast. Please meet him." The other doctor, the cardiologist said this time. He then motioned the nurse to assist them while they went in.

Dadi held her hand and went in. The rest of the family present there followed. Naina was in a fix. Should she or should she not. In what capacity should she go in? She was no more the family, but her feet betrayed her as they carried her in. After all, he was like her father once, who stood like a pillar behind them when Jassi was there and had taken up all their responsibilities so that they could live, a comfortable life. Only, the destiny was not in his hands or else he would've fought that as well.

Srishti's heart came to her mouth, looking at his frail form. The formidable looking Dada Ji of a few days back lay there helplessly. He opened his eyes and tried to remove his oxygen mask. Srishti held his hand laden with tubes. He held her hand, his grip nothing like she'd always felt before. He looked up at his wife and signaled her something. Dadi looked behind herself and seeing Vineet there brought him forward to give his hand in Dada Ji's. Dada Ji looked at Vineet, his eyes shone with satisfaction and put Srishti's hand in his, giving his approval for their relationship. Srishti could not take it and broke down while as Vineet held her back, shushing her. Dadi came forward and sat next to him. A relationship of over fifty years was coming to an end, but still; she managed to smile at him.

"Traitor." She just said feebly.

Dada Ji tried smiling as well. It must have been some old joke between them, something no one else knew about. He took out his mask finally. Srishti opposed, but Dadi didn't object and stopped her as well. She'd rather see his face and share a few words rather than prolong his life for a few more minutes.

"I'll be waiting." He said incoherently.

"I'll come as soon as I've done what you left for me to do." She said lovingly. Her old wrinkled eyes got misty. Dada Ji tried lifting his hand, but he didn't have the energy. She, herself lifted his hand and brought it to her cheeks to wipe her tears. A faint smile crept upon his lips as he did that. Their relationship appeared so complete where words had lost the meaning. They were an extension of each other's thoughts. His glance fell at Naina, and he gestured her to come closer. He clasped his hands and narrowed his eyes, mouthing an inaudible sorry, to ask for her forgiveness.

Naina came closer and held his hands and broke down bending to keep her head on his bed. He put his hand on her head to bless her before his body became listless. The heart monitor beeped and showed a flat line. The moment marked the end of an era for the family. The majestic old tree that held them together had fallen. Dadi closed his eyes and finally broke down. She had kept her ground so that it was not her tearstained face he saw, the last time he looked at her face.

The next few days went in a whirlwind. Srishti's uncles, Dada Ji's nephews, and their sons arranged his funeral. There was a sea of people who had come to take part in it. Her maternal Grandparents had flown down. Shivesh uncle also reached the morning of the funeral with them. The eldest of his nephews was called to light the pyre but suddenly Dadi, who stood there solemnly, came forward.

"He had wanted Srishti to do his last rites. Please let her do that." She told the priest who was performing the rites.

"But girls don't. It is against the Shastras. He will not get Mukti." He said gently.

"He won't if his will is not fulfilled. I don't know Shastras, but I know what my husband wanted. We are doing it for him. It has to be done the way he wanted." She then turned to her nephew and said. "Please take her along and assist her in doing what needs to be done."

Sanjot, his nephew did just that. There was a murmur among the people present there. Dadi knew that they would be the center of gossips for quite some time, but she had no choice. Her husband's wishes were paramount to her and in her heart; it would be what she would want for herself too. Srishti was the center of their Universe and if she could not give them Mukti, nothing in the world could.

Srishti did what was told to her along with her uncle between her sobs, but in her heart, she felt proud of her Grandfather who defied all odds all the times and even in his death, tried setting a precedence that might give way to the recognition of daughters as the torchbearers of a family's inheritance.

It had been five days since Dada Ji's death. The clouds of sorrow had engulfed the family leaving each one speechless. Srishti hadn't spoken a word to Naina yet. And Naina didn't try it either. Vineet had told Naina about what transpired at the hospital when one of her father's friends accidently told Srishti about her mother, about Naina. Naina felt terrible, but Shivesh was there to console her. Shivesh had wanted to move out into a hotel, but Dadi insisted that they stayed there.

It felt so awkward for Naina to stay in that house which was once her own. Back then, she could saunter from one room to another without a care in the world, but now, she was hesitant to even go to the kitchen. The huge lawn, where she and Jassi would spend hours together, holding hands, strolling or barbequing in the winters along with his friends and cousins, came so naturally. But standing there with Shivesh, it felt uncomfortable. She wasn't sure if she did right by asking Shiv to join her there, in a place that once belonged to someone else's son. She couldn't comprehend the plight of Jassi's mother, who endured the pain of his loss all over again. Things change, lives change as soon as the equation of our relationship changes. And there was Srishti. Her behavior was making Naina feel more uncomfortable. Srishti didn't say a thing but made sure, Naina felt unwelcomed in her house. She deserved that, Naina thought. Did she? She suddenly wasn't sure.

It was late in the evening. Naina sat on the veranda at the back of the house. It was her favorite spot back then. She loved sitting there whenever she felt lonely after putting little Srishti to sleep. The breeze was as good as always. The kitchen garden beautifully kept like before. When Jassi came over around that time, they would sit there drinking coffee and talking endlessly, making plans for their future. She felt at home there. Just when she was reminiscing and reliving the olden days, Dadi came along.

"It's good that you could come, Naina," Dadi said almost startling her.

"Oh! Yeah, I did. But I guess I got a little late." Naina said, standing up.

"Sit," Dadi said, sitting on the other cane chair and continued. "There is never a good time. Things happen at their own pace, and we can't do a thing to change them."

"I feel terrible. I wish I hadn't left back then. I shouldn't have left Srishti. I don't even know why I thought; I could not leave my job and my career to look after my baby. A lot of women do that. I could have done that too." She said as a stream of tears made way through her eyes.

"I know you do. But neither you nor I could predict that Jassi would leave us so early. Don't beat yourself for what was not your fault. You did no wrong." She said consoling Naina.

"But my daughter doesn't think so, Ma. She might be thinking that I'm an awful person. I left her. Do you realize what a sin it was?" Naina said.

"You didn't leave her on the stairs of a temple or in the bassinet of some orphanage. You left her with her Grandparents. Rather we kept her here with us. It was our fault if it was a fault ever. You did what you were told to do, like a good daughter and as a good daughter-in-law. In fact, this decision of Colonel Sahib had always weighed on our conscious, but I guess, we were too greedy to hold on to what was left of Jassi." Dadi said resigning.

"But I could have lived here with you and with my daughter," Naina said between her sobs.

"Don't be silly, Naina. You know, you couldn't have. You were young. You could not lead a lonely life holding on to Jassi's memories forever. Look at yourself today. Shivesh is such a wonderful person, the kind of a person every mother wants for her daughter. You have two sons. I'm happy that you are living a full life. Jassi must have wanted that for you too." Dadi said, keeping her palm on her knee.

"But where does that leave Srishti. I became Naina Masi for her. I orphaned my own child just as soon as her father died. What kind of a mother does that make me?" Naina said.

"It changes nothing Naina. Srishti grew up thoroughly loved and pampered. There was no life for you here and no job to match your caliber. To live here, Colonel Sahib would've pressured you to get married to someone here, so that you could retain your Resident status. Would you have gotten married for that silly reason, a marriage of compromise? My Jassi would've never forgiven us for doing that to his Neha? Don't take it upon yourself for what happened. The time was such. Circumstances were not favorable, and the emotions were high. Srishti is a wise girl. She's had too much to handle in the last few days. Give her time. She'll come around." Dadi said, getting up but stopped before she left and spoke again.

"Don't curse yourself for choosing to pursue your career. Your first duty is towards yourself, towards making yourself worthwhile in your own eyes. Being a wife or a mother is consequential to the decisions; we take to spend our life. If these decisions drown our own identity in them, they aren't worth what they are made out to be. Srishti is a woman now. Sooner she understands this, better it is for her as well."

Naina was awestruck listening to her mother-in-law this dispassionately. 'What a woman' she thought. She was right. It was she who hadn't let her give up her job back then. Her mother-in-law was the woman who stood up for her when her own mother couldn't, in helping her with Srishti.

She would've been marooned if she'd stopped working while Jassi was away. She was right in explaining as to how the life of a soldier's wife was so lonely and could turn her insane if she didn't do something useful with her time, thinking about his wellbeing, praying for his life every time some incidence of killings happened on the Borders.

Though, both their families were well provided for, it was she who insisted that Naina had to be financially independent, especially when she was qualified to be a professional. Her mother-in-law was always this strong and had liberal views, much like what Jassi had. She had groomed her son well, and Naina was now sure that she must have groomed Srishti just as well, maybe better than what she could've done herself.

Thinking this, she felt a lot better. She had to make an effort to talk to Srishti. Srishti might get angry first, but she was sure, her daughter would relent soon. She stood up near the pillar and looked into the starlit sky, trying to find Jassi in them. She was sure; he was looking at her from up there and smiling. She smiled back at him in the longest of time.

Living with Shivesh, being his wife and the mother of his children, she had felt guilty when the thoughts of Jassi came over. She'd tried blocking them, and yeah, they had faded away with time. Today, she felt, she shouldn't have. Thinking about the man she once loved wasn't a crime. She had not wished him to go away from her. Fate had snatched him from her. It was not her fault. But to have totally abandoned his memories, it sure was. Why couldn't the love of two people, the two most important men in her life co-exist in her heart? It's so ironical that she loved both her sons equally, both her parents, not one less than the other. People loved their siblings equally and a good number of friends at the same time. But when it came to loving the men in her life, she had to choose one above the other. Why was she repeatedly told to not bring up the subject of her slain husband in conversations with her current?

Why did she have to make that distinction between both her husbands, one gone, since long? Why did she lock the memories of her happier days spent with Jassi and left them at her parents' house when she left to go with Shivesh? Qucstions; that she had no answers for.

While Naina stayed behind, Dadi made an exit from the veranda to go to the living room only to come face-to-face with a perturbed looking Srishti, who probably had overheard their conversation out there.

Chapter 34

Dadi looked at her face. Srishti stood there quietly with the stance she had maintained ever since she'd known about Naina. She wanted to take Srishti in her arms and make her understand about all that was done in the past, but she'd no energy left. The over-exhaustive conversation with Naina had drained her, while she was still reeling under the loss of her husband, her anchor in life. She simply kept her tired hand on her shoulder briefly and left to go to the living room where she sat for all the days of the mourning.

Srishti was tempted to go to the veranda, to confront Naina but thought otherwise. She got back to her own room. Naina was another woman ever since she'd come this time. Her quirkiness, for which Srishti had always liked her, was missing. She looked lost. Srishti wondered if Naina still thought about her. Dadi's words from earlier had jolted Srishti out of her stupor. For last few days, Srishti had been angry with herself, with her destiny that took away her Father, her Mother who betrayed her and left and also her Grandparents who took upon themselves to raise her while it was something, her Mother should have done. She felt lonely among the sea of people who were her family, much like a feeling Vineet described once. This time, she forgot about what she preached him. She was the same old angry girl that she could not be when she was actually that age. The revelations had put her in a fix. She didn't know whether to be happy to have finally united with her mother, whose love she'd yearned for all her life or to be annoyed with her for the things she had no control over.

"Hey! Sera! Where are you lost? I've been calling you for a while." Vineet stood right in front of her and asked, shaking her so that she took notice of him.

"I...I'm...I'm sorry, Vin. Just a little disoriented." She said, trying to compose herself.

"Doesn't matter. Are you okay? Do you need anything?" He asked.

"No. I mean, Yes. I'm fine. I'm totally fine." She said, repeating herself.

"Okay, if you say so. Did you talk to your Mother?" He finally asked hesitatingly.

"She. Is. Not. My. Mother. Do you hear me? She is not my mother." She said in a raised voice.

"Does that admission give you happiness? If it does, let it be. But if it doesn't, there's only one way to get over it, is talk to her. Let her tell you her side of the story, Sera. It can't be that bad." He said subtly.

"There's nothing more to tell Vin. I know as to what happened back then, in parts, maybe, but I do. I'm just not able to digest the fact that how could my own Mother not stand up for me." She said in a very heavy voice.

"Still, give her a chance. It might make her feel light as well. Think about her Sera. Just think as to how she might have felt holding on to the truth in her heart for so long, something that you couldn't handle for a few days." He said.

"Okay. I will, maybe not now, not today." She said, giving in to his deliberations.

"Also, I wanted to tell you, rather ask you if I could go back to Delhi for a few days. I'll come back for the 10th day. I still have to make some submissions. Besides, Mom and Dad are coming over. I'll come back with them. They'd wanted to be with you at this time. Is that fine with you?" He asked, and she nodded in agreement.

Vineet left the next morning. It was one of the odd days when people didn't visit their house for mourning. Only the family members were there.

She sat in her room, looking over at the backyard. Her mind was numb. The blank wall of the kitchen garden had never gotten this much of her attention before. She'd always found it boring and asked Dada Ji to plant some beautiful flowering plants there. He'd always told her that flowering plants are not grown in the backyard. She never understood why, and he never explained. Today, she felt, there were a lot of things that he did omit to tell her about. His own love for her, for his home and homeland and for his inheritance was a lot bigger than anything else that mattered to others, so much so that it overshadowed the rest. She just became a commodity who needed to be passed on in the right hands for her sustenance and relevance. And her Mother; was she just as much a victim of her circumstances who got pawned in the power play of the misogynistic ethos, whoever set the rules for it.

In her extreme self-indulgence of thoughts, she didn't realize, there were repeated knocks at her door till it became too loud. She wiped her face clean of the mist; her tears had formed unknown to her and answered the door.

It was Shivesh Uncle to her surprise. She'd briefly met him earlier when he'd come to Delhi a couple of times and this time when he'd come to be a part of her Dada Ji's final journey. He carried a tray that had her breakfast in it; she'd forgotten to have. His presence in her room in such an informal way, it didn't add up, but she invited him nonetheless and excused herself to go to use the restroom before she sat with him for a conversation.

"Hey! I hope I didn't disturb you. We hadn't communicated much before as much as I might have liked to...aaa.. but I guess, we can talk if you don't mind." He said hesitatingly standing there, having kept the food tray on the coffee table and then gesturing towards the food, he continued, "Your breakfast. You haven't eaten since morning."

"You didn't have to do that. I was coming out anyway?" She said politely.

"Oh! Okay. Actually, your Dadi was bringing it in, but I thought, I should...I mean, I thought if we could talk for a while, (pause) only...only if you are fine with that." Shivesh sounded too hesitant, somewhat awkward breaking the ice. Srishti smiled at his half-baked efforts and motioned him to sit on one of the chairs and sat down herself.

"Why don't you eat first, Srishti? I can come back later if you want." He said, looking at the confused expressions on her face.

"No. I'm fine. Is there something specific that you wanted to talk about?" Srishti asked.

"This is no interrogation, Beta. I only wanted to let you know; I fully understand the turmoil that you are going through. A lot has happened, and a lot of revelations have surfaced in a matter of a very small time frame. It's complicated for anyone to comprehend it in better circumstances, but at times like these, it's hard to imagine what your state of mind is like.

I just want to tell you that though I don't come anywhere close to what your Dada Ji meant to you or what is the place of your Father in your life, I'm there, will always be there if you needed any help. I wish Naina had the courage to admit about her relationship with you, at least to me. I definitely would've made an effort to know you better and connect to you at a level our relationship needed to be. But I guess, she had her compulsions. She upheld the promise, she had made to your Grandfather more than being honest with you and me. Trust me, I don't blame her." He said.

"She didn't tell you either! What kind of a relationship is that where she kept an enormous part of her being hidden from you? You...you still trust her." She asked with disbelief.

"Relationships are not about being judgmental, Srishti, and trust is not a unidirectional entity. Each one of us is entangled in an assortment of varied relationships, much like a Venn diagram. There's only as much you can probably do to make them co-exist, but sometimes in keeping with the sanctity of one, the other would have to be kept at bay. Nothing is absolute as far as human behavior goes. Your honesty towards one might come across as dishonesty or betrayal towards the other, but it is you, who would have to decide where you stand as far as your relationships go." He explained.

"Isn't a husband and wife's relationship above any other? Should there be secrets?" She asked.

"You are a progressive girl, Srishti. Don't get caught in this caricature of unwarranted expectations, especially if it is with the person you are in love and are going to spend your entire life. Every relationship that we form with anyone must be just as sacred. But every relationship should have boundaries that let you be the person that you are. You should always be in your right to keep to yourself what you do not want to share with someone else, even if it happens to be your life partner.

I knew that Naina was married before and was a widow. I met her at a friend's place in California and fell in love with her instantly. She told me about her tragedy and how much she loved your Father and wasn't ready to move on. Back then, she thought, she might never get over it, but I pursued her. If I think back today, her reluctance to be in a relationship might have stemmed out of the fact that she cared about you and felt that she might get back to you someday or maybe the fact that she would have to share with me the secret; she so vehemently guarded having made a promise to your Grandfather. But yeah, I was able to soften her resolve, and she agreed to marry me on the condition that I would not ever ask her or try to dig up anything about her past marriage. Back then, I didn't know what was she protecting. She's a good person Srishti, and though I'm not pleading her case here, I can tell you from the perspective of what I know about her is that the happiness, I've seen on her face after having spoken to you or when she talked about you was something I always grudged. She must have loved you all these years, only she couldn't share it with you. Talk to her whenever you are ready." Saying this, he got up to go.

Srishti got up as well and hugged him. He hugged her back. How she wished, she'd known him earlier. If it felt like hugging her Father, she won't know. She had no remembrance, but she did feel secure and protected.

"Thanks so much. It meant a lot to me. I'll do whatever it takes to smoothen things out, now that everything is out there in the open." She said.

He blessed her, keeping his hand on top of her head and left quickly. He smiled to himself thinking about the things, he spoke to Srishti. Was he actually telling her what he said or was he reminding him of what he'd conveniently forgotten when he spoke to Naina back home? Whatever it was, he was sure, it would do good to all of them put together, only if Srishti talked to Naina like she promised.

Chapter 35

Srishti was restless after Shivesh left her room. She did promise him, she would talk to Naina, but it was harder than she thought. They had once bridged the distance between them easily as it only measured in terms of time and space. But today, the void she felt was in her heart, which was stemmed out of mistrust and years of misplaced belief.

Her mind believed her Mother, the trauma she might have gone through while the people around her were busy making life-changing decisions about her. The searing pain she might have felt, first at the loss of her husband and then being asked to give up her only child along with the memories of a life, she once thought was her forever. Her intellect reasoned, but her heart, her heart was acting like a three-year-old who wanted to cling to her Mother and not let go, how much so ever anyone wanted otherwise. It wasn't ready to relent. It wanted her, all of her, all for herself, only it was twenty years too late.

She stood in front of the mirror, and not liking what she saw, shook her head. It wasn't doing her any good. She wished that she hadn't come to know the truth ever. At least, she could mourn the death of her Grandfather peacefully. What was she doing, indulging in self-pity? In doing what she was doing, she was only disrespecting the memories of the man who had made her what she was today. If he did injustice to her and her mother, she never felt it, for all these years. All she'd felt was loved and pampered to the hilt. She shrugged the depressing thoughts and dashed towards the washroom for a shower.

She felt light having showered and ready to discard the excess baggage from her heart and head. In all of five days since his death, she hadn't thought about him or mourned him in totality. Her mind had been completely overtaken by the betrayal done to her by the very people she called her own. All of her waking time was spent in being angry with Naina.

In the rigmarole of events around her, she realized, her mind had forgotten to register an essential detail, and that was the demise of her Dada Ji. She wasn't going to see him ever again. Her mouth twitched, her heartbeat increased, and when the magnitude of the loss set in, a loud shriek came out of her throat. She swept the tray carrying her half-eaten breakfast with her hand, and it landed with a loud clank on the floor, shattering its contents before she sat down on the floor with a thud wailing uncontrollably.

Dadi came running to the room along with Naina and the others present in the house. She took her in her arms and let her cry her grief out, the two of them shared equally. Dadi gestured Naina to stay back while as the rest left to let them grieve together. Naina sat there helplessly, watching her writhing in agony and sorrow while she could do nothing to relieve her pain. She, herself was a cause of her pain. Srishti sobered down after a while as her cries turned into hiccups while Dadi kept rubbing her back.

"Are you better now?" Dadi asked, and she nodded.

"Everything will be all right, Srishti. We all have to go someday. It was time for him. With you having grown up into a woman that you are, he's gone a happy man. Just forgive him if you think, he wasn't just towards you. It's only because there were things, he strongly believed in and had never thought twice before sacrificing anything for them.

But always remember that he hasn't loved anything or anyone more than you." Dadi added sobbing herself.

"I know that, Dadi. I do, and I'm sorry for behaving the way I did. I'm sorry, this happened because of me." She said sobbing again.

"No. It did not. It was Colonel Sahib's guilt; he'd lived with all his life. It was his guilt that in our selfish love for you, he had kept you away from your mother and her from you. It was his time to go. None of us have the power to make people live or die. Don't blame yourself for what is not your fault." Dadi said, looking into her eyes and added. "You take rest now. Sleep for a while, and you'll feel better."

Then looking at Naina, she said. "Stay here with her Naina while I go outside and sit with the rest. I'll send the maid to clean up the mess." Saying this, she left.

Both Srishti and Naina were in a fix. This was the odd time to fix their relationship. Naina got up awkwardly and bent down to make her stand and dragged her towards her bed. An eerie silence surrounded them while Naina made her lie down, in a dilemma whether to sit beside her or pull a chair next to her. She cursed herself again to have let so much of distance come between them. She finally decided to pull the chair so as not to push Srishti when she was at her most vulnerable time. She was about to turn when Srishti held her hand. Naina looked at her in surprise.

"Sit here with me. Can't You?" Srishti whispered.

"Yeah. I can. I..I want to." Naina said and sat next to her on the bed, almost raising her hand to keep it on her head but pulled away. She didn't know as to how Srishti would react to it.

Srishti looked at her, pain visible in her eyes, came closer and put her head in Naina's lap circling her waist while as the barrage of her pent-up emotions broke loose through her tears washing away the misery, she'd felt in last few days.

Naina held her instantly in her arms and the agonizing ache and distance of years dissolved in the warmth; the mother within her could never let go off.

"I'm sorry, Srish. I'm so terribly sorry for failing you. Please forgive me if you can." Naina said sobbing.

"No. I'm sorry for misunderstanding you, Mom. I'm so very sorry for being angry with you when it wasn't your fault." She said.

The words ceased to matter; apologies turned irrelevant once the hearts were united. Srishti lay there clinging to her mother like a little baby that she was when she left her. Naina was glad that she'd finally gotten her daughter back and at the same time was able to keep her promise; she'd given to her father-in-law.

She was sure that Jassi, her Jassi must be proud of her today that she was able to make amends with the most beautiful of the possessions they had created together; their daughter. She was missing him today after ages, and for once, she did not feel guilty of betrayal to Shivesh. She felt at peace with herself. She felt complete having come a full circle from where she began, and she promised to herself, she would protect her daughter from here on. She would not let her become a victim of the circumstances like she once became.

Srishti slept like a baby for hours together. One of her aunts had come to call them for lunch, but Naina sent her away saying, she would when Srishti got up. Later, they spent the entire evening catching up with each other on the veranda at the backyard. Shivesh joined them too for a while.

The happiness of uniting with her mother had come at a very wrong time.

Chapter 36

Vineet got back on the morning of the 'Kriya' along with his parents who he had put up in the same hotel as her Granny and Grandpa stayed in. He hadn't spoken to Srishti after he'd left; instead, she did not reciprocate his calls whenever he called. He didn't think too much about it. After having settled his parents in the hotel, he made way for her house. Srishti was busy performing Puja for the 'Kriya' much to the displeasure of the priest and some distant relatives since it was the duty of the boys. Dadi stood her ground and did not buckle under pressure making it clear that it was what she had decided with her husband long back. Srishti was their sole heir, and she needed to perform any ritual, which required to be performed, be it for her husband, her son, or even her whenever it happened.

By the next day, all the guests had left. It was only Dadi and her along with Naina and Shivesh in the house. Naina was leaving for Delhi in two days along with her husband. The house felt eerily silent. It used to resonate with Dada Ji's loud voice from time to time and his throaty laughter whenever he was happy. She looked at the wall where his picture hung now, keeping his son company.

Her maternal Grandparents had come from the hotel they were staying in before they left for Delhi. Vineet's parents were coming home as well, along with him to meet them before they left too.

Though Srishti had made peace with Naina earlier and had come to terms with Dada Ji's death, she was jittery for a few days since then. She often looked lost, kept to herself, and was engrossed in deep thoughts.

Naina and Dadi couldn't decipher as to what was going on in her head. Shivesh had told them to leave her alone. She was probably processing the truckload of information, she had gotten in last few days, and though she responded positively to it now, it was still raw, and her subconscious was sure to rebel and reason before it became a part of it.

What Dadi worried about was her cold and distant behavior, her indifference towards Vineet ever since yesterday when he got back. It could possibly not be because he left to go back for a few days. What changed in a matter of one week?

Vineet's parents came over. Srishti was courteous towards them but averted her eyes as soon as she came face-to-face with Vineet. He wasn't ready for this. Vineet had no clue as to what had transpired in the last few days for her to be behaving the way she was doing. Did she expect him to stay back with her for all the days of the mourning? If so, she could've easily told him, and he would've managed it somehow. He hadn't known Srishti to be someone to whom things like that mattered. But he knew that the people behaved differently in times of grief. It could just be that passing phase, and he was sure he would soften her as soon as they were together.

Navneet, Vineet's father, came forward and greeted Dadi.

"We are extremely sorry for your loss, aunty. I wish I could meet uncle, to ask for Srishti's hand for Vineet. But I guess, the destiny has its own way of doing things." He said.

"Yes. I wish that too." Dadi said in a very heavy voice while as Srishti held her with her arm around her.

"I know, this is not the right time to talk about it, but since everyone is here, I want you to tell me how should we go about it. We can come back later if you want." Navneet said, looking at her and then at his wife, who gestured him not to speak on the issue.

But before Dadi could say something, Srishti butted in.

"I.... I know that you'd especially planned this visit keeping in mind my degree completion and I do respect that uncle. But, with what happened now, I don't think, I'm in a state of mind to think about relocating, much less get married. I can't leave Dadi on her own." She said with a little annoyance and a flutter of incredulity at her own words. Naina closed her eyes in disbelief while as the rest looked on with an expression of shock.

"Srishti!" Dadi reprimanded her trying to do the damage control. "Why don't you leave it to the elders to decide these things? Go inside."

She looked at Vineet; the shock was written large all over his face. In her heart, she sympathized with him and with herself as well, but she could not run away from her responsibility now.

"I can't, Dadi. This life is mine, and I want to be the one taking a call on it. For all the days gone by, I've been thinking about it, and I've decided, I can't leave this place. Dada Ji didn't want me to. There's a whole lot of work that needs to be done here, the things he'd wanted me to take up. I can't let him down now when I know what it is all about. I can't quit." Then looking at Dadi, she continued, "You only said that I would undertake every ritual, every rite towards this family that the tradition demands. Allow me to take up the responsibilities too."

Dadi came closer and held her hands, looking painfully into her eyes. "Don't do this to yourself, Beta. Don't do this to Vineet. Don't worry about me. I can come and live with you when I need to be taken care of. There is my extended family to help me live the rest of my life. Don't sacrifice a full life for the few days that are left of mine. I wouldn't be able to live with the guilt." She said.

The air was thick. Vineet felt as if someone has sucked out the oxygen from the room. He didn't come back to hear Srishti, his Sera say this about their relationship. He loved her too much, even to the extent of leaving everything to come here and live with her only if she asked. But she was on a spree of taking unanimous decisions about their life. He felt like shaking her up.

Yes, she was grief-stricken, and he could excuse her for that but be taking such life-changing decisions was more like a knee-jerk reaction. If she had said that when they were alone, he would've reasoned it out with her but, here, in front of their entire family, he didn't know as for how best to contain her.

She looked at Vineet. He shook his head, signaling her not to go any further. She walked up to him and stood in front of him with her head bent, and her eyes closed. Srishti took a deep breath to muster up the courage to speak to him. She looked up piercing into his now cold eyes and said,

"Look Vineet. I'm sorry for what I'm doing right now, and it has to be done now when I'm overcome with emotions. I know, this is not a practical decision as far as my professional abilities go, but I have to take it if I want to live with my sanity intact. Last month or so, had been very enlightening about the facets of life, I had no clue about, and it's all because of Dada Ji. I can't let all the work that he'd been doing go waste." She paused for a while, looking hopefully in Vineet's eyes.

"This place is my home, Vineet. Even though I know, I would be committing professional suicide if I stayed back, I would have to. I know, it would be selfish of me if I asked you to do the same for me, but I'm still asking because, few years down the line, I don't want to sit and wonder as to what you would've said if I'd asked. So, I'm asking you now. Would you still want to marry me if I decided to stay here? Would you be able to give up your dream job, the prospects of lucrative and fulfilling professional ambitions? Just say no if you have an iota of a doubt so that I could move on without any regret that I......" She never got to complete what she was about to say any further. Vineet instantly pulled her into his arms, exhaling the breath, he was holding for a long time and said.

"I thought you'd never ask."

"Vineet." His father shouted this time. "You can't take such an irrational decision. You can't simply sidestep your dreams, your ambitions. People work relentlessly to achieve this. You, too have. You possibly can't let go of something that you have earned so painstakingly."

Vineet left her and came to his father.

"Yes, Dad. I can't. I can't let go of what I have earned so painstakingly, and that's her. I can work anywhere. It's just a job, something to earn a living. I can't let go of my life for something so trivial. She's my life, who's made me understand what love is. She taught me how to love Dad, to love you and mom without judging you. We'll figure out the logistics in our relationship later, but what I have with her is priceless, and I'm not letting it go." Vineet said firmly.

"Mind it Vineet. It is a long and lengthy battle. You sure, you can cope up?" Srishti asked.

"I'm the son of an officer who never buckled under pressure, Srishti, I sure can battle it out." He said, glancing at his father sideways as a feeble smile broke on his father's face. He did manage to trick him and melt him.

The atmosphere in the room thinned out as the clouds of uncertainty started to disappear.

In a while, everyone left, leaving Dadi and Srishti alone, promising to be back whenever they could. Naina wanted to stay, but Shivesh had insisted that Srishti needed to be left alone right now. Vineet left promising, he would be back over the next weekend once his parents had left.

"You didn't need to do this Srishti," Dadi said, putting her head back on the headrest of her bed.

"I know. I didn't need to, and I didn't want to do that earlier. But right now, I want to. Dada Ji was right. If everyone, who has the ability to fight, takes the easy exit, the battles can't be won. Battles are not won just with passion or a sense of duty alone, we need to have the aptitude and the capability to undertake the task. I'm a born fighter, Dadi. I carry the genes of those who stood up for what they believed in. Even if I quit, it changes nothing, but if I stayed back, I could at least try to bring in the change, to take the battle ahead.

I want to fight for the rights of all the women who are muted on one pretext or the other. **I'm not a commodity that my relevance depends on the suffix that states my father's name or my husband's to render me legitimate. Their names are for my identification among all the Srishti's of the world, an address of sorts. They can't become my identity**. I'm my own self, and I want my rightful place under the sun. With Vineet on my side and the blessings of Dada Ji and Dad from above, my struggle would not go down unnoticed." She said.

"You know that it's not easy. It's a process that's long drawn. It wears the people down. Fighting with a system is stressful. You won't find many who would back you." Dadi said.

"I'm aware. But I can't quit without trying." Srishti said leaning back and closing her eyes.

Epilogue

Srishti had passed her exams in distinction as always and had gone to Delhi to politely turn down the job offer citing her inability to join in the event of her Grandfather's death. They had been courteous enough neither to object nor had given harsh reviews on her CV.

She got married a little after a year of her Dada Ji's death. She wanted a small ceremony, but Dadi won't relent. She insisted it held at a scale that Dada Ji had wanted it to be. Srishti gave up to her wishes.

Naina had come a month before her wedding, and Shivesh uncle and her half-brothers joined her a week before. Granny had called her over to help her shop in Delhi. Vanya, who lived in Dubai, had joined her a week earlier and so did the rest of her friends.

Dada Ji's absence tugged at her heart, but she braved it out for Dadi. Vineet was super-elated. He'd wanted to leave his job, but Srishti stopped him, not to be in a hurry. They could manage to shuttle between two cities for a while till they planned their next action.

It was an emotional moment for everyone when Pundit Ji called out the parents for 'Puja.' She looked at Dadi's face. Dadi looked reluctant to come forward and insisted that Naina and Shivesh performed the ritual. It would have been her Dada Ji along with Dadi otherwise, but now Dadi hesitated. Being a widow, she didn't want to let Srishti start her life with bad omen. Srishti cringed at the shallowness of the thought. She pulled her along and made her sit next to her, making her participate along with Naina and Shivesh uncle.

"Come forward for 'Kanyadan,'" Pundit Ji asked when the time for it came.

Srishti looked up, looked at the happy faces of her family and her friends, and then at Vineet's.

'Kanyadan.' The word felt insulting and demeaning. She shuddered at the thought of being given away in 'Daan' as alms as if she was a commodity, mere cattle. She couldn't be reduced to being a hand out that passed her off from one master to another. She wanted to marry Vineet as an equal and not be given to him as a responsibility. She had to voice her opinion. She had to change that to liberate her from the pseudo pragmatism, the rule of thumb that went on unchallenged for the years gone by.

"There would be no 'Kanyadaan' Pundit Ji," Srishti said firmly. The chill ran down Vineet's spine as a stunned silence enveloped the chilly December night in the lawns of her house.

"What? You don't want to get married." Pundit Ji asked.

"I want to get married to him. I just don't want to be given away as 'Daan'. Please change your mantras to suit the occasion." She said, smiling looking at Vineet's now relaxing expressions. She did scare him and all the rest. Naina smiled and shook her head in disbelief, sharing a similar expression with her husband. Her daughter was a force to reckon with, and she was proud of the upbringing, her Grandparents had given her. Dadi looked a little puzzled earlier but smiled at her proposition now, understanding where it came from. Pundit Ji was in a fix. This was new for him. He tried convincing that it was how it should be done, but Srishti didn't move. He finally gave up.

They weren't sure if he knew of any substitute mantras but who cared. Their vows of love were taken a long time back, and they knew what mattered to them beyond what was written ages ago.

They went to Delhi where her father-in-law had given them a warm reception with who's who of the diplomatic and political class was there. Dadi went back with the rest of her extended family, instructing her to stay at her new home for a while.

They went for a weeklong Honeymoon to Bali.

Srishti had started looking after her Grandfather's Agro-based business and was getting the hang of it before she made sweeping changes to take it to another level. On the sides, she started taking a keen interest in the social organizations where her Dada Ji worked for the benefit of the people living in the Border areas and other neglected classes. Vineet was planning to set up a Financial Services Consultancy with its base in Delhi so that he could leave his job in a few years once they plan to start a family. That would give him the independence to shuttle between homes, their home in Jammu and Delhi. Srishti had applied for a Ph.D. at Jammu University so that she could be eligible for the teaching job in the University or at IIM that is yet to come up in the outskirts of Jammu.

The socio-political conditions remained as fragile as always, not that she was expecting anything to change in a matter of months. The cease-fire violations on the Border were at an all-time high. The conflict and rhetoric about the ongoing conditions was still the talk of national debates on TV in high decibel conversations. The plight of the people in Jammu due to discrimination was as is. The pseudo-secular brigade in the political class and among the activists who voice their equivocal support for Article 370 was quiet, rather evasive about the lodging of 40,000 Rohingya inhabitants in the outskirts of Jammu. The administration that stands guard for upholding of the ethnicity of the people of the

State holding Article 35A as a shield and had been depriving the West Pakistan Refugees, the legitimacy to be the Subjects of the State for 70 years is allowing the citizens of another country to settle down on the grounds of humanity. Sounds bizarre, doesn't it. The humane approach is suddenly found missing when the very own Kashmiri Pundit Community struggles to live a dignified life.

In the past five years, the baton of governance changed hands from one party to another both in the regions of Kashmir as well as in Jammu but conditions at both the places remain much the same. And now with legislative assembly suspended, the state was under the Governor's rule. A state that could have been the pride of National Tourism is reduced to being a begging bowl that was sapping the resources of not only the State itself but of the hard earned money of the tax-payers across the rest of India. The acts of sedation were rising in Jammu as well, the miscreants testing the waters with scarce incidences of misbehavior in Jammu University or at other places to incite the locals. Jammu is quiet, a disquiet brewing among the people against the administration, and against the non-committal attitude of the authorities.

Srishti was trying to understand as to what's happening around her. She looked into the vast library of her Grandfather and is reading about the inception of the conflict like Dada Ji told her about. She wants to be well equipped with the required knowledge before she went head on and fought the system. She planned to file the writ-petition in the court for legitimate rights, the Right to Equality for the women of her State at par with the male counterparts.

Uri and Pulwama were sad days in the history of turmoil in the valley where 18 of the Army and then 44 of the CRPF men died in the ambush followed by few more on the following days. But the Heroics of Surgical Strikes and Balakote had her thinking that the political will to tackle the situation in her state was there in the right place after years of denial and empty condemnations. She and the people of her State did have some hope with the current political dispensation; she knew would come back with a raging majority for the next term too. The Iron fist; she remembered like her Dada Ji had put it.

There was a lot of clamor about going in for Assembly elections by the Kashmir based parties and by the Opposition at the Center but she wondered; if all the regions of the state were not represented correctly in the Legislative Assembly, what good it did for the Democracy we so wanted to uphold.

Life is not what she planned it out as, but the beauty of life lies in its unpredictability, the exuberance that accompanies the surprises, the fear of unknown and the passion that drives us uphill to conquer what was thought to be unreachable, an Eldorado before someone got there for the first time. She'd chosen the rocky path straddled with the age-old mindset, the misogynistic ethos and the laid-back attitude of the society that paid little attention to things, which didn't matter to it in the short term. Knowingly she'd taken it upon herself to dismantle the hurdles she felt on the way creating a concrete road for the rest to follow, for how so long she could go.

Now on this day, the historic day of **5th of August; 2019**, little did she know, she wouldn't have to graze her knees to make that happen and a mere power of vote, the right vote that puts the Right people at the position of power is enough to make the pain go away. **It happened; it happened finally that the dignity of the women of her State was restored with a single stroke of change of Law, the Mighty Article 370 and 35A, the archaic law that had lived long enough, much past it's expiry date**. She wished that it had been revoked earlier, a couple of years back; so her Dada Ji might be alive today and she hadn't had to pick up that fight with him. Damn it, if it was revoked a couple of decades earlier; she might not have been separated from her mother. But that goes on. All she had were a few questions in her head making her restless.

Do the Lawmakers, when they make Laws factor in the effects of those very Laws on the lives of people going forward?

Should the Laws we make at some point in time, come with an expiry date, the best before such 'n' such time? After all, people change, societies change and so do the aspirations.

Srishti once thought that it was battle she had to fight with her Grandfather to do what she wanted to do, but it was a mere tiff if she thinks back in time. The real BATTLE began after she confronted the truth of her existence, both as an abandoned daughter and a prospective Bride. Just as she readied herself to go head on with the system to ask for her Rights, a new beginning was what she is promised today, the biggest Impediment to her social existence, revoked. With all her optimism intact, she does know that the fight was far from over. She could already hear the Bugle for the next Battle in her head - DELIMITATION for the end of years of discrimination against her region, the region of Jammu and she knew; it was not far. Only if she and the others geared for the impending Battle, THE BATTLE AHEAD..........

About The Author

Dr. Sonia Sharma is a doctor turned author. After a sojourn of twenty-three years as a Cosmetic Dentist and an Implantologist, creating artworks to put a smile back on the faces of her patients, she has let her words do the talking.

Her writings are all about viewing life through its different perspectives, which finally define our emotions towards a person or a problem.

She's the author of 'AFTERLIFE', 1st of the series of 4 books and 'IMPERFECT LIVES - A Collection of Short Stories'

Her books promise to tickle the human sensibilities to accept our flaws as our uniqueness and help explore the realm of desires, one beholds in the sub-conscious, raring to explode and express at the smallest of persuasion.

The work that's closest to her heart is this book titled 'THE BATTLE AHEAD...', a story of the struggles of a girl born in her home state of Jammu and Kashmir, the troubled child of Independent India.

Other books by the Author

AFTERLIFE

AFTERLIFE is the story of a young woman Anna, who has forgotten to live her life after she's come out of her failed marriage. Her life revolves robotically around bringing up her daughter and pursuing her profession for survival, both financially and otherwise, until the day, her twisted destiny brings her face to face with Kush, another of her kind. Their similar past and their unbounded chemistry makes it challenging for them to resist each other and just when she thought that her life had more to do than breathing, her past appears in the most unexpected ways.

How they deal with fighting their inner demons, giving in to their sexual desires, addressing their children's psychological fears, while balancing the past and present, thereby achieving the ultimate Nirvana is what the book comprises of.

AFTERLIFE is the first of the series that takes us through the lives of people in different backdrops, who have stopped living for themselves after their failed relationships and how a spark of a second chance at love rekindles that fire and incinerates/cremates the misgivings of their dead past to bring them the divine light of a new life, their AFTERLIFE

Order @ https://www.amazon.in/Afterlife-Dr-Sonia-Sharma/dp/8193653580/ref=tmm_pap_swatch_0?_encoding=UTF8&qid=&sr=

THE IMPERFECT LIVES

'THE IMPERFECT LIVES' is a collection of short stories that depict the lives of people who are less than perfect in their attributes.

The gradations of grey in the monochromatic zone withhold the unspoken truth about the human lives that lie hidden beneath the vibrant spectrum of life that's out on display.

Pragmatism wins with a dash of emotional seasoning where the fault lines separating the right and wrong are blurred. Thus leaving one guessing as to how far would we go in passing judgments about people without being aware of their fears, insecurities and probably a fragmented psychosis.

Available @ https://www.amazon.in/Afterlife-Dr-Sonia-Sharma/dp/8193653580/ref=tmm_pap_swatch_0?_encoding=UTF8&qid=&sr=